THE
WHITE
ROSE
B. TRAVEN

Translated from the German
by Donald J. Davidson

Published by
Lawrence Hill & Company
Westport, Connecticut

THE

WHITE

ROSE

B. TRAVEN

TRANSLATORS NOTE

THOUGH THE WHITE ROSE originally ap-
peared in Germany fifty years ago, in 1929, and has been translated
into many languages since then, this edition is the first to be
published in the United States in the English language. About fifteen
years ago, in 1965, a British publisher, Robert Hale, Ltd., issued an
English edition, but it was an incomplete version and was never
published or distributed in the United States.

The version of the novel printed here is based on the last German-
language edition of *Die Weisse Rose,* prepared and published in
Traven's own lifetime—the Rowohlt Verlag paperback edition of
1962. For various reasons the text here differs slightly from the

Rowohlt edition. Traven continually revised his own work, changing the wording here, deleting a passage there, adding a scene or moving it from one place to another. In the instance of THE WHITE ROSE, not all such corrections were incorporated into German editions. Specifically, in the early 1960's he prepared emendations to the 1951 edition of *Die Weisse Rose* for Krüger Verlag (his hardcover publishers) to incorporate into subsequent editions. Krüger made most, but not all of them. For this first U.S. edition Traven's widow provided the publisher with Traven's own "corrected copy" and the relevant corrections have been incorporated in the text.

There are also a dozen or so other short alterations to the Krüger-Rowohlt text. For instance, I have restored to the novel two paragraphs Traven deleted from the original editions, and I have deleted several short passages involving implausibilities in his description of American life in the Roaring Twenties. In minor instances I have changed the surnames of characters to accord with names actually encountered in the States. I have also identified the aged industrialist who appears in a key scene in the book as John D. Rockefeller, Sr. A few other points may interest the reader. In the German original Traven made frequent use of English, much of it slang, and a considerable part of that dated or incorrect. I have translated it into American idiom. Traven's Spanish was taken over into the text intact.

At the heart of the novel lies a concept that is difficult to translate into English; *die Heimat*, "country" or "nativeland." Neither English word alone does justice to the German, which often connotes the region, rather than the whole country, along with feelings of deep attachment or love for it. I have translated the word in different ways in different contexts: home, land, soil, homeland, native land, native soil, and so on.

THE WHITE ROSE is well grounded in the facts of American history, though Traven, like every novelist, makes his individual use of it. For example, the anthracite strike that is the source of Mr. Collins' power takes place when he is not yet thirty years old, and the plucking of the White Rose occurs when he is in his fifties, a lapse of more than twenty years. And the plucking occurs during the Huerta rising of 1924 and 1925. This dating enables us to connect the strike of the novel to the great anthracite strike of 1902. And the basic element of that strike—reduction in wages, refusal of management to deal with non-miners, non-recognition of the union, importation of foreign laborers, confusion within the union on aims, the spreading of the strike's effects to the national economy—are accurately reflected in THE WHITE ROSE.

Similar parallels can be drawn between other events of the novel and events of the first quarter of the twentieth century, involving stock manipulations and bank panics, orgies and scandals, Sugar Daddies and chorus girls. There was a sensation-seeking press, incipient film censorship, Palmer raids, suppression of reds and radicals. Traven did not invent this background of human greed and human folly, but many readers, especially those under fifty, may miss these echoes of an earlier age.

In the end, however fascinating THE WHITE ROSE may be as a witness to the times, it is still a novel. It is, and will remain, one of the most interesting and controversial of Traven's works. Surprisingly enough, it has never before been available in America. As Traven so often said, what matters is the work itself, not who wrote it or why. Here it is for you to enjoy and to judge for yourself.

Donald J. Davidson

THE
WHITE
ROSE
B. TRAVEN

CHAPTER ONE

AMONG the large American oil companies that had extended their operations into Mexico, the Condor Oil Company was neither the largest nor the strongest, but it had the best appetite.

Not only for the development of a person, but also for the development of an entire people, a healthy appetite is of vital importance. It is even more decisive in the development of a large capitalist enterprise. Appetite determines the pace of development and the means employed to reach the goal, which is to become an influential, even dominant power in international economic affairs. In its structure, its essence, its goals, its methods, a large modern business differs little from a nation-state. The single visible difference is perhaps this: a large capitalist enterprise is usually better organized and more rationally and cleverly run than a state.

The Condor Oil Company was the youngest of the companies fighting with and against one another in Mexico, where the struggle for market leadership was being waged. Since it was the youngest, it was the most voracious. In the selection and application of means to secure an influential place in competition with the older, more powerful companies, it recognized no restraints or inhibitions. If it had any slogan at all concerning the kind of war it was fighting, it was: the war fought in the most brutal manner lasts the shortest time and is therefore the most humane.

In this it found at the same time a moral excuse for its actions. It could say in its own defense that it was waging the most humane war. There would be peace again as soon as it had won the war.

An oil company's power depends not only upon the number of producing wells it possesses; it depends as much or more upon the land it owns or controls. Three kinds of land are involved here: land definitely having oil; land that in the geologists' opinion ought to have oil; and land that oil experts instinctively believe should have oil. It is the third category that makes speculation possible and permits millions of dollars to be made without so much as a single barrel of oil having to be produced.

So went the war of the companies to acquire more and more land. They worked with greater enthusiasm and will to acquire all the land that might have oil than they did to exploit with every scientific and technological method, down to the last acre, the land they already had.

Since the Condor Oil Company, given its small capitalization and the number and richness of its producing wells, could not rival the great oil companies, it had to take the second course—namely, to secure more land suspected of having oil than any other company. The company possessing an enormous amount of land that has or could have oil, especially if that oil is needed to satisfy the demands of the market, can determine the price and exercise a certain control over other companies even though they seemed to be invincible, uncontrollable, because of their enormous capitalization.

So it can quite readily be said that there wasn't any misdeed or crime that the company's land agents would not have committed to get the desired land if it seemed necessary.

The Condor Oil Company had eighteen rich running wells. When it so much as smelled land having oil or land another company was perhaps thinking of acquiring, it was johnny on the spot. Of course, in the ruthless business of driving people off the land, no one from the company took part, not the directors or any of its high officers. It seldom even allowed an American to work in that branch of the business. Only when the land the company wanted was already in the hands of someone who had bought it for the company did the officers become involved. The company, in every case, was the second purchaser. Mexican or Spanish or, sometimes, German or French subagents arranged these shabby deals.

The Condor Oil Company had its headquarters in San Francisco. Its Mexican headquarters were in Tampico, and it had branch offices in Panuco, Tuxpan, and Ebano, and it was preparing to construct two more offices, one on the Isthmus, the other in Campeche.

It had excellent American, English, and Swedish geologists working for it, and paid them well. It employed a comparatively large staff of surveyors to survey and inventory the tracts. They were less well paid than the geologists, for their work was less highly valued. That's why the surveyors often ran around in shabby, torn clothing like vagabonds. The geologists were certainly closer to the company directors, professionally and economically, because they could pass on to them valuable tips about rich oil fields. The surveyors, on the other hand, were closer to the proletariat, and though they would not willingly admit it, because they had gone to college, they had to work longer and harder than the workers did. It did not matter to the workers whether they were treated like proletarians or not. There were plenty of surveyors, and they were fired much more quickly than the burly riggers, who were as bold as bandits. The riggers were not ashamed to pack tomatoes occasionally if they couldn't build rigs or if they were fired because of a thrashing they gave a foreman.

In the region where the Condor Company was operating lay the hacienda La Rosa Blanca. The hacienda was almost completely surrounded by rich oil-bearing lands, all of which were on lease to or in the possession of the company.

The hacienda, about two thousand acres in all, belonged to the Indian Jacinto Yañez.

Its products were corn, beans, chile, horses, cattle, hogs, sugar cane—and therefore sugar—and, finally, oranges, lemons, tomatoes, and pineapples.

The hacienda did not make its owner rich, nor even well-to-do. For everything was grown and managed in the traditional way. The work on the hacienda went on leisurely and at a comfortable pace. No one got excited. Nothing was rushed or driven, and if, once in a while, there really was a burst of bitter words, it was only to provide a change. Life would certainly become monotonous if the valves didn't pop open occasionally.

The hands on the hacienda were Totonac Indians, like the owner. They weren't paid much. They certainly weren't. But every family had its hut with a roomy patio. The family could keep as many cattle as it liked, and in proportion to its number raise on the land whatever seemed necessary for its support.

For generations the families residing here had lived on the hacienda, and nearly all of them were related by marriage to the owner. Several of the families, in fact, owed their origins to the great procreative ability of one of Jacinto's ancestors. Jacinto was the godfather of nearly all the children born on the hacienda, and Señora Yañez was the godmother. In Mexico *el padrino*, the godfather, and *la madrina*, hold a vitally important position in the family circle. This stemmed from far in the Indians' distant past. In spite of the frequent marriage of Spanish men and Indian women, many Indian habits and practices survived in the customs of the Mexican people—especially where they involved house, kitchen, and family relations, all those matters, in fact, affecting the wife's domain, where the husband is usually passive and neutral.

In the old Mexico, Indian Mexico, the godfather meant as much to the child as his own father—and that is still so to this day. In many cases if the father dies or, for whatever reason, proves himself incompetent to raise the child, it is the godfather who assumes all the rights and duties of the father. The godfather has to see to the child's welfare. Even if public law does not compel him to fulfill his duty in regard to a child who needs help, he still cannot avoid it, for that would then cause him to lose prestige and respect, just as if he had done some other evil deed that the law excuses but his own social circle does not.

The child's father calls the godfather "compadre" and the godmother "comadre." Both godfather and father call each other "compadre," and godmother and mother call each other "comadre."

For these reasons the child's father and the godfather regard themselves as brothers, and the relation between them is often more affectionate than that between blood brothers, because the choice is a voluntary one, depending on the sympathy two people feel for each other.

If the Indian farm worker chooses the patron, the master of the hacienda, to be godfather of his child, then the patron accepts. He is never too proud to accept, for he considers it an honor to be selected as godfather. That runs in the Indian blood. And from that moment on, the patron is addressed by the worker, the father of the child, as "compadre." And the patron no longer says, "Hey, Juan!" to the worker, but calls him "compadre," though the strictly economic rank of the two has not changed. From now on they are brothers and treat each other like brothers.

This relation exists on all the Mexican haciendas where the owner and the people are of Indian descent. Such a relation produces situations which are perhaps found nowhere else on earth.

The hacienda belongs to the patron. It belonged to his family even before Columbus was born. For the forebear who was founder of the family was an Indian prince, a chieftain of a Totonac branch having its home in the region. The patron considers himself as only the beneficiary of the hacienda. He feels responsible for the welfare of everyone who lives on it. He does not dress better than those who work on the hacienda. He wears the *tilma*, as they do, and sandals. He eats tortillas and frijoles like all the rest. But the relation between them is nonetheless quite different from the patriarchal relation existing on the old European farmstead, where farmhand and milkmaid sat at the same table with the farmer and his wife.

On haciendas where the patron is a Mexican of non-Indian families, their own households. The patron is judge of all their affairs, their advisor, letter writer (if he can write at all), doctor, lawyer, defender against authorities who ask the impossible. He is their provider after bad harvests and the guardian of their widows and orphans. Still, he is never *the* master. He never enriches himself at their expense. He has more cattle than the others, more corn, more beans, and a bit more money. A bit more, not much. For far too many families live on the hacienda. The families procreate. They increase plentifully. And all the young couples starting new families want to stay on the hacienda. Lands and means must be provided for them all, and they are provided. Indeed, the patron must have a bit more than the rest, for he has twenty times the responsibilities of the rest.

On hacienda where the patron is a Mexican of non-Indian descent, matters are completely different. Then there are masters and servants, for money has to be earned. The hacienda must be made productive so that it can be sold at a thousand percent profit to someone who would like to sell it in turn for a thousand percent profit. On those haciendas, of course, there are no compadres and no comadres.

Jacinto Yañez, the patron of the White Rose, was indeed an Indian. And because he was an Indian and followed the old Indian laws—without knowing their wording, since he carried them in his blood—any clash between him and an American oil company had to lead to tragedy. Against a giant business that needed to make millions in order to guarantee to its stockholders luxury yachts and buying sprees in Paris, the weapons he knew how to use, and was accustomed to using, had to fail.

The Condor Oil Company had already acquired the other haciendas in the area in the usual way. These estates had been divided into lots, numbered from one to seventy-eight.

But one pearl was missing from the crown of the Condor Oil Company. That pearl was the most beautiful of all, the hacienda Rosa Blanca, the White Rose.

All around it was oil land, where the richest wells poured out in thick streams the black gold, streams so powerful that at the first blowout they shot five hundred feet into the air with the ear-shattering roar of fifty locomotives blowing off steam simultaneously. The richest of these wells lay on the borders of the hacienda.

The Condor Oil Company had to gain possession of the White Rose, even if it had to bring about a war between the States and

Mexico in order to do it. In any case, the company's directors would not go to war. They were too old for that. And even if they hadn't been too old, their doctors would have said they were run down or diabetic or had heart defects.

Señor Yañez was offered a lease at ten dollars an acre each year for twenty years, along with an eight percent share of the profits.

But Jacinto said to the agent: "I can't do that. I can't lease the hacienda. I have no right to it. My father didn't lease it. Nor my *abuelo*, my grandfather. Nor his father. I must preserve it for those who will follow after me. They'll also need to eat. And they will have to preserve it for those who come after them. It's always been like that. I got the orange and nut trees from my father. And I wouldn't have them if he hadn't planted any. So I must replant seedlings so that those who will be alive after I'm gone will have oranges, lemons, and nuts. So it has always been on the hacienda. Surely you can understand that, Señor Pallares?"

Of course Señor Pallares, the buyer for the Condor Oil Company, could not understand. He had never owned land, and his father had never owned any. He was only a *licenciado*, a lawyer, as his father had been.

He returned to the company and said that Jacinto was crazy.

At that the manager said, if Jacinto was crazy, they could get him sent to the nuthouse.

Jacinto would not have been the first person sent to an insane asylum to rot away and die there because an oil company couldn't get his property in any other way. Dozens of Mexicans had been sent to institutions because they refused to sell. Obviously, anyone who refuses to sell his land for a price that is a thousand times higher than it was before oil was found in the vicinity is crazy.

Another agent arrived. Again he was a Mexican. And again he was a lawyer—Señor Perez.

He arrived with a large money bag, bringing the glittering gold along with him. Not all of it, but indeed a considerable part. He was hoping the sight of all that beautiful coined gold would cause Jacinto to weaken.

Licenciado Perez was not offering a lease. He was going to buy the hacienda outright. That paid more, and therefore it presented a greater temptation.

"But I really cannot sell the hacienda, Señor Licenciado," Jacinto said in his calm, stoical way. Since time had no definite meaning to him, he never allowed himself to be rushed when he was speaking. "I really cannot sell the hacienda. It doesn't belong to me at all."

"What!" Señor Perez said. "Doesn't belong to you? That's news to me. The records show it's your property."

Jacinto laughed. "Naturally it belongs to me, Rosa Blanca. Just as it once belonged to my father. But it doesn't belong to my father anymore. I mean, the hacienda doesn't belong to me in such a way that I can do with it what I like. It also belongs to those who will be alive after I go. I am responsible for them. I am only the steward for those who will want to live, and will live, later. Just as my father was only a steward—and his father and his father's father, and so on back into the past, and so on into the future."

"That's silly, Señor Yañez. Let the others take care of themselves. You can surely give the money to your children or leave it to them. They can become doctors or lawyers, or they can buy a nice shop where they can earn a lot of money and buy themselves an automobile."

"But they still won't have any land," Jacinto said stubbornly. "They'll still have to eat. How are they going to eat if they don't raise corn?"

"Don't be so dense," Señor Perez said. "Your descendants are certainly going to be able to buy corn for the tortillas. They surely will have enough money."

"But corn still has to be raised. Someone has to plant it. And land is needed for that. An automobile is perhaps pretty enough, but it certainly isn't corn. And it isn't meat, either. Or beans or peppers."

Perez gave up trying to deal in this way any further with the stupid Indian. He attacked from a different direction.

"You're getting old, right?"

"No," Jacinto answered. "I'm not growing old. When I grow old, I'm dead. I'm not growing old. My father didn't grow old. He dropped dead the moment he thought he couldn't work anymore. He wasn't old. He worked up to his last day. And, I repeat, I can't sell the land because those who come after me must also have land."

He began to recite all over again what he had already said to Licenciado Pallares about the orange trees and nut trees and how subsequent generations would reproach him if he cared for them badly or if they had to starve because he had given the land away.

But even as he was speaking, he recalled that he had told all this to someone else once before. And he could see that his words were making not the slightest impression on Señor Perez. He realized that Señor Perez, though he was an educated lawyer, understood nothing at all about land and duties and all the things that seemed so important to Jacinto. Then a new thought occurred to him. Until that moment he had thought only of his own descendents when he spoke of those who would come after him and need to eat—and not at all about posterity in general.

But now, as if someone had told him purely by thought transference, it dawned on him that he had still greater obligations. They were greater than those he had to his own descendents: what would become of the compadres and comadres? What of the sixty families who lived on the hacienda? If he sold it, all of them would be disinherited, dispossessed, uprooted. They all were his children, wards, protégés, charges. How could he abandon them and deprive them of the land? They were his flesh and blood, just as much as the offspring of his own body. "No, I can't sell the hacienda, Licenciado." He said it now with greater assurance than before. "The hacienda doesn't belong to me. It belongs to my compadres as well. What would they do then?"

Senor Perez lit a cigarette and played with the matchstick for a while, as if he were searching for the best answer so that he could defeat Jacinto with a single sentence. When he had completely splintered the matchstick, he said, "The people? They could all get work in the camps. And earn much more there than they earn here on the hacienda. What do they get here? Fifty centavos a day? Maybe eighty. People in the camps earn five pesos and work only eight hours. And have it a lot easier. Buy themselves boots and silk clothing and shoes and perfume for their wives. If they save up their money and don't drink it all up, they're soon able to buy themselves a store."

Jacinto didn't understand this. He knew nothing of what was being said. In his mind there was a single thought, one simple thought. But it was so strong that it encompassed and explained to him the whole world and all its problems. All problems were definitely solved in this one thought. He could not express it in the pretty words of a poet or the elegant flourishes of a scholar or even the numerical confusion of a sociologist. He could only repeat again and again in one short, simple sentence: "But they won't have any land, and then they won't be able to raise corn."

The word "corn" had for him, the Indian, the same meaning that the words, "Give us this day our daily bread," have for the European. Today, today, dear Lord, for we cannot wait until tomorrow. We're hungry today, and if we don't have bread today, we'll be dead tomorrow.

To the lawyer the continual repetition of the same sentence was boring. In fact, Jacinto didn't know any other sentence. All his wisdom was contained in this sentence, just as the wisdom of all mankind was rooted forever in these words: "Land is bread, and bread is life!"

But Licenciado Perez knew that corn could be bought everywhere. Only money was needed for that. And a person could earn money. Easily. With the money the company had promised him if he agreed to the sale, Jacinto could buy himself a shipload of corn. Corn, corn, and more corn. The stupid Indians thought of nothing else.

Still, with all his cleverness and legal learning, Licenciado Perez never gave a thought to the fact that someone surely had to raise corn if people wanted to have it or buy it. Corn still had to be grown somewhere. But the lawyer inhabited another world, a world where land and corn could be separated without his ever seeing the problems that developed from the separation. In his world the connection of corn and land, man and land, was completely severed. In his world people no longer thought of "corn," but only of "product." In his world people said, "What do those who come after us have to do with us? After us, the end of the world, with television in the bedroom. Land? What is land? We need land only for the production of oil that goes into feeding our automobiles. Corn? Land for corn? To hell with this crazy Indian. If we need corn, we'll make it with machines and sell it in tin cans."

"Jacinto," Señor Perez said confidentially. He was speaking insistently, as you might speak to a brother who has run away from home to persuade him to return because his mother is crying her eyes out. "Jacinto, be reasonable for once! I won't cheat you."

"I didn't think you would," Jacinto answered.

"I am going to buy the land from you honestly, for a good price."

"But Señor Licenciado, I really cannot—"

"Stop! Stop!" Señor Perez broke in, in a tone that one uses to address a sick man who must not be agitated. "Sure, Jacinto, you cannot sell it."

"No, I can't," the Indian said as stubbornly as before. "I haven't any right to do it. The land doesn't belong to me."

"Don't repeat that nonsense again. I've found the records and read through them. The land does belong to you. The title is in excellent order. I've never seen such a good, clear title before. The land belongs to you and you can do with it whatever you like—lease it or sell it or give it away."

"But my compadres and those who follow . . ."

Señor Perez, practiced in the wiles of clever lawyers, gave the Indian no time to get set in the old persistent thoughts. He already knew what was coming, and so he attacked at once. "All the men of the families you have here on the hacienda will get work in the camps of the Condor Company. I promise you that. I'll make it a condition in the sales contract. They'll be paid no less than three pesos a day, and if they are skillful and learn on the job, four and even five pesos."

"Yes, I believe that," Jacinto said, "that the peons earn that much in the camps. The muchacho of José here worked in a camp, and he received four pesos. Pedro's youngster also worked in a camp; he needs to earn money because he expects to get married, and the father-in-law is asking a cow for the girl. But Marcos, he worked in the camps, and he has come home again. He says he'll never go into a camp again even if they pay him ten pesos. He'd rather stay here on the land. He says he was always sad in the camp, and here he is always laughing."

"He's simply a blockhead, that kid. You have to be able to take it if you expect to make money," the lawyer said. And, like all those in his profession, he was right.

He now turned the conversation in another direction. "When you have all this here money, Jacinto, you'll be able to buy yourself an automobile."

"I don't need an automobile," Jacinto said indifferently.

"But, *hombre,* then you can get to Tuxpan in half an hour."

"I've never wanted to get to Tuxpan in a half hour. I like to speak to people along the way and see how the corn looks and what the little ones are doing—I know them all—and I want to look at the branches of the blue flowers up close. I want to know whether the big turtles in the lagoon have laid eggs in the sand. And there's that heavy mahogany tree that snapped off four years ago and fell across the road and still won't rot away. I've already built two fires under it, to burn through it. But the job's still not done. We always have to ride round it."

"Stupid, stupid," Señor Perez said, half aloud. And then, out loud: "But, you see, in an auto . . ."

"When I want to go to Tuxpan to sell hogs or bring back a new hat for Nazario, I take the yellow *macho* and ride early, around three thirty, and I get to Tuxpan by nine. That's just time enough. And I've seen everything along the way. I've talked to Raphael, who has been putting a new thatch roof on his house because the old one leaked. Moreover, I still arrive in Tuxpan plenty early. I don't need an automobile. I really don't, Licenciado."

Once again Señor Perez saw his plan frustrated and it was a visible effort for him to find a new way to make possession of a lot of money enticing to Jacinto.

Before he could conceive of something new that would perhaps increase Jacinto's understanding of the financial world, the Indian found an answer to the lawyer's offer to find places as workers in the oil fields for all the compadres. He hadn't been able to work it out in his head as quickly as a lawyer, who was practiced in that. It took him longer, but he hit the mark all the same. And he hit it more exactly than Perez had expected.

"That's really very good if the men here are going to be working in the oil fields. Maybe they really can work and make some money. But once the wells are drilled, there'll be no more work here for those people. And they won't be getting any more money, either."

"The company isn't drilling wells just here. It has a lot of land. So the people from here will be sent on to the new fields."

But now Jacinto was definitely on the right track. "But in that place, where our men will be sent, surely there are people on the land who will want work. What are they going to do?"

Señor Perez felt trapped. Without pausing to think about it, he blurted out: "Those people will have to go even farther to see where they can find work."

"But once the land really has been bought up from them, how will they be able to live when our men arrive there? They surely won't have land any longer. They'll all have to starve to death. And drilling doesn't go on forever. A day will come when there's no more oil. And by then all the men will have forgotten how corn is raised."

All problems are simplified when there is land enough and the people know how to cultivate it, but the simplest questions suddenly became complicated as soon as people are torn away from the soil. Señor Perez himself grasped this now. The Indian had completely thrown him from his secure position in society. Jacinto had challenged all the wisdom that Señor Perez had spent a lifetime acquiring. If he had been facing another lawyer, an educated man, even a businessman from a large city, he would have been able to dispose of these problems one way or another. With another man who lived in the city, with the prospects offered by bourgeois society, he would have been able to settle the questions. They would certainly arrive at a solution that satisfied both, since they both spoke the same language. They would have been able to talk about laws that were needed, of parliamentary acts and presidential proclamations, of the possiblities of better transportation, of the mass production of essential economic products, mass production as a result of sweeping applications of efficient machines and scientific theories. Yet the question remained open. Where will we get land? Making corn from petroleum by-products or coal slack—that seemed a bit farfetched even to a lawyer.

Señor Perez felt quite helpless against the startling simplicity with which Jacinto viewed the problems of society and human existence. He could not get through to the Indian. It was as if the Indian were on another planet, and the lawyer could never cross over to it.

The Indian wasn't aware that he had bested the lawyer. He didn't know that anyone could think differently from him, the Indian, who lived in and through the soil, a product of the soil. Like a tree.

That is why he could not be overcome by the weapon that the lawyer, considering it his strongest, had saved for last.

CHAPTER TWO

SEÑOR PEREZ took the fat canvas bag in his hand, weighed it thoughtfully, and then, with a quick movement, shook out the entire contents, ten-peso gold coins—hidalgos, because they were stamped with the portrait of the Mexican freedom fighter.

Perez began to count out the money as if the sale were already concluded, stacking the coins in little columns, laying fifty hidalgos one on top of another. It all looked very pretty.

At last he had arranged four hundred such columns like soldiers in rank and file.

Pleasantly, almost reverently, he surveyed the regiment and said: "The company is paying you two hundred gold pesos for an acre.

Two thousand acres is four hundred thousand pesos. There are only two hundred thousand here. So you'll get another pile just like this. Tomorrow if you like."

The impression Perez had hoped to make was not forthcoming. The Indian had absolutely no appreciation of so much money. If someone had plunked a mountain of corn or five hundred hogs down in front of him he would have understood that. Of course, he wouldn't have sold Rosa Blanca for them. The corn would be eaten up soon enough, and the hogs, too. And then what? Those who were to come would begin to die of hunger. A man can rely only on the earth. It produces forever and ever, in inexhaustible liberality, ever and again repeating the cycle of virginal purity, trembling love, hot reception, exultant bearing, contented decline, and then, once again, the quiet and holy new germination of touching virginity, trembling love, and so on eternally, like the rising and setting of the sun, the waxing and waning of the moon.

But coins, corn, hogs—as many of these as there were—they existed but once, and never again.

Jacinto really knew the value of a hidalgo very well. It was, depending on the market, two hundred or three hundred or sometimes only one hundred and fifty pounds of corn. It was a full-grown hog of medium size. A hidalgo, ten pesos, was a lot of money, a great deal of money. But this regiment of gold coins marshaled out across the tabletop made no impression on him. Their value did not impress him. It was a magician's illusion. Such a value did not exist.

"They look very pretty, Licenciado," he said at last, in polite acknowledgment of the lawyer's trick.

"It all belongs to you, Jacinto," Perez said, suddenly using the familiar "thou" to seem right brotherly. "It's all yours, plus this much more, for this is only half of it. For Rosa Blanca."

The lawyer might just as well have been offering the money to Jacinto in exchange for the right to chop his head off.

As it happened, that golden regiment did not come alive for Jacinto. It did not awaken any hopes. These columns had no hold over him, and could acquire no hold over him, because there before his eyes stood something greater, something higher, holier.

What he had, he had taken over from his father, not to possess it, but to hold it and someday pass it on to his successors. What he had was only borrowed, was his only to preserve for coming generations. It was his solemn duty to give the borrowed estate back undiminished when the time came. What could he say when he someday met his forefathers in the happy hunting ground and they asked him, "What did you do with our estate? What did you do with the property of our grandsons and great-grandsons?" He would have to creep away in shame into the darkest, remotest corner of the woods, where the sun never shone and the moon never let its soft silvery rays slip in. And then what if all the fathers of his compadres came and asked him, "What did you do to our sons and daughters?" And that would go on into the farthest, sempiternal time. Every thirty or forty or fifty years new men would arrive in the verdent hunting ground and ask him: "Where is the estate that your father entrusted to you for us?" They would drag him out of his secluded corner and toss him back again when he could not answer. So it would go on for ever and ever. With never any rest. Never.

And so, as the coins before him remained lifeless, Rosa Blanca received, at the same instant, even as it was being fought over, all life. It took on form. It spoke to him. It smiled at him. It became a person. He heard it singing.

He could bear it no longer. He stood up and stepped into the open door.

Standing there, he surveyed the patio. Today, as usual, it looked untidy. He was always going to change this or that a hundred times already. He was always going to change it when he saw it, and always it was forgotten and stayed the same as before.

There in the corner, right by the fence, lay an old broken cartwheel from a mule cart whose existence no one at the hacienda could recall.

That cartwheel was rotting away slowly because it was made from good iron-hard wood. Every Saturday it should have been cleared away, and every Sunday morning when Jacinto stepped out onto the portico the cartwheel was still lying in its corner.

Jacinto recalled that it had been lying there when he was five years old. His father had said: "That old cartwheel can also be burnt. Manuel can chop it up tomorrow evening and carry the wood in to the women in the kitchen."

His instructions were forgotten and the wheel was not chopped up.

Then the father said again when he saw it: "Maybe that wheel can be used for something. I'll talk to Manual about what he thinks can be done with it."

When he was about eight, Jacinto had climbed about in the spokes with the intention of making his body supple like that of a snake.

For a while it served as a place to leash a young coyote he and other youngsters had found. They were going to tame the coyote and turn it into a dog. But one night the coyote chewed through the leash and disappeared.

Then, once again, the wheel was going to be burnt. Then again, with Manuel's help, it was going to be used for something. Then, as a young man, Jacinto had sat on the wheel in the evenings—this was during his courting days—and dreamed of the girl who was now his wife. Sitting on it, he had hummed sweet ranch songs to himself. And many a night he had squatted on it and quietly cried to himself because he believed she would not have him.

Then, a bit later, he had cuddled on it with her in the night, and in ten places or more he had carved notches for the hugs she gave him—or for whatever else it might have been. He knew very well what he cut the notches for.

Then the father died.

But the old, broken cartwheel still lay there. And always in the same place.

Then the old major-domo also died—Manuel, who so often had been given the task of chopping up the wheel or using it for something.

Still, the wheel was not disturbed by the death of either man. It lay there and lay there.

And so, for years, when the courtyard was cleaned up every Saturday, Jacinto gave the order to get rid of the wheel for good. And every Sunday morning when he stepped out on to the portico to look at the weather, the cartwheel still was lying there. Until next Saturday. But something certainly would have been missing from the patio if the cartwheel was not lying there on Sunday.

And so it was still lying there now—peaceful, imperturbable, enduring, proud—and waited for the final decay.

Now Jacinto's eldest son, Domingo, often sat, alone and lost, on the wheel and carved notches, as his father had readily noticed. He also knew who the girl was.

Indeed, what Jacinto knew even better was that the cartwheel would still be lying there when he himself was called away. For the wheel was no lifeless hunk of decaying old mahogany. The wheel was a symbol—a symbol of the race that peopled the Republic, a race that was, is, and always will be the same. It could not be moved. The cartwheel had become ageless.

Turning his gaze away from the wheel, Jacinto saw Emilio, the cook's son, squatting on the ground with a wicker basket in front of him. He was shelling corn off the cob with another cob. That was the way corn had been shelled here for five thousand years—more, twenty thousand. A cornsheller could shell more corn in five minutes than the lad could shell in two hours, but it cost sixty pesos, or forty-five at least. It should have been bought back when the father was still alive. Jacinto had intended to buy one a hundred times. But perhaps they could still do without it for a while. It's been like this for fifty thousand years. Why, then, did he have to buy one this week? What was the hurry? The machine could wait. Emilio really had nothing else to do; he was always going off to hunt rabbits. In that case, he might just as well shell corn. At least he would develop strong hands and fingers from that, and they could be useful to him later in life.

Over there, near the wall that enclosed the wide patio, Margarito, the hacienda's major-domo, was standing, doctoring two mules whose backs had been chafed by packs. He was carefully washing the sores with black soap and hot water, singing as he worked.

He was singing a *corrido*, an ancient ranch song about a beautiful Indian maid who loved an Indian lad, oh so much, so very much. But then there came rushing along a Mexican with a big red hat and heavy silver spurs, oh so proud, so very proud, rushing along on a white charger, oh so white, so very white, rushing along. And the proud, masterful Mexican on the white charger and with the heavy silver spurs spoke many honeyed words, oh so sweet, so very sweet *palabras*. And he seduced the Indian maid who was so afraid, so very afraid, of the proud Mexican in the big red, oh so red, so very red sombrero. And so the Indian maid got a small child, an oh so small, so very small a child, and then the Indian maid, *la mamacita tan morena,* died with her little child in the deep, oh so deep, so very deep woods. And a blue flower, oh so blue, so very blue a flower, fell on her grave, which the ants, oh so busy, so very busy, had built over the dead maiden.

Even as Margarito is singing the hundred and twentieth stanza—or however many there may be—Jacinto hears in his soul, in a half minute, the whole long song, for he knows it all, and sang it while courting, with tears constantly in his eyes. And as Margarito sings and repeats the rhyme, devoutly, fervently, he interrupts himself at times and cries out to the mule: *"Caramba,* damn it, you sonofabitch, you bastard, stand still now or *por la santa Purissima,* I'll really kick you right in the damned ass, you stinking son-ofabitch!"

But these occasional lapses into the brutal reality of the hard working life do not interfere with the Indian's lyrical outpouring. After this earthy lapse he sings along again without noticeable dissonance in a calm melodious way about the beautiful Indian maid who was seduced and deceived by a proud Mexican in a red hat, on a fiery white charger. Discordant notes are foreign to Margarito. Everything goes together, and everything is in harmony.

Jacinto is Margarito's *compadre.* He is godfather of all his children, and Margarito's father is godfather of two of Jacinto's children—the oldest, Domingo, and Juana. Margarito's lineage is not entirely clear, or so everyone pretends. But everybody on the hacienda knows it—and anybody else who wants to know it is told—Jacinto's father is also Margarito's father. Margarito himself regards this as likely. In any case, he never denies it. And his mother, who is still alive, tending the chickens on the hacienda and helping in the house, says nothing one way or the other. She is neither proud of the rumor nor ashamed of it. If the Lord did her the great honor of blessing her with children, the identity of the father was immaterial. Fathers are sent as a means to an end. The question of feeding the children does not arise, for corn and beans grow on the hacienda in plenty, and everyone who lives there has a right to the corn and beans and chickens and hogs. Whether there are twenty or fifty additional children eating there, parceled out among the families, with their father considering it an honor and a blessing from heaven to be their father—even if he isn't—all that is unimportant. The patron doesn't even notice. The children, all the children, are sent from heaven, and so they have a right to live. If there isn't any father, there is still the patron. He feeds the children, must feed the children according to Indian law, and does feed them gladly, law or no law. Laws that do not exist deep in the blood haven't any value in any case.

And Jacinto looks across to the scattered huts and the sloping adobe houses where they all live. A small people, but a genuine people with a genuine king. But the king here is not a despot living in luxury on what his people slave to provide for him. He is nothing but a steward, an advisor, and his entire kingly prerogative consists of being responsible for the welfare of those his fathers entrusted to him, not as slaves, but as equals. Over thousands of years his forebears came to an understanding: only one family should manage the people's land at any given time. With this decision they prevented rivalries and wars among the tribesmen over the position of manager and over leadership of the next generation. The people here have no time for such conflicts, no time to calm the hatred that endures in people after such conflicts. Such small people are always disturbed in their order—what seems to us their primitive structure and cohesion—if a clan or tribe of city dwellers, of city builders, makes it appearance. Cities must absorb men en masse in order to survive and flourish. And since these masses inhabit less land than is needed to feed them, they invade the people who are directly attached to the soil. They then construct a system in which the townsman turns into tyrant and the farmer into helot.

From the huts the smoke of the ovens drifted out through the ever-open doors and gaps in the walls. In front of several huts women were kneeling before the *metate* and grinding corn. The pigs, chickens, turkeys, burros, birds, and animals of the woods and jungle that were domesticated and accustomed to the house, small deer, raccoons, dogs, and cats, ran loose around the patio and pressed against a woman who was squatting before a *metate*. When she straightened up a bit to wipe the sweat from her brow, she would throw a bit of cornmeal among the hungry guests in the yard. As they began a wild battle over it, the woman laughed and went at her work again with renewed energy, work that a handmill does in three minutes, and at which the Indian woman sits for an hour and uses all her strength. But a handmill cost fifteen pesos, and what was going to be done with the time left over when the chore was finished in three minutes. It was a much greater pleasure to have all the animals around, and all the children among them. In those three minutes at the handmill, the animals could not gather, the children couldn't scamper about and scream and yell with the animals, nor could one see and experience as much. When the raccoon went at the cat or the dog was annoyed by the turkey, that was life. The handmill wasn't life or laughter. With the use of a handmill it would have been impossible for the wife to tell her husband, when he came home from work, all the comical incidents that happened while she was grinding corn.

In an old barrel hoop near another hut a parrot was sitting. It was not tied down. This parrot played the most insane tricks on the children, cats, dogs, and pigs. When he sat there on his shelf during meals and received his two tortillas, he ate only a bit. He dropped most of the pieces for a certain pig that he favored. It was a small, fierce, gray, nasty pig. But Loro the parrot loved it. He only dropped the crumbs when that pig stood under the shelf. If another pig was there or if chickens were running about to snap up a morsel, then Loro did not drop anything. The pig so beloved by the parrot looked up to him as to a god given to the world. The family living in the hut had seen this a thousand times, but every day at noon the children trooped out to see it again. They couldn't see it often enough. If another pig caught the tidbits the parrot dropped for its pet, the parrot cried out like one possessed: "*Cochino!* Pig!" This was the only word he knew, aside from "*Como estas?* How are you?"

Now, standing on the portico, Jacinto heard the cry, "*Cochino! Cochino!*" He knew it, knew the parrot, knew the family, knew it all, everything. The squawking of the scolding parrot came to him not as a single sound, but as a note, one among the hundred thousand in the eternal, familiar, native song of Rosa Blanca. Every noise, every tear, the lowing of the cattle, the grunting of the pigs, the cackling of the chickens, the crowing of the roosters, the gobbling of the turkeys, the shouting of the children, the whimpering of the infants, the occasional barking of a dog, the flapping of tortillas in the huts, the buzzing of the flies, the gossip and chatter of the women in the kitchen, the cursing and abjurations of Margarito as he tended to the mules, the squeaking of the cabin door opening just then, the sobbing of a youngster whose mother had boxed him soundly around the ears because he had smashed a jug, the call of an Indian away off in the fields, the chirping of the locusts and crickets, the soft soughing of the sun-shafted blue air above him—all these blended for him into a single song, the eternal song of a Mexican hacienda. Here it was the inimitable song of the White Rose.

Far beyond the huts he saw women coming up the hill with jars on their heads, carrying water home from the stream. The women went barefoot, with their black hair, freshly washed in the river, hanging loose. They were wearing long red-and-green striped dresses twisted round their slender hips, and white blouses with short sleeves and red embroidery on the bodice. His wife dressed the same way. Only when Jacinto took her with him to Tuxpan to the *tianguis*, to the marketplace, did she wear a calico dress and shoes. But she never had a hat. Never in her life. Never anything but the shawl of the land—the *rebozo*.

From the fields the men were leisurely sauntering home to dinner. Some were carrying machetes in their hands, and others mattocks over their shoulders. Several were smoking. Several were whistling. The youngsters who had been out with their fathers were squealing and playing tag with one another. The door of the little chapel was decorated with fresh flowers for next Sunday's fiesta.

All this Jacinto was seeing now as though for the first time in his life. Never before had he heard the song of the White Rose sung so perfectly. And never before had he felt so strongly that he was the heart of the whole thing here, that if he should be released from his responsibility, then everything would collapse. The families would destroy themselves, ancient ties would be ruptured, the son would no longer know his father, the nephew his uncle. Rose Blanca would no longer be the ancestral home of a people. It would exist in the memory of the ranch's children only as a place where their fathers once worked. Nothing else would connect the children to Rose Blanca in its soul. Rose Blanca would be like the factory in the city where the father works, something necessary, but something to which one has no personal connection. The families would travel from place to place until the father found work that would assure his family its daily bread. Nothing could be more certain than that. Today a good salary, tomorrow unemployment. But as long as the sun rose and set, Rosa Blanca had work and food. But that there exists in this world something that guarantees a man the certainty of food and life—this fact the children will have forgotten. Sustenance will come only from the factory, the oil field, the copper mine, the textile plant, where all the workers are numbers and wear badges that are hung up on a board when they leave the factory in the evening.

Jacinto did not know all this. He knew only that when his compadres, when all those here who were more or less his children, no longer had a Rosa Blanca, then something horrible would happen to them. It would be something like what happens to a fish when it is cast up on the sand, or to a tree when it is dug up and left to lie on a rockpile in the sun.

For fewer than five minutes Jacinto had been standing there on the portico trying to figure out whether there was a way out. Those five minutes seemed to him like an entire lifetime. In those five minutes he had lived not only with the present, but also with the future. He had talked with the forefathers, with whom he was not acquainted, but of whom he knew they were his forebears. He had talked with his descendants, of whom he similarly knew they were his blood, his race, even though he was not acquainted with them. It had already become more difficult to find the descendants. He had had to search them out in spirit far from Rosa Blanca, abroad in the Republic and even up in the United States.

For they were no longer living on Rosa Blanca.

Rosa Blanca had become Lots 95 through 144 of the Condor Oil Company, Inc. Rosa Blanca was a plot of ground dotted with tall, dreary oil derricks.

Where orange and lemon trees once stood, where the crowns of papaya trees once waved in the flickering light, bathing the ripening fruit in the sun, where once there were green cornfields, where once the golden spikes of ripening cane whispered unending fairy tales, heavy trucks with caterpillar tracks groaned and rattled pitilessly over the quaking ground, which buckled in pain here and crunched in anger there as it was squeezed between the steel treads.

A maze of iron pipes covered the fields. And above it was a grid of electric cables and telephone lines.

Wherever one looked clouds of steam were hissing, puffing out like thick clouds of fog. The ground, muddy and marshy with oil, stank dreadfully and befouled the air.

Everywhere there were shouts and orders, curses and tears. Steampipes howled. Cables screeched shrilly above the creaking wheels and rollers.

Files of pipe-carrying Indians marched about the fields like slaves on chains, spurred on by cursing overseers.

The sun-shafted air, once so full of jubilant song, was now filled with the groaning and gasping, the rattle and clatter, the stamping and thumping of machinery and pumps.

Of Jacinto's descendants none remained here, except one. And he was stumbling along in the line of pipe-carrying slaves who received two pesos fifty a day—and who were let go if they were not obedient or had crushed a foot when a pipe fell on it.

This one of his descendants Jacinto encountered in spirit. He stopped him: "How do you like it here, *hijito,* my son?" The descendant answered: "Good, padre, thank you. I get two pesos fifty. In Pachuca, in the silver mines, I got only one peso seventy. I have eight children. It is hard to raise them. Corn now costs twenty-two centavos a kilo and half is holey from maggots. But I can't stand here talking to you any longer, *padrecito mio,* for if the foreman sees me standing here gabbing away, he'll chuck me out. It's not so easy to find other work. And I have eight children." He bent down and kissed Jacinto's hand. Then he quickly sprang back into the line of marching, pipe-carrying slaves.

Jacinto really should have had nothing to think about. He was indeed the legal owner of Rosa Blance. Still he considered it a good idea to deliberate for a while. He knew from other rancheros: Once an American petroleum company wants your land, it is difficult to defend it. You can't pay your lawyer as much as the company pays its lawyer. And you may even have to defend yourself against your own government, and that is just as difficult as defending against an American oil company. The government gets large revenues from oil export taxes, so it sees to it that a lot of oil is produced and exported. The government needs the money to build roads and schools and to pay a high per diem to the deputies in the parliament in order to keep them as friends. Being a deputy is a business, just like distilling whiskey or handling silk or publishing a newspaper.

The deputy cannot work for a *centavito* when he is obliged to deliberate on the welfare of the people. Just as the church cannot save souls and the teacher of the true faith cannot preach for nothing. On the wages of God—of which it is said they are so sweet—only those who will never grow wise will wait. Deputies and soul-savers, however, belong among the wise. For hath not the Lord already said: Be wise like the serpent and take it when you can get it, for truly, miserable are the heavy-laden, and if thine is the power, the others will have to be slaves unto you, so that neither is the widow's mite to be despised.

Jacinto awoke from his daydream.

"*Oye*, compadre," he called over to Margarito, who was still tending to the mules with black soap, hot water, and ranch songs. "*Ven aca,* come here."

"*Que paso*, compadre?" Margarito answered as he sauntered across the patio. "What is it?"

When Margarito was standing before him, Jacinto said: "There is a *caballero* inside in the *sala*. He is looking for workers for the oil fields. Would you like to accept?"

"Me? Take a job? What do you mean by that, compadre?" Margarito asked in amazement. "Who would be major-domo then?"

"We'll manage to get along all right."

Margarito thought for a moment. "How much is he paying, then, this fellow?"

"Four pesos a day."

"A day?" Margarito asked in disbelief.

"Yes, a day."

"Good money. Really, good money."

"*Claro.*"

"How long does he have work?"

"As long as you like. Three months, six months, or forever," Jacinto said.

"That's too long. I don't stay away that long. I'm willing to go for three months. Then I'll be coming home again."

"No, you can't do that," Jacinto said.

"What? Not come back? What then? Not come back. Why?" Margarito could not understand not being able to return to Rosa Blanca, to his homeland.

"The caballero is taking on workers only if they are going to go on working with the company. Forever. When the work is finished here in the neighborhood, the people will be sent along to other camps." Jacinto was simply telling the bare truth.

"Never return to Rosa Blanca. Never?" Margarito mused. "No, in that case I'm not going. Four pesos a day. Damn. But never to return here, to have to stay forever in the camps where it stinks so much and the people are always fighting and beating up on each other. No, compadre, tell him I'd just as soon not go. Four pesos is very good money. But no, I can't go. You can also tell him—that gentleman—he won't be able to get any people here if they can't come back again and have to stay away forever. He can get enough workers in the city. No one from here will be going."

"Three youngsters have gone already," Jacinto recalled.

"Oh, sure," Margarito said. "But one, Marcos, has already come back. He's not going to go out into the fields again. He says nothing should be like that. Just work, and never any fun. The foreman is always behind you hounding and scolding no matter how much you work. Pedro's boy is still there so he'll get the dowry for his girl friend together quicker. And José's kid may never come back because José won't let him into the house any more. He got mixed up with a B-girl there and was going to marry her. So that's the situation with him. Four pesos. *Olé!* Well, I'm certainly not going voluntarily. There is so much stench there, and shouting and complaining. And what are the mules and the horses going to do if I'm not here? They really only listen to me. And I won't be able to see anymore whether the calf is being weaned from the cow, and how the steers are fighting it out to see which is the strongest. And then the little pigs and chickens on top of that. And the children will also be left alone. If I take them with me to the camp, they have no place for them there, and I wouldn't know what they were doing all day long. On the whole, compadre, if I can't come back here to Rosa Blanca— You can certainly tell the caballero that I won't go, and neither will anyone else from here. We belong here. And now I have to go see to the mules over there, who look bad and have to be well tended to. Javier should have been paying better attention. He knows nothing at all about how to load animals."

Margarito sauntered back across the patio, whistling the song of the Indian lover. As he came nearer the two mules and saw that one was trying to bite the other, he interrupted his song once again and cried: "Macho, you damned coyote! I'm going to kick you in the—" But when he did pass behind the animal, he didn't kick him, but merely led him away from the other mule so that the biting stopped of itself.

What could Jacinto do after this conversation with Margarito? It was exactly as he knew it would be. They belonged here, every one of them. They all were children of Rosa Blanca. They and Rosa Blanca were a unit that could not be separated. A child can be taken away from its mother. But these men could not be taken away from Rosa Blanca. If they were, then they both ceased to be what they were. La Rosa Blanca would remain a ranch or hacienda, but then it would no longer be *the* Rosa Blanca. It would be one more hacienda just like thousands of others. And all the more so if it became an oil field. And if the people who were rooted here for centuries left it, they would not be the same any more. They would then be nothing but confused, homeless, dispersed workers on the land or peons in the camps or beggars on the streets. They would be the uprooted who have lost their purpose in life because they no longer belong anywhere. They would lose not only their link to the soil, but something much more important. They would lose their hearts and their souls, which were as one with Rosa Blanca. Their history was rooted here; their cradle songs, love songs, earth spirits, fairies, and elves and tree nymphs were born and lived here.

Margarito had merely confirmed for Jacinto what he knew long before and what his father and grandfather and all the ancestors had known: Rosa Blanca did not belong to him, he was not the owner, he was only the manager of the property of all those who were living here and who had lived here since time immemorial and probably longer. Everyone would want to return to Rosa Blanca because he had to. He could work anywhere else, make money anywhere else, but he could only live here. Therefore Jacinto had no right—no exclusive claim—to Rosa Blanca. And if he had called together a council of the men—as was done nearly every month when the work was discussed—to lay before it the question: "Shall we sell Rosa Blanca and get a lot of money for it?" they all would have answered: "We can't do that: there are still the children to think about."

Jacinto went back into the house. The lawyer was still sitting at the table, religiously contemplating the golden columns in front of him. He had not dared leave the table to go out on the portico for fear that a gold coin might be stolen, and he would have to pay it back from his own pocket. But whether there had been one gold coin or ten or a thousand lying on the table, he might have left them alone and unattended for an hour or half a day and he would never have needed to count the coins when he returned. Nothing would be missing. But he was a lawyer. So he didn't trust anyone farther than he could see him.

"Well, now," Perez said when he saw Jacinto enter, "it's all settled. Here, count the money."

Jacinto did not sit down. He said calmly: "Rosa Blanca isn't sold. And it won't be sold, even if you put ten times as much on the table. That money there is of no use to me. Land really can't be swapped for money."

"To the contrary, all land is exchanged or sold for money," Señor Perez protested, just to have something to say.

Jacinto, still standing, responded: "Land is eternal. Money is not. That is why you can't exchange one for the other."

"All right, then," the lawyer exclaimed angrily after a pause. As he bagged the coins, he added: "You're a crazy old idiot! That's what you are. You should be sent to the nuthouse, to the *castenada*. That's where you belong. And we'll get Rosa Blanca yet. You can be quite sure of that. And we'll get it cheap, believe you me. Much cheaper. You've missed your chance, *hermanito*. I simply have to tell you that. We'll get you yet."

"All of you together can never get me," Jacinto cried out, now also becoming a bit angry. "You can kiss my ass every time—that you can! You can't frighten me, ever. Not you. Or anyone else. And you're also not getting one man from Rosa Blanca to work in the camps. I have to tell you that. Would you still like a *copita?* A small drink? Or a good havana from San Juan Bautista?"

He brought out the glasses. The lawyer said: "*Salud!*" Jacinto raised his drink and answered, "*Salud!*" And they tossed the drinks down.

The lawyer tied up the bag, called to his *mozo* to bring the horse, mounted, said good-by with all the courtesy a Mexican never forgets, even when he is vexed or disappointed, and rode away.

As Jacinto stood on the portico and watched the lawyer ride off, he was thinking of only one thing: "How can he send me to the nuthouse? I'm certainly not crazy. I'm entirely reasonable, quite right in my mind."

Then he sauntered over to Margarito, watching him doctor the mules for a while, and said at last: "Next week we could drive the calves into the corral and brand them. And on Sunday we'll both ride over to Concordia. Don Federico has an excellent jackass he's willing to sell. Can pack a load of a hundred and fifty pounds without a hitch. We'll start a fine breed of mules with it."

"I've been saying that to you now for five years, compadre," Margarito said. "Mules are quite favorably priced now, and breeding mules can pay off."

"Leave these two sick mules here in the pasture for two weeks without working them so they'll recover properly," Jacinto said.

And with that he went into the house. From the portico he called out to his wife in the kitchen. He would like to have a bit of coffee.

A girl brought the coffee, followed by Jacinto's wife, Concha, his name for Doña Concepcion. She was swinging a towel on which she had dried her hands.

"Take a good look at me, *mujer,*" Jacinto greeted her. "Does it look to you like there's something not quite right with me?"

"Something wrong with you, Chinto? What do you mean by that?"

"Do you think I'm crazy and should be sent to the asylum?"

"Crazy, you? Yes, I really do believe you must be crazy if you think such crazy things about yourself. And, you know, I thought the Licenciado was going to stay for dinner."

"He couldn't. He was too concerned about his coins. He would have been trembling constantly during the meal for fear someone was perhaps spiriting a coin away from him."

"Here? In our house? This fine lawyer must really be crazy through and through if he can believe something as impossible as that. It's not you, Chinto. He's the crazy one, even if he is a lawyer. And now leave me alone. I have more to do than to listen to such crazy nonsense."

She went back into the kitchen. As Jacinto watched her go, he said half aloud to himself: "I'd like to know how the Licenciado can think such a thing of me. Crazy."

CHAPTER THREE

THE REPORT of Licenciado Perez arrived at the headquarters of the Condor Oil Company in San Francisco.

"Who does this filthy chump of an Indian think he is? Who does he think he's dealing with?" Mr. Collins, the president of the company, said. "There isn't any land anywhere in the world that I can't get if I want it. Nothing in the world is more certain than that. If I want it—even if it's on Jupiter—I get it—as sure as death."

Within the company this remark was taken to be a great witticism because it came from the president. The *bon mot* made the rounds of all the offices, and every salaried employee felt obliged to laugh at it. Only the youngest office boy, an impudent fourteen-year-old simpleton, refused to laugh, but said to the youngest office girl, who was just as sassy as he was: "What a clod! And he calls himself president! How is he going to run up to Jupiter? Some joke! He'd have to tickle me on the belly, and even then I'd begin to cry." Then the two giggled together until the chief bellowed: "Quiet there, you silly kids." These two brats did not need to laugh at the president's joke. They had no families to support, and could earn their four dollars a week just as easily somewhere else.

Mr. Chaney C. Collins, president of Condor Oil Company, who considered himself one of the most indispensable persons on earth, nursed his business sense on a few dozen mottos he had picked up here and there along life's way. They showed him the way to go forward, hitting the rough spots as little as possible. Several of these mottos were clearly not meant for him personally, but were intended for his visitors.

Among the latter, two especially were worth mentioning because they shed a clear light on his character. The first stood in a very pretty frame on the massive desk. It faced away from the president and was turned directly toward the visitor sitting before him. It read: "Honesty is the best policy." By turning this motto dripping with cheap drivel toward the visitor, Collins was clearly saying that it was the visitor, not Collins, who was expected to conduct himself honestly in the management of business.

The second motto intended for the visitor also hung in a pretty frame on the wall in back of Collins. It hit the visitor sitting in front of him right in the eye. In large, bold letters it spread the wisdom born of hectic modern life: "Your time, like mine, has irreplaceable value." "Time is money" had become too old-fashioned to interest anyone.

On the table Collins also had a portrait of his wife, who had already grown rather fat. And a photograph of his daughter. She was not yet fat, but even from the picture you could tell that this world could put nothing over on her. Furthermore, she looked just like a movie actress who was living her life fast and hard.

In a drawer on the right, hidden among business papers, he had also placed a few photographs of chorus girls intermixed with dirty French postcards. From the pictures the girls looked saucy and expensive.

In the same drawer was a photograph in a portfolio. On this

picture was inscribed: "To my beloved Daddy, from your Flossy." He wasn't Flossy's father, of course, but it was nice of her to say this so pleasantly. Flossy cost him six hundred dollars every month and that did not include the gifts and the evenings he spent with her in the clubs or in the hotels along the highway outside the city.

The chorus girls had not written anything on their pictures. He had not known them for as long as Flossy, but they were even more expensive because of that. In her time Flossy had been a chorus girl too. She had forgotten this and didn't like to be reminded of it. That would drive her into a frenzy and was always very costly to Mr. Collins.

Then there was still another girl, of whom he possessed only a miniature that was found in a small, prettily worked, heavy gold frame. It lay in the left-hand drawer in an ebony chest that was always locked. Occasionally he placed this small portrait on the table before him when he had to concentrate on his work and would not be disturbed except by his executive secretary. If a completely unexpected visitor appeared—especially his wife—then the picture disappeared quickly into his hand or his vest pocket.

Last week he had had to buy this woman in the expensive golden frame an auto. And not a rattletrap for twelve hundred dollars. That wasn't for her—not if he wanted anything from her. The auto was a high-class affair having every luxury, its interior more like a boudoir than a vehicle. It cost sixteen thousand dollars. It was at the time the most elegant auto west of the Rockies. Now that she had the car, she was pestering him four times a day on the telephone because she also had to have a garage where she could put it. And the garage had to have a mansion joined to it.

Twice a week, late in the evening—it was at night, actually—she teased him about it pleasantly, but in the daytime on the telephone she called him a stingy tightwad because he wasn't quick enough with the garage. He talked his way out of it by saying he still hadn't found anything suitable. But that would do only for a short time. Then he really had to find the garage—and the mansion that went with it, of course—or he might find himself forced to write the auto off as a loss. For if he was too tightfisted to produce the garage, she could easily find someone who considered it an honor to provide it.

Two of the dancers who were a bit closer to him were also

complicated affairs. In business and in every other respect, too. Each had her special requirements, and they all had to do with expenditures, all of which he had to meet.

So you will readily see that the president of a large American oil company does not lie on a bed of roses. He has his troubles finding his way in the world and making both ends meet. Being president of an oil company requires all of a man's ability and wisdom. And if he is going to stay president, the difficulties he encounters have to be solved and solved well. The reproach must not be made that the president of an oil company is perhaps a blemish on the fair white body of human society. That would do no harm to oil, but to the shareholders. The president of an oil company represents an idea, a principle. He bears responsibility for the stability of one pillar in the structure of the state. That's why an ordinary member of a church congregation has more freedom than the pastor. A church member may stray. That does no harm to the church. But if the pastor kicks over the traces, then the entire church can begin to shake—even the foundation on which the church rests.

What is a paltry salary of $150,000 a year to a pitiable oil company president who is so pestered and harassed? That amount scarcely pays for the salt in his soup. So perhaps life isn't so plain and simple as a poor half-crazy Indian thinks. Life is more complicated by far. Worse, it is truly complex. How, after all, is a person to make his way through it?

There is the imposing house in the city, since the president cannot live in an Indian hut. Why else should one be president of an oil company? There are the servants. These people are not slaves. They are hired help, domestics, household staff. They have to be paid well.

The house has to have the best furniture, and a lot of it. The house has to have a garden—a well-tended garden worthy of the president of an oil company.

There has to be a useful auto for himself and a fashionable auto for his wife. She has to have a chauffeur, for the car has to be cleaned, new tires put on, new spark plugs installed, the battery charged, and a host of other tasks performed.

The daughter also has to have her own elegant auto. She wants to go out with her friends to provide them pleasures that, without an auto, could be associated from time to time with all kinds of troubles. We weren't put in this world just to sit around in the corner all the time and mope. The daughter does not have a chauffeur. She drives the car herself. And she does it well. But the tickets for ten, fifty, or a hundred dollars rain down on her with a vengeance—for speeding hell-for-leather through a stop sign or thoughtlessly parking the car near a fire hydrant. Occasionally, she drives around to a peddlar who deliberately gets in her way so he can be run over and sue for damages. There are plenty of lawyers who have nothing better to do than bring damage suits on behalf of those who have been run over, since they receive twenty-five or even forty percent of every award. Since the plaintiff, poor devil, cannot pay his fee, the lawyer goes shares with him, and the lawyer always gains for his own pocket. And if the president doesn't pay, then the insurance company pays, and it does not do so without good reason. In the end it is still the president who pays.

Every month the wife wants a check for a thousand dollars, for pin money, though she never takes either needle or pin in hand. But there is the ice cream, the masseuse, the dancing master. She also gambles, and gambles a lot. At a bridge party with her friends, the wives of other presidents, she loses three thousand dollars in two hours. The bills for her Parisian clothing, her New York stockings, her Viennese shoes, are sent to the president's office. These are extra expenses. And so are the hats—which she wears only for two days each. Whiskey and French liqueurs are also expensive.

The daughter gets only a hundred dollars a month for pocket money. But to tell the truth it always comes to three hundred. Certain expenses aren't counted. They come from the miscellaneous account. The daughter when she is short of money again—and she runs short four times a week—flits quickly into her father's private office; and Mr. Collins, lucky fellow, is glad to be interrupted at his boring work. It gives him an excuse to prattle inanities and trifles with his darling daughter on his knees. And he fancies that the dreary office is filled with sunshine when she strokes his neck and kisses him on the tip of his nose, chattering constantly: "You are the sweetest, dearest daddy in the whole world." And so she extracts two hundred dollars today, fifty dollars tomorrow, and twenty the day after, and then another hundred. "Dear sweet daddikins. Today things are really bad for you. I need five hundred dollars today, but I'll be good for the rest of the month." Three days later, the month is over, according to her, even if the calendar on the table has to develop stomach cramps because it no longer knows its way about and loses confidence in itself. But it costs him another fifty dollars all the same. Even having sunshine in a president's office costs money.

But Mr. Collins thinks of one of his mottos: "Smile and give to the poor." So he just smiles and gives to those who need it. Anyone who is needy is poor.

And the chorus girls of the Follies are poor.

Not having a chorus girl is a disgrace that would make him a laughingstock at the club. His friends would jump on him every day when he appeared, using the sympathetic tone a person uses to speak to the sick: "Hey Greasy!"—his nickname at the club, in reference to his job as president of an oil company—"Hey Greasy! Care for a tube of get-up pills?" So it would go every day with everyone he ran into at the club. For once they have latched on to something they think is witty, they trot it out for such a long time that a person can go crazy. Generations can pass before these men who can and do earn millions with the wave of a hand make up a new joke, to say nothing of finding and understanding a joke that has a hint of wit or humor. Life is truly complicated.

The need to use tonics and pills is a sign that one is old or is approaching old age. But an oil company president can never let it be suspected that he is old. An old man can become President of the United States—in which office neither wisdom nor youthful vigor is needed, where these things are hindrances, as the majority of examples prove—but he cannot be president of an oil company.

The office of the president of an oil company requires robustness, recklessness, remorselessness, unscrupulousness. Neither an aging man, nor a philosopher, nor a poet need apply.

So, to avert the suspicion that he needs to use remedies—unfailing fidelity to one's own wife simply is not believed—and to avert the other suspicion that he might not be unfavorably disposed to rouged young men, chorus girls enter into the care-laden life of the president. He doesn't receive them in a bad humor. Not at all. Although he is a good Christian who remains true to the Methodist or Baptist or—if he wants to hold a very high poisition—the Episcopal Church, he is still of the opinion, as a man and as a husband, that Mohammed was truly a great prophet: He understood the soul of man so well that he made laws that ought to bring relief from man's countless sorrows.

Mr. Chaney C. Collins is a powerful man in the oil industry. In only a few days he can so convulse the market that a hundred other branches of industry will begin to totter and several to fail. A panic will break out in Wall Street among the owners of small- and medium-sized industries and that will overtake the large, and they will then begin to become restless, spend sleepless nights, and have to send ten thousand dollars' worth of cables circling the surface of the earth to stabilize the market again and restore the calm in which alone the giants can develop their great businesses in safety.

Mr. Collins needs only to hold back a million barrels of oil and the market will go wild because the speculators don't know what is going on, rumors immediately will set in and cause mischief. Or Mr. Collins can dump on the market a million barrels of oil that he is holding in reserve for such speculative purposes and provoke a price war that will whisk away with it all the value in the market. For in this system today all values and products that mankind has created are so involved and interwoven that a change in the value of oil immediately brings about changes in the value of products that have no relation at all to oil. A decrease in oil prices can generate an immense increase in the price of wheat or cotton or the shares of railroads and steamship lines.

This happens very logically. Much more logically than in roulette. It happens so very logically that a clever man who has sufficient capital in reserve and who has thoroughly studied and knows well the laws by which the movements are logically bound to happen throughout must always win. But not even the greatest has the imperturbable composure needed to carry out his plan with mathematical precision. Even the greatest, because he is a human being and is susceptible to human suggestion, allows himself to be swept away by the panic. He is swept along by the panic just as the calmest and most thoughtful person is seized at a theater fire by the panic of those who struggle toward the exits, although they all could reach the outside uninjured if they went quickly, without elbowing, through the nearest door, and once outside, did not crowd together out of curiosity to see whether their relatives are following them.

CHAPTER FOUR

WITHOUT A DOUBT Mr. Collins was a power-
ful man in the oil industry. But in comparison with the four women in
his life he was just an ordinary man, who differed from the rest at most
in that he could pay more without getting more for his money than
any man should get from a woman. What a man can get from a woman
is always the same. No woman can give more than she has. And when
she has given what she can give, the man arrives at a great truth, that
all women are alike in this respect—which is all that matters. Women
undoubtedly think the same of men. After much experience, the man
at last comes to the realization that of all the women he has known the
first he had was best. For the memory of her lies farthest back and is
nearest the memory of his youth, and that seems romantic to him

because it is the past. And for the woman the man who she loved first is usually considered best, the one whom she will always love, because he is no longer in her way. The reasoning is the same as with the man.

One most treasures that which is most expensive. Even the prostitute truly loves only the honest fellow for whom she has to earn money and who beats her occasionally to boot.

Among the four pieces of evidence that Mr. Collins has at his disposal to prove to his male friends that he is brimming with vitality, Betty was at that moment the most treasured, because she was the most costly.

Flossy, who got her check for six hundred dollars every month with the regularity with which a spouse has to pay money for the household expenses, stood in his mind's eye and experience very nearly on the same level as his wife, Mrs. Alice Davis Collins. He bickered with Flossy, quarreled with her, felt himself competent (and entitled) to criticize her; and the nights he spent with her were exactly determined and regulated. He regularly left her house at four in the morning when he had fulfilled his conjugal obligations, because he wouldn't be able to go home later and still be able to say he had stayed at the club. As with his wife, he treated Flossy to two trips a year—a trip to Palm Beach, Florida, in winter, and in summer a trip to Canada or Europe. Naturally, he visited her dutifully in Palm Beach, spent some ten days with her, and then went over to Havana, taking her along with him. Then he would go to Tampico, and he would not take her along. Since he had to travel to Tampico on the company's behalf, the entire trip was written off to the account of Condor Oil—thereby considerably reducing the cost of Flossy's special summer holiday. He really might have been able to take Flossy with him to Tampico as well, but it was cheaper to send her back to Palm Beach from Havana. Besides, it made his life easier. In Tampico he always found what he needed on the first evening. And he could recover from Flossy pleasantly with a girl of another color. Indeed, he did not understand what the brown-skinned girl in Tampico said to him of love. But that was not necessary. They both knew what they wanted of each other, and for these desires the language is international. In any case she could pronounce the word "money" in damned good English, and numbers, too, which she associated with the word "dollar." She didn't need to know more than that. Neither did he. After he had been with Flossy continuously for ten days to two weeks a period of recuperation did him a lot of good. For Flossy was beginning to become more and more like his wife. In every way. In bed. In speech. In dress. In nagging. In sermonizing. He was not philosopher enough to know that two women who come under the influence of the same man for a long time gradually become like twins.

Flossy was—if Mr. Collins had ever made out a final accounting—the cheapest of his women friends. That's why she was also the most faithful. And that's why he sometimes felt just as bored with her as with his wife.

The two chorus girls who were of more recent date were not yet taken fully into account, though they already had cost more than Flossy, solely because of the trinkets he had had to give them. For the time being, both seemed to have obligations elsewhere, though they intended to free themselves of them once and for all when they knew exactly how much Mr. Collins was worth. Not how much he was worth intrinsically, as a man or a lover, but how much he was able to pay and was willing to pay. Naturally, neither of the ladies knew about the other, that she was also being courted by him. Mr. Collins knew enough to keep that under his hat, for as soon as the two began to fight over which one could have him, it would become more expensive for Mr. Collins. For the lady who was edged out would begin to make difficulties for him in order to salvage what could be salvaged. And that always amounted to a hefty sum. It was usually enough to restore the virginity alledgedly lost in the struggle to its original pristine condition.

That was done very easily, after a formula tested by Mr. Ayres, president of Grannis and Cosland Refining Company.

One morning Mr. Ayres arrived at his office to find a letter from Simmons & Simmons, Attorneys at Law, waiting for him. The attorneys were writing to tell him that Miss Minnie White, singer and dancer at the Vanity Theatre, was thinking of bringing a suit for breach of promise. Miss White had figured the damages she had sustained at one hundred fifty thousand dollars, a sum that, considering Mr. Ayres's comfortable circumstances, had to be regarded as ridiculously small.

Mr. Ayres had never promised to marry Minnie.

Minnie knew this quite well, and it goes without saying, the lawyers did, too. Mr. Ayres also knew very well that the lawyers and Minnie knew he hadn't promised to marry her. But Minnie, the lawyers, and Mr. Ayres knew that in America a woman who knew how best to present her case to the jurors almost always got what she wanted. That's why telephone calls and conversations went back and forth, and Minnie, relenting, was persuaded to consider her damages good for one hundred thousand dollars. She would keep only sixty thousand dollars for her pocket, since the lawyers were claiming forty percent of the amount sued for. If the suit were lost, she would get nothing at all, because Miss Minnie indeed had nothing. The lawyers were assuming the risk.

Mr. Ayres could not pay the hundred thousand dollars himself without breaking into a bank. His salary was good, but not so good that he could readily spare a hundred thousand. He had a family.

So the suit was filed. Now the lawyers no longer expected Mr. Ayres to pay the full amount; for if he could have paid he wouldn't have let it come to court, and would have settled. The suit had to be brought in order to find an opportunity to get the matter into the newspapers. As soon as it became a judicial matter, the newspapers could be expected to co-operate.

Mr. Ayres belonged to so-called society, and his position as president of a powerful company made him an interesting person to see entangled in a scandal—one who satisfied to the highest degree the wives' need for sensation and longing for gossip. The poor people to whom smutty films, prurient novels, spicy comedies are forbidden (or so censored as to have an effect as tame and boring as the Wednesday-night sermon in a Methodist church), these poor people all at once find fresh, stimulating excitement in their barren lives when they can savor a spicy story on page two of the newspaper. The censor cannot interfere here, for this is a legal matter. The courts are public, as they must be in a true republic to prevent corruption and unjust verdicts.

What the newspaper reporters made of this simple story was admirable reading. It allowed everyone to forget what the censors had forbidden their wards to read and see in the last twelve months.

In enormous boldface type in two even rows across the front

page of the morning paper ran the news that the president of a large company had been seen with a dancer who was wearing nothing but silk stockings.

Underneath, in smaller boldface: "PLEDGE OF MARRIAGE SEALED WITH RING. The unidentified company officer denies the allegation, saying the ring was only a small token of friendship, a gift that had no significance at all and in any case was not meant to be a promise of marriage. He is already married and has three children. The oldest daughter is attending the university. The dancer is expecting to experience the joys of motherhood soon and is demanding three quarters of a million dollars as damages."

In still smaller letters—but conspicuous nonetheless—followed:

"The names of the complainant and the defendant are still being withheld temporarily by special order of the court. However, they will be made public very soon."

This withholding of the names is a special trick of lawyers who want to give Mr. Ayres time to come to terms and pay up. But the newspapers likewise have an interest in the practice, because Mr. Ayres can be brought to terms with them, too. Newspapers are incorruptible, especially in the States. But they are very sensitive to advertising; and a large company frequently has expensive ads to place, even if they are the annual statements, and they often can be repeated arbitrarily in order to produce fat advertisements. Newspaper people are also incorruptible, and nowhere more so than in the States. But they listen readily to solid tips that permit them to speculate successfully in the stock market.

So far the court has decreed absolutely nothing at all, not even about the withholding of the names. To this point the court knows nothing about the matter, and the judge reads the newspaper on the streetcar with the same pleasure as the rest. But he surely reads it with more human understanding, and more sympathy, especially for the poor president, since he, the judge, can be sitting in the very same soup tomorrow. He doesn't have a dancer from the Vanity—he can't afford that—but he has a stenotypist. And if she should, one fine day, suddenly take it into her head that a secretary's existence is too ridiculous for words, then the judge, too, can find his misdeeds described and his steno's brassiere in boldface type in the morning papers. In the meantime he doesn't know what it's all about. No one from the court knows it as yet. So far the lawyers have done nothing more than file a complaint for damages, Jane Doe vs. Richard Roe, Simmons & Simmons, Attorneys at Law, giving file number G916 to the court documents.

Mrs. Ayres, the wife of Mr. Ayres, likewise relishes the juicy story, and she also reads it avidly, with almost sensual pleasure. Indeed, she does not know that it is her faithful husband who is here accused by the reporters of bigamy, at least prospectively, and so she can treat herself with rapturous eyes to a story that is spicier than any she can find in French novels.

In the evening, with her husband sitting at the table, this sensation is, of course, discussed thoroughly, so that the taste and smell of the earthly joys offered by such a story can be enjoyed down to the last exhalation of a sigh. With him she guesses randomly at the identity of the president and the dancer. He really ought to know the president, especially since he belongs to the Rotary Club and Elks. Wouldn't it be delightful if their pictures could be seen in the newspapers? She had on silk stockings and nothing else when she was seen with him through the window, and the curtains weren't drawn tight. That was definitely known. But it would be nice to learn what her face looked like—and, in general, what she was like above the green garters. Maybe the newspaper will soon publish a picture of her in a swimsuit or in the costume of the chorus girls of the Vanity, who all go without stockings during a performance, and wear only shoes, a bit of lace around the hips, and across the breasts, two patches of fabric trimmed with glittering beads.

Mr. Ayres, knowing, of course, who is involved, because his lawyer had already asked him by telephone that morning whether he had read the newspapers, lost his temper over the craziness of newspapers and lectured his wife because she was so anxious to read such sensational stories in the papers and was willing to sink so low as to seek the pictures of these people.

That morning, and for the next day, people in the city and the surrounding area buy newspapers like mad. Everyone hopes to find the names made public. Everyone is interested in the question whether the expectant mother is so far along that she can't perform any longer. Everyone hopes she isn't. If she can appear a few more times at least, she can be seen in the flesh. As soon as her name is known, the ticket sellers at the theater will immediately sell out the entire house and raise the price of tickets by as much as two hundred percent.

In the expectation that the names will be published, newspapers are now bought in large quantities so that it is no longer necessary to publish the names. Meanwhile a new scandal comes along, just as fat and juicy as that of the president and the dancer, and they are forgotten. If, someday, the names should subsequently appear, scarcely anyone reads them. By then there have been so many scandals, cases of corruption, political swindles, successful and unsuccessful ascents of the Himalayas, bank robberies, attempts at assassination with bomb and revolver in Chicago, train wrecks in Mexico, murders of American missionaries in China, that a week later one really cannot know for what reason in fact the names of a president of an inconsequential copper company and a dancer whose name has never been printed on a theater ticket are made public. At the moment there is more interest in how many thousands of dollars Ma Ferguson, the governor of Texas, has made in the building of a state highway and what she plans to do with the money.

But Simmons & Simmons, Attorneys at Law, cannot wait for this swing in the opinion of the newspaper reader; they cannot wait for Mr. Ayres to explain to his wife what the trouble is and be absolved by her at relatively low cost; they can't wait for Mr. Ayres to persuade several members of the board of directors of his company that this is only a shabby case of blackmail and for them to warn the newspapers not to push the matter to the utmost. If they do, the newspapers are stone-cold dead, for among the directors are a few who could wring a newspaper's neck within eight hours and do it so thoroughly the newspaper would forget what it called itself yesterday and who its managing editors were.

Simmons & Simmons cannot wait for such unforeseen events. They must work as quickly as the devils of hell who fish out the poor soul who has fallen through the ice and drowned and warm him up so that hell, too, fulfills its purpose.

B. TRAVEN

The lawyers exploit the prime hours after the newspapers appear. If they don't succeed at their game in this period, it can be a long story. Of course, they will be victorious, however long it takes. Still, the money can elude them. Mr. Ayres merely has to take the risk and secure everything so well that there is nothing much to get. He waits out the scandal in Europe, and when he returns the affair has become so cheap that it is no longer worth the lawyers' while. What becomes of Miss Minnie is, was, and always will be of no concern to them.

Little in the entire story is true in any event. It is only meant to satisfy the reader's hunger for salacious stories which, as a result of censorship and prudery, can be satisfied nowhere else. The newspaper profits from that.

Whether the president loses his position or the wife decides to separate from him or the dancer drowns herself matters not at all to the newspapers. It only cares when one of these results makes it possible to publish another sensational story.

Miss Minnie White was very often together with Mr. Ayres when she was wearing nothing more extensive than her silk stockings. Usually she had on much less than that. But then no one had been able to see her through the half-closed curtain. She was much too cautious for that. Not from innate modesty but from simple utility and convenience. If you have the feeling that you can be observed, it has an annoying effect and distracts from the business at hand. But Simmons & Simmons is prepared. They keep a private detective in reserve, and he can and will swear at any time that he has seen a woman clad only in silk stockings and a man wearing not much more together in the same room. Miss Minnie has only to name the place—that is, the house—where what the detective saw could have happened. The private detective and Messrs. Simmons will take care of the rest. Then either a washerwoman or a chauffeur will come forward to swear they have seen Miss Minnie and Mr. Ayres go into that house. No one can contradict the washerwoman. She is honor and truth personified. Mr. Ayres, resting so perfectly on the blazing grill, will have to admit it is true. He will be careful not to swear to the contrary, for he knows other persons have seen him there.

Miss Minnie is certainly not expecting a baby. Mr. Ayres is

49

perfectly well aware of that. Miss Minnie is much too clever to allow such an accident. Children are always an accident; they are no blessing from heaven. She knows this from her youth in Minneapolis. She had five sisters. Neither her father, who worked in a suitcase factory, nor her mother, who worked in a dress factory, ever spoke of a heavenly blessing, but only of the brats, the bastard brood, who ate so much and tore up so much and always and eternally cried that they were hungry.

Messrs. Simmons & Simmons also know that Miss Minnie is not expecting a child. They would have told her right to her face that they considered her cleverer than that, for she was certainly not a baby and ought to know better.

The papers knew better than anyone else that Miss Minnie White was not in a family way. If she had really been expecting a baby, the papers would have been very careful not even to refer to it. That could have led to inconveniences of all kinds. The newspapers had only written that the dancer felt herself a mother so that the story would be the juicier. Besides, the lawyers had hinted at something, and the reporters had only inferred what they thought proper. Such a report only served a purpose. Names really weren't named. And if it should come to that, Miss Minnie could make out at her future appearance in the Vanity that it was a reporter's trick.

Although there was very little truth in the whole story, the attorneys still attained their goal. Mr. Ayres was thrown into a panic. He had to be afraid that a great scandal could arise. He didn't really know how far the lawyers intended to go. It was scarcely necessary that the dancer's name be published. His name would be enough. By publishing it they could show their readers how unafraid they were, and how busily intent they were to protect the American people from the lewdness and depravity in which individual unscrupulous citizens sought to entangle it. This was one of the chief tasks of newspapers, and they did not show consideration to anyone even if it involved members of the upper class. One should be prepared to excuse the working class and this poor girl, the dancer, who certainly belonged to the working class, much sooner than these magnates who believed they could do in the free republic of righteous citizens what they wished only because they had more money. Of course, the newspapers would say that only after they were positive the board of directors of the company of which Mr. Ayres was president desired that Mr. Ayres should be smashed because they wanted to oust him, for these and other reasons, and couldn't get rid of him in any other way.

Indeed, Mr. Ayres did not always know how he stood with the board—whether they were keeping or dropping him. Mr. Ayres couldn't let it come to a decision. He also didn't know how his wife would take it. He knew even less how it would be taken in the clubs to which he belonged. Such a scandal could cripple him for a long time, and he would then have to work devilishly hard to rise to the top again.

He considered all such possibilities, and he went to Messrs. Simmons and Simmons and began to negotiate. For the expenses they had been put to he paid the gentlemen ten thousand dollars.

At that Messrs. Simmons and Simmons invited Miss Minnie White down to their offices.

Mr. Henry Simmons greeted Miss White: "A half hour ago we had a longish conversation with Mr. Ayres. He said he definitely isn't going to pay anything and that he's perfectly willing to risk not only a trial but also a scandal. He says, and I believe him, that he's right. If we go so far as to cause a scandal, he'll lose his job and then he'll be unable to pay anything at all. And the same is true if a trial should come about. He has sworn to us here with tears in his eyes that he loves you sincerely, and asked us to put in a good word with you in his behalf. He cannot live without you. He is going to buy you that Stutz Bearcat you've been wanting for so long. I really don't see, Madam, why two people who are as nice as you two are should not love and cherish each other. What sense does such a battle make? You're also a bit to blame, Madam. Don't be so hard on him. He has his trials and tribulations, too."

Tears welled up in Miss Minnie's eyes, real tears, since there was no longer any reason to pretend in order to squeeze out a settlement.

"He's also pestered and harassed and harried, poor man. As we all are. You, too, Miss White."

She cried a bit more because she was now receiving sympathy for herself. She, too, was plagued and pestered and forever pursued by people who wanted money from her. Everyone thought a girl in the chorus at the Vanity had millions to give away. Other women bought shoes for fifteen dollars; they cost her twenty-five. So it went with stockings, undies, hats. And all those who got tips expected from her triple what they got from other people. And if she didn't pay it, she was viewed disdainfully and treated like a common streetwalker.

Who is master of life? The president of an oil company? Or the attorney who undertakes the meanest divorce suit and extortion maneuvers? The dancer in a revue? Rockefeller? Sinclair? Morgan? The President of the United States? None of those who seem to be masters of the world. Those who can buy and sell continents, create republics and destroy them, crown kings and depose them, start revolutions and throttle them, none of these is master of life. They are all caught in the machine that is called The Modern Age, Our Contemporary Life. They are whirled around, and tossed about, like little grains, now up, now down, now in-between, now in the corner, now on the right side, now on the left.

Perhaps Jacinto, the Indian who owned Rosa Blanca without owning it, was master of life. He was master of life right up to the day when it was discovered that Rosa Blanca bore oil in its soil.

At that point Jacinto ceased being the master of life, for now he, too, was becoming a grain spun around in the machine.

Perhaps Margarito was the master of life. Margarito who doctored the mules, who understood the language of mules, who could swear terribly and sing sweet ballads in the same breath.

Perhaps the compadres of Rosa Blanca were the masters of life, until they lost their native soil.

Perhaps the lion in the jungle was the master of life. Yet the flea was stronger than he, for it pestered him and the lion couldn't resist it; a thorn that he stepped on was stronger than he for it made him lame; the poisonous snake that bit him on his nose if he was not careful could lay him low, which is why the snake was stronger than the lion.

Perhaps the master of life was the colorful butterfly fluttering from flower to flower, concerned about nothing, enjoying life to the full until it found itself caught in the web of a spider which was stronger than it.

Perhaps the master of life was the class-conscious worker who knocked down and thoroughly thrashed his foreman because the foreman, thinking himself the stronger and more powerful, had yelled at him. But the industrious worker produced more than the market could absorb, and the factory couldn't pay the man and had to let him go. So his children tore at the worker's body because they were hungry and believed they were masters of life and their own father had to be their slave and serf.

From her lawyers' office Miss Minnie White telephoned her friend, Mr. Ayres, and offered her apologies for all the trouble she had caused him. She'd been insane, she said, and had let herself be goaded into it by a friend. Whether or not he was going to be her friend again, she loved him more than anyone else.

Mr. Ayres also apologized to her for all that he had done to her and declared that he alone bore the blame. He was delighted to be allowed to call her his again.

Two days later the two traveled to San Diego in his touring car. The day-long trip on the romantic drive along the Pacific Coast brought the two together more closely than they had ever been before.

The discord was put aside and forgotten. This could be done after the lawyers got what they wanted for themselves.

For the time being the further adventures of Mr. Ayres and Miss White are of no interest, neither to Messrs. Simmons and Simmons nor to the newspapers. The commercial side of the affair had been satisfied, and interesting oneself in the private lives of two people from whom, at present, money cannot be made, is unfair. No one can say of an American that he is unfair. He is helpfulness and kindness personified.

CHAPTER FIVE

MR. COLLINS frequently had to give a thought now to Mr. Ayres's affair. Mr. Ayres was an intimate friend. They had attended the same high school and belonged to the same clubs. For that reason Mr. Collins knew all the particulars of the affair. A precise knowledge of that history was useful to him. It helped keep him on guard.

But how is one to guard against the demands of the lower half of the body when they're greater now than at the age of twenty? At twenty one has romantic ideas. The many purely natural desires of the body seem sordid. One believes in the chastity and purity of love. This is so not because the man is nobler at that age, but because he is more fearful than the woman. He suspects there are mysteries he can never penetrate without exposing himself to serious danger.

At the age of fifty, after one has more or less cheerfully and successfully survived twenty-five years of marriage and fifty occasional infidelities and the accompanying storm and stress, the practice of the mature man takes the place of these romantic assininities. Without exception, everything in life is now considered unemotionally, in purely detached fashion. Gone forever is the belief that woman or even love might conceal a mystery. A woman may indeed offer surprises at times, but only because you never know where you stand with her, and she is always on the lookout for things to do that you would never in any case have expected of her. It is this single mystery that makes a woman bearable, especially when it is the woman to whom you are married. Bearable by the average man to the degree you can expect to see after a long marriage. All the quiet, contemplative amusements that are delightful at sixteen or seventeen have completely lost their appeal, and with them their attraction. Nothing remains but pure detachment and cool sobriety. You now have to follow custom. So it is with the husband, and so with the wife.

To expect to be loved for one's beautiful eyes, or youthful ardor—this hope vanishes entirely. If a woman or a girl should mention it, you feel flattered, but you no longer believe her. The wisdom of the philosopher, which is what you have become, no longer permits such strong convictions. Your understanding of womanly beauty has been purified. You're no longer taken in by every pretty face. You have become selective and now would be very careful in the choice of a partner in marriage.

Whether, in fact, you find everything that the philosopher lays claim to—that is, womanly beauty, wit, or in lieu of wit, conversational ability, taste, savoir-faire and, never to be forgotten, a well-groomed, willing body—depends only upon the ability to pay that you have acquired in the meantime.

Indeed, very seldom now—no, to tell the truth, it never happens that you find all these things in one and the same woman. Because that is contrary to the laws of nature. It is only possible to believe this between the ages of sixteen and twenty-five. And that is when you commit the greatest mistake, that is, you marry the wrong person.

Because all these virtues are not to be found in one woman— you have now attained to this wisdom—the mature man whose urges and desires have become more violent as his wisdom has grown must apply in his private life the specialization he has learned over the years to use in his profession or business. It is only as a specialist in his profession that he is able to produce the means that he needs in order to become a specialist in his private life as well. He does himself good by patronizing one woman for her beauty, though she lacks wit, and another for her wit, though she lacks desire. And to get that, there is yet another woman.

That's why we overlook the facile reproach of the devout, that Mr. Collins might have been called a rake because he had, in addition to his wife, a Flossie, a Betty, and two chorus girls who for the present were still waiting to be ranked where they belonged according to their special qualifications. Mr. Collins was a product of his times. A grain that was swirled hither and thither in the great machine "Our Modern Age" without being able to protect itself, without being able to do anything about it.

Betty had said to him on the telephone that she had to speak to him urgently. He had replied to her that he couldn't talk to her then because he was in a conference with top-level company officers. That meant nothing to her. At once she rushed down to the Condor Building. The receptionist told her that she couldn't speak to Mr. Collins in any event since he was in a meeting.

Nobody could do that to her. Not to Betty. Meeting or no meeting, she was going to see Mr. Collins when she wanted to see him, even if he was dead and buried. Uninvited entrance into the sanctuary of the conference room is punishable by death. An important meeting of the directors of an American petroleum company is many times holier than the holiest Tibetan shrine.

Anyone who knows the works has to admit that such a conference is, in fact, holier than anything having to do with religion. And that is said here without irony. From such conferences, and not from the White House in Washington, there can originate, and have originated: the rejection of foreign ambassadors; the changing of its own envoys; sickness and resignation of secretaries of state; armed intervention in the affairs of Bolshevik Russia; the abolition of freedom of speech for communists; the plotting of a new Mexican revolution; support for the Turks against England; twenty-year minimum sentences for Wobblies; free trade for whiskey smugglers; the dispatching of pocket battleships and Marines to Colombia; the entry of American troops into Peking; the stuffing of starving Greek and Armenian children with trashy canned goods that could no longer be fed to American soldiers because of the precipitate peace; unlimited land and water rights for America in the independent Republic of Nicaragua; lively hope that the Habsburgs and Hohenzollerns would grasp the scepter in their hands again; the dismissal of two thousand mayors and their replacement by others; the taciturnity of the American President; the firing of the political editor of the New York *Times* and the economic editor of the New York *World;* the forced sale of the Chicago *Tribune;* a glut of anti-Semitic articles in the newspapers, the exchange of professors between Columbia, Chicago, and California universities; the reduction of Bible prices; the granting of more long-term credit to German industries and to Bolshevik Russia; the deportation of pacifists and similar peace-pipe smokers; the building of eighteen new battleships and one hundred fifty submarines; a treaty among all peoples not to make war without first asking Washington's permission; the League of Nations against Mankind and for Profit; congratulatory telegrams to Germany for delivery of military zeppelins; propaganda for the uplifting of morals among the working class; the banning of two-dollar prostitutes; the encouragement of mobile prostitution to revive an auto industry struggling for its life; support for the installment plan and similar ideas for the enslavement of the people least able to pay; the denial of credit to cooperatives and unions that build houses to rent at cost; and a few other things.

If you reflect on all the consequences that can follow from the deliberations and decisions of conferences in large companies, especially steel and petroleum corporations, you will understand there are holy things here. No god was ever so powerful that he could carry out schemes as complicated as those devised here. Peoples and nations are at issue, Christian, Jewish, Mohammedan, and Buddhist religions, gods and demons, the moving of mountains and piercing of continents, the joining of oceans that do not belong together, and the partitioning of lands and peoples who have grown up with each other since time immemorial. What it would take God a million years to do is done here with a resolution. Wherever such a resolution is passed, whether in heaven or on Olympus or in the conference room of an American petroleum company, there is the Holy of Holies. The sanctuary of mankind has to be there and nowhere else.

On the conference room door a small placard was hanging. Written on it were these words: DO NOT DISTURB—KEEP OUT. This went for office clerks, businessmen, the American President, the King of England, and Jehovah. But it did not apply to Betty. She wanted her garage, and the house that went with it. She had to have it, and what is more, she needed it at once, because she had told her friends she already had the garage and the house and was going to give her housewarming party on Monday evening. The party would cause the kings and queens of Hollywood to burst with envy. And there had to be a swimming pool filled with warm water. Around one o'clock at night she would propose to her guests that everyone should change for a swim in the pool. She would have elegant, light silken bathing suits at hand. Then when the men and women were in the pool she would quickly gather up all the clothing, mix it up, and hide it. For the rest of the evening people would dance only in their swimming suits.

"I don't see what the joke is," one of Betty's friends said to her. "The film stars do that in Hollywood every day."

"Just you wait and see what happens afterward," Betty said.

Indeed, everything Betty was planning still existed only in her imagination, because the house was still missing. She had thought up many other amusing surprises that would increase everybody's pleasure.

It has to be admitted that Betty had an artistic taste and an excellent imagination as well.

To the company's governors, the stockholders who have influence without their names being known to the public, Princess Betty is partly like a business partner and partly good publicity. The Princess adds to Mr. Collins's prestige and power. And a company having a prestigious and powerful president, who is respected and feared at the same time, has greater assurance of winning the game than a company having as president a stingy, withered, pessimistic, timid, faint-hearted, little old man. The shrewdness of the latter is

·worth a lot. But Mr. Collins with his lust for life, bearing the burden of earning several millions a year in order to support his princesses and ladies-in-waiting, can best the skinflint with a wave of his hand. The tightwad drives his car cautiously because he doesn't need much for himself and doesn't want to lose a sure thing. Mr. Collins is rough and reckless in his car. Because he can never lose anything, he has to win, no matter what it costs, no matter who or what gets ruined in the process. He is not in the least free. He is a product. He has not *made* himself. He was *made*. But he is not to be blamed for this. Only his parents are perhaps to be condemned. But his parents are the times. You curse the times if you think you have to curse at all.

Just as the minister of the First Baptist Church demands admission into the Kingdom of Heaven and gains it from heaven's terrified board of directors, who are anxious to preserve the Olympian tranquillity and dignity, so Betty, when she stood in front of the doorway to the American Holy of Holies and saw that placard, announced her arrival, surpassing the minister by several orders of magnitude.

With the heavy golden handle of her short umbrella she knocked twice, hard and heavy, each irreverent blow landing as if it were meant to blast a hole through the door.

The receptionist, when she saw what was happening, turned pale, thinking she was about to lose her job.

Without waiting to see whether anyone inside would perhaps call out, "Come in!," Betty flung open the door. With a blaze she burst in on all those present, who were sitting together as solemnly as cardinals at the election of a pope, as if she were going to say: "You are all fired!"

She took one more step, slammed the door closed behind her with a crash, and shouted at the chairman of the conference: "Mr. President, where are you keeping my garage?"

Betty spoke carefully and elegantly without ever sounding affected and unnatural. And as a rule she spoke calmly and thoughtfully. For a young woman she had a deep voice, but it was gentle, warm, and resonant. Indeed, when she was very excited or wanted to give her words especially strong emphasis, she talked slang. But not because she let herself go or lost her head. She used slang on purpose in order to attain a greater effect, just as a hard-working businessman, though he has attended college, lapses into slang when he is trying to sell something to a stubborn customer. We are all taken in by slang and become less cautious.

Betty came from Seattle. Her parents were still living and believed she was a private secretary for a San Francisco newspaper publisher. Betty wouldn't have cared if her parents had not believed this. Her father was a ship's chandler, and the family was well off, living in comfortable circumstances. Betty had majored in literature and history. She spoke French and a bit of Spanish. For a while she had been a schoolteacher in a small California city, but was fired for bad conduct by the school board—she told her pupils that the Biblical story of creation was not to be taken literally; mankind had evolved slowly over several million years from a beastlike creature to its present form. With pink slip in hand, she naturally could not find a new teaching job in cities in the west. And in the large cities of the north and east, the jobs had been given out for years to come. So she became an editorial secretary at a daily paper in San Francisco. One of the younger editors asked her out to dinner at a nightclub, and that evening through a friend of Mr. Collins, who was coincidentally an acquaintance of the editor, she met Mr. Collins. Subsequently she lost her job at the newspaper by twice refusing the editor-in-chief's invitations to dinner. After the second refusal she was told her work was not satisfactory—she couldn't take dictation fast enough—and she was invited to look for another position. As she was looking for a job one day, she met Mr. Collins in the street. Remembering her from the nightclub, he spoke to her and invited her to lunch. She accepted the invitation.

Up to this time Betty was an American girl like any other who has received a good education but then has to earn her own living. In association with Mr. Collins, who seemed to earn hundreds of thousands of dollars for no other purpose than to spend them liberally, and under his tutelage, she flowered, within four months, into one of the most elegant ladies in San Francisco, without ever being classed among the demimondaines. Mr. Collins was her one and only, though she perpetually led him to expect that he would have competition any day now. You couldn't say she dominated him. In fact, she even avoided letting him think she dominated him. But she got what she wanted. She was far better educated and cleverer than he, and she also possessed greater intelligence. And her essential character was more aristocratic and discreet than his. For him she was the inspiration a powerful man in industry needs as much as an artist does. Breadth of mind and genius are the same in art as in business. As the true love of an artist Betty would have lived on his income and certainly been just as happy as she was now living the luxurious life corresponding to the income of an oil company president. She honestly loved Mr. Collins. And only because she really loved him, it never occurred to her that her position could be viewed differently from the way she saw it. She was persuaded she would stand by Mr. Collins even if he should lose his exalted position. For his generosity she had respect, and she admired him for it. For his rank, on the other hand, she had no respect at all. And so it was a matter of indifference to her whether she disturbed him by her impulsive intrusion into his business sanctum. She believed in his invincible might, that even if he should fall, he would always land on his feet. If that was too difficult for him to do by himself, she was capable of encouraging him so that he would pick himself up again, even against his will. Still, she knew she would never marry this man, even if she had the opportunity.

Even if Betty took everything from him and wanted everything from him, there was one thing she did not want under any circumstances—a child. The father of her child, she thought, should be someone with a soul. And, at the very best, he should have the soul of an artist. But that was exactly what Mr. Collins lacked—a soul.

But still, Betty was not so perfect that she radiated light. She had her dark side, which had already been present when she was still a child. As she grew older, she had had to lighten up a bit in order to get on in life unhurt. Yet under Mr. Collins's influence that dark side, which would perhaps have vanished entirely, took on heavier, deeper shadows.

In his profession Mr. Collins was a genius. A genius can be a genius anywhere, as an artist, a general, a shoemaker, a banker, an oil magnate. Often enough, there are criminal geniuses, too, those people whose creativity can find no scope within the law. Fundamentally, every genius is a criminal, because every genius violates and defeats existing proven laws. That's why geniuses are always feared by the good burgher, because the genius threatens his existence, which is rooted in dogged perseverance.

Now a woman who is going to be and remain the lover of a distinguished man must be in many ways the unalterable opposite of that man, and yet be as similar to him in other ways as though she were a part of him. Lovers should not understand everything about themselves, so that each will find in the other, again and again, the new, the unexpected, the strange. That prevents monotony, which sets in in a well-made marriage when one is sure of the other. On the other hand, lovers should be like enough to understand one another immediately by the wink of an eye or the tone of the voice.

In education, taste, sensibility, and outlook, Betty was Mr. Collins's perfect counterpart. Because of these qualities, he admired, respected, and feared her, and fancied himself wretched in comparison, and he never forgot he was a gentleman. She, however, admired him for his relentless business drive, his daring, the assurance with which he sized up business matters, took in economic events, and forecast events in the market clearly and precisely.

Those were their contraries.

Their similarities lay in material things. Both loved luxury, both wanted it to be conspicuous and brilliant. He had said there wasn't any land anywhere in the universe that he couldn't get if he wanted it. He meant this literally. After the world war he had even wanted to buy Germany, but when he heard that a matchstick cost five billion marks there, he dropped the plan. Nothing could be ventured with such incompetent, inefficient businessmen as the Germans.

With Betty it was the same, but even more so. If she wanted to have something, and had satisfied herself that it could be got here below, she had to get it. In her determination she was ruthless and implacable. And she was like him in temperament, though he was more reserved since he knew he might make stupid mistakes if he got carried away. And in business situations mistakes are not permitted. Still, he had a temper, and it would flare up once he had already settled a matter in his favor to a degree that insured no further mistake could be committed.

Betty had this temper and a stubbornness about getting her way even in childhood, and gradually, in school and as a teacher and a secretary, she had had to suppress it. But under Collins's influence these traits at last developed splendidly.

Collins had bought the auto Betty wanted—the smartest on the market. As to the garage, he said he'd see about it. He repeated this "We'll see" so often that Betty became bored with it. And she became so tired of the repeated excuse, "I haven't been able to find anything just right yet," that the catastrophic intrusion into the national sanctuary had to occur—forcibly amidst rolling thunder.

Betty had never set foot in Mr. Collins's home. She avoided his wife. Not because she felt any fear of her, but because that could cause complications, perhaps even lead to a divorce. She wanted to avoid that. A man newly divorced after a long marriage to which he has become accustomed usually acts quite helpless, like a child that has lost its mother. This helplessness might even trap her into marrying him. She didn't want that under any circumstances. So it was for reasons of sheer good sense that she never mixed in his married life. Nary a word. She even urged him not to neglect his marriage and his wife too much. It was not known for sure whether Mrs. Collins was aware of Betty's existence. But it may be assumed she was told, and that she also wanted to avoid any scandal. At her age a divorce wouldn't do her much good. Sure, she could sue for alimony, but her social standing was better with Mr. Collins at her side than without him. So she acted as if she knew nothing about Betty. And if a friend dared to allude to her, she said: "Nonsense, it's nothing but gossip. I know him better than that. He has his little amusements. That's all. I don't begrudge him that. He has to work hard. Have you seen the new styles at Boiret & Martin? I bought four of them this morning."

Betty was still standing close to the door. She waited, or seemed to be waiting, for the first faint sign that those present in the room were awakening, for everyone seemed stunned by her bolt from the blue.

Collins was not presiding over the meeting today, but had turned the chair over to a senior vice-president in order to be freer in the handling of the topics on the agenda. He was standing erect, holding a sheet of paper in his hand, and he appeared to be reading aloud from it just at the moment the thunder rolled. The men all rose in the presence of the lady, pushing their chairs back, either to stand up more easily or to seem to be willing to offer her a chair, although there were enough empty chairs in the room.

Mr. Collins's executive secretary, who was taking dictation at the conference, glanced up at him. When he blinked slightly, the secretary stood up, not so much rising as gliding from her chair like a snake and quietly, inconspicuously, and altogether noiselessly, slithered out of the room, as if she had done something wrong. No one noticed her departure. Some of the men knew Betty, or more properly, Miss Betty Cuttens, very well. They had once met her, accidentally, in a nightclub with Mr. Collins. They were accompanied by their lady friends, and Mr. Collins was there with Betty to spend a pleasant evening. So it happened that they all shared the same table. And the result was that every single one of them danced with Betty at least once that evening, and in polite retaliation Mr. Collins swept around the small but elegant room with the friends of each of them in turn. He was a good dancer, and he made ample use of his ability to dance well without faltering because he believed, probably with good reason, that dancing kept the body lithe, and therefore young. In any case, he was sensible enough to leave his presidency in the drawer of his desk when he wanted to celebrate with his employees and associates.

Betty was as well respected by Mr. Collins's friends and business associates as if she were his wife. They could not take any liberties with either Betty or Flossy, just as they would never have dared to do so with Mr. Collins. On the other hand, they could easily tell jokes in Betty's or Flossy's presence that could not even have been hinted at in Mrs. Collins's presence. Of course, that is not to say that Mrs. Collins wouldn't listen to a juicy story just as willingly as the next woman who, to establish her own respectability, feels an obligation to blush at the proper point when she hears a joke, but none at all when she retells it to her friends.

But the real difference was that with Betty one really could behave much more freely, gaily, cheerfully, than with Mrs. Collins.

The champagne bottles kept under the tables because of Prohibition and a desire to maintain appearances could be unconcernedly taken out and displayed. It could be openly admitted that this was honest champagne, and not Canadian ginger ale, that would-be harmless poison substituting for the only genuine article. The champagne, whiskey, and Benedictine bottles stood under the table as a precaution. For if the Prohibition agents made a raid, then everyone could deny ownership of a bottle of champagne, for no one is responsible for anything that is standing under a table without his knowledge, and surely not when it was already there before he entered the room. Obviously it had been left behind under the table by other guests lacking in religion, morals, and respect for the law. The champagne was served in crystal glasses because, of course, it was officially accepted that it was ginger ale. Whiskey and dry martinis were served in mocha cups, with sugar bowls and cream pitchers, as though they were really chocolate. Anyone entering and surveying the room could get the impression he was at an innocent dance festival sponsored by a teetotaling institution. Sometimes agents really did investigate because the host's dollars had not sufficiently mollified them, or the department had got a new and greedy chief who was seeking acclaim, and his price had not been established yet. Occasionally the agents had to raise hell to show the good burghers how seriously they dealt with violators of the Prohibition laws and how necessary it was to raise the budget for enforcement and, by the by, the department chief's salary. So then the club would be searched. When it was, the cups were emptied at a gulp and black coffee, already present on the table for this purpose, was poured into them to kill the smell of whiskey. No new-born lamb could be more innocent than the good people gathered here to enjoy themselves quietly and legally after the exhausting daily grind. Anyone who was found drunk here had obviously gotten drunk somewhere else. He was drunk before he entered the building, and the host had tried in vain—as could easily be attested—to get rid of the man or couple without causing a big scandal. This hadn't succeeded, so the host had finally allowed them to stay as long as they conducted themselves properly. The host really couldn't be held responsible for what a couple did and drank in another club.

Betty was a good sport, that is to say, she was ready for

anything. She never spoiled other people's fun or disturbed their good humor. In her presence the men might carelessly kiss their lady friends at the table. One might even announce airily that he was already a little bit tipsy. But every one of them knew just how far he might go in Betty's presence.

But when Mr. Collins showed up with one of his new chorus girls, things became wilder by far. And often enough it came very near the point where you couldn't tell exactly who was whose woman. Of course, it could very well happen, in time, that one of the chorus girls might also have to be respected nearly as much as the wife. But for the time being, neither one could rise so high. Both were standing, so to speak, in the waiting room and it was still not to be guessed which one of them would continue her journey in luxury. Perhaps neither would ever board the sumptuous carriage.

All the men on the board of directors gathered in the sanctuary had heard of Betty. And when she came thundering in, everyone knew—even those who didn't know her personally—that this woman had to be Betty. For the president's wife would never have dared to do what Betty had done. The wife would have waited outside, in a special anteroom, until her spouse had a minute for her. And without exception, all who were now seeing the much-discussed princess in person for the first time were terrified.

They had always considered princesses to be very special beings. If it was said of a magnate's girl friend that she looked every inch a princess, definite ideas were formed immediately, ideas and notions shaped by the movies, in films in which a former salesclerk in a tie store is made up, painted up, dressed up, styled up, gussied up, until, at last, she meets the ideas stenographers and payroll clerks have for princesses.

But what they were seeing now was no film star. To the film queens there always clung, inextinguishable, ineffaceable, the smell of the office or box factory or warehouse from which they had come. To Betty there clung none of the odor of her trials as a teacher and editorial secretary. Perhaps because she had never really felt like a teacher or a secretary.

Betty was born a princess, and was never anything but a princess. And a princess had to deal in this way with subjects who have provoked her displeasure. Now, in America, a woman may always do more, dare more, than a man even allows himself to think. She is the freest of women in the freest republic in the universe. She is the freest as long as she is well dressed and doesn't carry a red banner in a socialist parade, and isn't a striking textile worker, and doesn't nag and prate because her husband was shot by the militia as a striking mineworker, and doesn't make pacifistic propaganda. As soon as she does these things her skull is fair target for the policeman's nightstick, just like her husband's. Even in the freest state in the world freedom cannot go that far. Even freedom must finally have a limit. Otherwise we wouldn't know where freedom begins, nor what it really is.

If Betty had been a mere worker who wanted to ask the directors why she had to live on fourteen dollars a week while the company had an annual surplus of a million dollars, she would never have dared to come in like Betty. If she had, she would have got sixty days in the workhouse or reformatory for disorderly conduct and drunkenness.

But Betty could do as she wished. She was a woman in the freest republic, where women are not treated like slaves, as they still are in Europe and Asia. For Betty was in the right in this case. She had to have her garage, and the house that went with it. And the gardener, who would also wash the car and take care of all the occasional maintenance. And if the house already was attached to the garage, and the gardener to the house and to the car, then a Chinese or French housekeeper also belonged to it. She could be helpful to Betty in personal matters so that she wouldn't have to make her own bed or draw her bath or wash her stockings. Since Mr. Collins would be dining with her occasionally, she also needed a black or Irish or Swedish cook in the well-equipped kitchen, where nothing would be lacking, and where the dishes would be washed by electrically driven machines.

When the men at the conference heard what was involved, they understood perfectly why Betty was compelled to burst in here with a roar. Certainly she was not to blame for having disturbed this holy conference with such profane matters. The guilty party was Mr. Collins. How dare he deny something to Princess Betty?

Betty was justified in every respect.

The men had recovered in the meantime from the thunderclap, and they not only understood Betty and fully forgave her this wild intrusion, but even conceded that it was her duty to pommel Mr. Collins about the chest and shoulders with her fists. They had wandered from their chairs in order to see Betty up close and undress her mentally.

Thereby Mr. Collins grew in the directors' esteem. In the eyes of those who were seeing Betty for the first time Mr. Collins took on a supernatural greatness. If, before this, he was very powerful in the company, he became overpowering after this event, and his position seemed unassailable.

CHAPTER SIX

Now MR. COLLINS was really not in any sense an employee of Condor Oil. That he was not. Though he was president of the company, he didn't hold office in the usual way. He was president because he had founded the company and was one of the principal stockholders. Still and all, he could lose his job as president. If he was involved in a scandal, so much so that he was at its center, then he would have to resign, since a scandal involving the president damages a company's reputation and its business suffers. To the public the president must appear spotless, a model of respectability and chastity, as much for the good burghers who are going to invest their money in the company business as for, especially, the communists and similar malcontents and revolutionists.

Those feeble agitators who lack the ability to grasp the fundamental problems of the so-called capitalist system and to radically attack them fall too easily into the folly of investigating the private lives of capitalist giants in order to prove through this how rotten and near to collapse the capitalist system is.

Workers delight in gossip and bedtime stories about others just as much as the middle class. The good burghers are too stingy and anxious to stage a good juicy scandal of their own, and project their immorality on to others; the workers aim at the big capitalists and the monarchs. And the agitator is more certain of getting the applause of his listeners when he can dish up a scandalous tale than when he speaks about and analyzes the problems of the system.

But in order not to mislead the worker into dissipation and goad him into desiring higher and higher wages and demanding his share of what he produces, the belief must be maintained in public that the large capitalist, who in the opinion of agitators fattens on the sweat of the workers is a model of moral strength, thrift, and respect for the law.

Thus an embarrassing scandal can bring down a great man because his peers, to protect themselves and preserve and even increase their power, must let the man fall in order to show publicly that they have nothing in common with him, that they aren't like him.

If Mr. Collins should have become involved in a scandal, he would not have been able to continue as president. But he might still have remained a powerful force in the company and done much more for it by working in the background.

Through his personality and the prestige that Betty lent him as his mistress, he could achieve results for the company that were unattainable by many other company presidents. He could bring about the construction of roads that were useful only to his company because they created a quick connection to its oil fields, roads that served only the company and that the company would have had to build for this reason, but which the state now built. For the governors of states, members of congress, mayors, city fathers, did what he decided. If they didn't, they ceased to be what they were. Without caring about it at all, he influenced policy. The politicians who busied themselves professionally with policy did not know they were doing exactly what Mr. Collins wanted. Most of these politicians considered themselves to be free and independent, serving the interests of the commonweal. By their own lights, many of them were respectable and honorable men.

Early in life Mr. Collins had learned how to conduct politics without the politicians' feeling that they weren't free to act but that they were led by an earthly divinity in their volition, thinking, speech, and actions. He had taken a fancy to the idea when he grasped and correctly analyzed with his brilliant perceptiveness and observational ability the true background of a great strike of construction workers in Chicago.

Mr. Collins stemmed from Harrisburg, Pennsylvania. His father owned a grocery store there. It wasn't very remarkable: Annual income less than three thousand dollars. Mr. Chaney C. Collins had to work and starve his way through college. He helped out as a waiter, painter, messenger, porter. Every month his father sent him a check for forty dollars, and on several occasions it was reduced to only thirty.

After leaving college without getting a degree, he got a job in a bank through the intervention of a canner who sold his tins to the elder Collins and wanted to preserve his friendship. Mr. Collins began at the bank at seventeen dollars a week. After a year he was raised to eighteen. So he changed over to an insurance agency. There he started at twenty-two, and after three years he was making forty.

Then he got himself into an advertising agency, beginning at forty dollars. Four years passed, and he was bringing home a hundred a week. A quite extraordinary salary, but he earned it, because he worked out several good ideas and proposals for publicity for a toothbrush, a facial cream, an electric toaster, a new cigarette, a brass polish, a collapsible carrying-case for a child, and a newly discovered roofing compound that consisted of a mixture of cement and tar. From his ideas the firm made a clear profit of forty thousand dollars. When he learned this from the books one day, his financial wisdom teeth burst through. He realized that up to then he had been an ass.

So he decided to begin for himself. When he announced he wanted to leave, the company offered him one hundred fifty a week, then one hundred eighty, and finally two hundred dollars and a five percent share of the profits from the sale of his plans.

He declined it all, because he was not going to concern himself with trifles any more.

His concern with working out advertising plans for the new roofing compound had put him in touch with home-building and building speculators. He was even thinking of engaging in real estate and building houses himself. But then the great building trades strike broke out in Chicago.

Quite by accident he learned from one of the speculators, who was drunk and bragging about how smart he was and how he had led all the blockheads around by rings through their noses, the true story of that strike.

At the time there were two magnates in Chicago real estate, both fighting for supremacy. Because the person who had supremacy decided policy in Chicago. And whoever made policy decided where the streetcar lines should be routed, and where not, where the stations would be built, and where, in the interests of the inhabitants, they were forbidden, where the city had to build a hospital and where the district was unhealthy for healing the sick. Whoever had this power knew a year in advance where a streetcar line was going, and thus he was able to buy up land cheaply from those who did not know a trolley line was planned and sell it at a five thousand percent profit as soon as the rails were laid. As it was with the stations, so it was with the hospitals, slaughterhouses, schools, tenements, with everything that was dependent on real estate.

Both magnates had several blocks of private homes, tenements, office buildings, and shops in the works at the same time. There was a single object at stake, and it ran into many millions of dollars.

Whoever finished his building projects first was the winner. He could keep all the leases which were already signed, while the builder who wasn't finished on the appointed day had to pay a sizeable penalty to the home buyer and renter. Whoever finished first got all the renters who were waiting for homes; whoever finished last might have his houses standing empty for a month.

Because the need was filled for the next month, no one was buying then.

So the magnate who first got the idea and was most willing to lay out money on it went to the construction workers' trade union and bribed the secretary for ten thousand dollars. Under the illustrious influence of the great labor leader Samuel Gompers, who long ago had the honor of being born among the decent, hardworking, proles of the Amsterdam ghetto, leadership of a trade union became as good a business as the mass manufacturing of ready-to-wear men's suits or badly sewn women's dresses. A union leader of this kind, one who at his death couldn't leave to his various weeping widows and orphans a bank account of several hundred thousand dollars, had misunderstood his calling. He was a dolt who got out of prison one day only to return there the next, all because he believed a union had something to do with socialism.

The bribed secretary now discovered that a ten-hour workday was too long, and seven dollars a day was too low. Now, in the middle of this intense building activity, the hour had come at last when they would achieve what the anarchists had been hanged for in Chicago several years before. To do this successfully, as the secretary told the convocation of construction workers, they could not strike everywhere at once. They had first to strike the one magnate, and then the other. When both had been vanquished, the construction workers would at last be masters of Chicago. He knew how to make it all beautifully clear, and the workers believed it all, for he was, after all, their secretary.

So the strike began. It was conducted with all the fury and hate that can be evoked in workers who are getting, instead of their seven dollars a day, only meager strike support payments. There were pitched battles with strikebreakers; strikers and scabs were stabbed; police fired into the aroused crowds; and many prison sentences were handed out.

Finally the magnate who had bribed the secretary was finished with his building program, and the one who, because of the strike, was not ready lost his money and was eliminated from the race for supremacy in Chicago real estate.

The workers talked themselves half to death in their meetings about the power of the speculators and the indomitable might of capitalism, and they drudged away in a united campaign to strengthen their organization and to sign up the last unorganized man. For only a strong organization was necessary to smash capitalism or, if the socialist world order was perhaps not going to be seen in the very near future, at least to get an adequate living wage.

It was knowledge of the true story of this strike that was the basis of Mr. Collins's power.

Mr. Collins remembered a fellow student from his college days whose father was vice-president of one of the large anthracite companies in Pennsylvania. Through this schoolmate he succeeded in getting an interview with the vice-president.

After the vice-president had grasped the plan that Mr. Collins submitted to him, Collins was invited to attend a meeting of the company directors and present his plan.

Collins's plan was so clever that though he was a nobody, he could not be cheated out of it. For if the company tried to use it without coming to terms in advance with him over the cost, he had only to go to a newspaper and the plan would be defeated. And there was always some newspaper that would look into indiscretions in order to have an exclusive on a sensational story, and pay well for it to boot.

The directors saw this at once, and so they began to enter into serious negotiations with Collins.

Collins demanded eight percent of the net proceeds of the deal. They agreed at last on five percent, paid ten percent in cash and ninety percent in company stock. Furthermore, Collins was admitted to membership on the board of directors and for the duration of the maneuver was appointed private secretary to the president at a monthly salary of three thousand dollars. For practical purposes, he had little to do, since the executive secretary stayed on to handle current business. He had only to be present at all times to give advice on the necessary tactical movements.

At the time he was not yet thirty years old.

CHAPTER SEVEN

THE MANEUVER began. As it turned out, it went off exactly as Collins had foreseen.

The chief trick consisted in not saying one word about it beforehand.

The company operated all the pits on overtime. There was overtime and more overtime. There were generous bonuses for the miners for efficiency. Thousands of new workers were dredged up from Europe.

All the storehouses were filled to the brim with anthracite and large fields were rented to hold and store the mined coal.

No new customers were taken on. To prevent suspicion from arising, only current contracts with the railroads and steamship lines and coal dealers were honored. The action was conducted so cleverly, in accordance with Collins's advice, and went off so smoothly and inconspicuously that no other company even so much as suspected that what was being prepared here was one of the most tremendous coups ever seen. For the maneuver was carried out in that calm, contented period that precedes deep economic crises. At such times people dare not risk anything foolish since the normal course of business yields sufficient profit. A too risky speculation could only lead to an insecurity that at the time is unwelcome. People keep to the fat contracts they have and don't much care what others are doing, because, having the contracts in hand, they can put on airs and afford to be glad that others have something.

And one day, after everything had been prepared for several months, the great blow was delivered.

It began quite calmly as a gentle caress. The Anthracite Company informed all the workers that after Friday of the next week all piece rates were being reduced by twenty-five percent and all day rates by fifteen percent.

The company was operating according to a new system. It was *not* bribing union secretaries. It did not need them at all. The effect was much greater without their co-operation, since the secretaries would have perhaps messed up the maneuver. Besides, some secretaries of the mine workers are unreliable. They are honest fellows and keep to the workers. They stand on their soapboxes and cannot be silenced until they are knocked senseless with stones by agents of the coal magnates. The tens of thousands of company workers called a meeting at once, but nothing came of it. They still expected to earn enough through the bonus system, even after the pay cut, if they slaved away harder and worked still more overtime than before. A few directors began to become uneasy. But Collins stayed calm. In this situation he showed for the first time his talent as a great leader among the magnates.

"We are only just beginning, gentlemen," he said. "Don't get upset yet. You can condemn me to death if everything doesn't turn out right. I'll even execute the sentence myself. I'll shoot myself if that suits you. But see it through." So they let him proceed.

A month later the bonus system was abolished.

A week after that, all overtime was canceled, and the workers who in the meantime had adjusted to the bonuses, the overtime, the high pay, who had gone into debt, bought lots for houses, sent their children to college, and done so much more that now threatened to strangle them in debt, began to become confused.

A stringent new system was instituted in the pits. Anyone who arrived at the seam so much as a minute late was not permitted to work that day, yet he had to stay in the shaft because there was no cage to take him up. He had to wait until his shift left. In addition, on the next day he did work, a half day's pay was deducted for the minute he came too late.

That wasn't all. The coal was inspected more carefully. If more than four stones or half a shovelful of slack was found, or if the weight was short more than four pounds, the entire wagonload of coal was not credited to the miners, and they were not paid for it, though the company took the coal anyway. At this point the union was implored to step in. It had already been called in when wages were reduced, but then the trustees decided after long deliberation that they first wanted to wait and see whether it was only a company maneuver. According to reports the secretary had studied, business in anthracite was booming.

When the union delegates requested a meeting with the company, management pointed out that it couldn't deal with people who didn't work in the company mines. Three days later, when the system of not recording coal at its full weight was being applied even more ruthlessly, specially elected delegates—men who did work for Anthracite—requested a conference.

This time the request was granted. Immediately after an exchange of pleasantries the miners were told they would be fully compensated for the time lost during the meeting. That would be entirely proper.

This generosity disposed the delegates to be docile. They had come to show how aroused they were, firmly bent on acting at the conference like voracious tigers, but when they were offered excellent cigars, and were courteously invited to sit down in the deep, soft easy chairs, they became so tame that the president could have placed his head in the jaws of their tiger and never felt a tooth.

It was made clear to them that the company had such a surplus of coal on hand that it intended to shut down the mines for a good long while. Only the pumps and the maintenance crews would stay on the job. They even went so far as to produce the ledgers on existing inventory for the delegates to examine.

The miners didn't know how to read such books, because they dealt with credit and debit, and the delegates didn't know sales from inventory. But they leafed through the books, pretending they understood it all. In the end they had to admit that there was an enormous supply of unsold coal on hand.

During the meeting, in which the delegates said very little, they were always addressed like gentlemen. Without their wanting to admit it, they were befuddled by this courteous treatment. Deep down, they felt as if they were members of the board of directors and had a say in deciding what was going to happen in the mines.

When at last they were standing on the outside again, they realized they were no wiser than before. In the union meeting that afternoon it was terribly hard for them to give an account of what they had accomplished and to report on everything that was discussed. Among their listeners were those who would have done exactly the same if they had been chosen to go to the meeting, but now they shouted out angrily at the delegates: "You cowards, you raggedy asses, you've let yourselves be thoroughly buttered up and sweet-talked again. We ought to tar and feather you all." Another miner cried out shrilly: "How much'd lousy dogs give ya? Now ya can pay f'ya phonograph, eh, Billy?" At that remark laughter filled the hall.

On Wednesday of the next week the company announced that all union members would be laid off at the end of the week. Only those workers who handed in their union cards at the company offices would be allowed to continue working. All the others, those who did not turn in a union card, would have to sign a statement declaring they were not members of any union. If it got out that anyone had signed and nevertheless had remained in the union, he would be laid off immediately without being paid the wages due him, and would have to leave the company town with his family within forty-eight hours. If he didn't, he would be handed over to the police for trespass on company property.

On Saturday morning the strike broke out in all the Anthracite Company mines. It was exactly what the company needed to collect its profits from the maneuver. As here, so always: Workers rarely strike when it suits them. They usually strike when it is convenient for capitalism. Not out of stupidity, but because they are obeying iron laws. Whatever the workers do, they will do within the capitalist system, and whatever they do within the system will be useful to capitalism because they are a part of it. They are bound up with it, during the system's supremacy, body and soul. The active person performs, the passive suffers. Within the system it is the capitalist who acts. He knows what he wants. He wants to make a lot of money. The worker only wants a share. He wants to make it just like the capitalist, he wants to have more than his fellow rabble. If the baker strikes and succeeds, bread becomes more expensive for the shoemaker, and the baker then has to pay more for his shoe soles. Within this system everything serves capitalism. Not because one is a cruel exploiter, the others are starving, and the rest traitors to the working class, but because they all are caught up in the same machinery.

Mr. Chaney C. Collins knew this law, and he used it to his own advantage. That was the entire extent of his wisdom.

Now the Anthracite Company began to collect. It was the first company to use modern ideas about proletarian rights and freedom movements to make hundreds of thousands of dollars in profits. Since then it has become a habit, even a respectable business practice. But at the time, when Collins was thirty years old, this business was still not worn out, and it had no rivals. For that reason, no single company has ever since taken in so many millions by this trick as the Anthracite Company took in at that time.

The strike at the Anthracite Company had begun, and it involved some twenty thousand miners. The major newspapers sent special correspondents to the company to learn from it everything about the strike and its origins that could interest the newspaper reader and be magnified sensationally and so made into bold headlines.

The company directors assigned Mr. Collins, at his own request, to satisfy the reporters' hunger for thrilling stories. Mr. Collins had thought out carefully, long in advance, how he was going to deal with the newspapers. The success of this tactic depended upon their remaining ignorant of the fact that they were being used to further the plans of the Anthracite Company.

The reporters were told that the company was greatly overstocked and that all its warehouses were overflowing with coal. Sales had fallen off steadily, and the company did not know what to do with the surplus while demand was lower than production. This was clearly proved with the aid of the inventory ledgers and sales contracts that were shown to the reporters.

Mr. Collins said that an unprecedented drop in the price of coal was imminent. For this reason they had decided to lower wages as the only way of withstanding the impending fall in prices. The workers, however, had not seen the necessity of this reduction in wages, which was certainly understandable since, after all, they weren't well enough trained in economics. He declared that the company couldn't deviate from the reduction in wages, since maintaining the former scale would ruin the company, and even the entire American coal industry. So far as the company was concerned, it would not yield, because it could not, without committing economic suicide. When asked why the company had forbidden the workers to belong to a union, Mr. Collins explained that the workers were willing to work for the reduced wages but that the union wouldn't permit it. Outside interference in the company's economic affairs could not be permitted without thereby surrendering all the rights and liberties guaranteed to business and labor by the Constitution. The company would recommend that its willing workers establish a union to which only company employees would belong. Only this union would be regarded as the legitimate representative of the company workers. But it seemed, Mr. Collins added, the workers were not willing to take the company's thoroughly legitimate and essential wishes into account. Therefore he could predict confidently that the strike would last ever so long, six months at least, and perhaps even eight to fourteen months.

The reporters thanked him for this informative explanation of the reasons for the strike so far as it concerned the company.

Reporters serve only the truth, and regard it as their sacred duty to seek it out, even if it is to be found in the sewers of the people and between the bedsheets of the individual person. For it is the singularly exalted task of a newspaper to report the truth and nothing but the truth to its readers. That is why the newspaper is

God's earthly instrument, the scourge of liars and all corrupters of the people, of agitators, Jews, conspirators, foreigners, and European immigrants who, filled full of anarchistic and similar pacifistic ideas, alight on the shores of our beautiful land to contaminate and destroy our glorious republic. That is why the reporters also went to the union to hear the other side. Here, however, as they later told their readers, they did not find the calm confidence on aims they had seen among the company directors. Instead they found unrest, nervousness, nonsensical speeches, anarchistic brawlers, unclear concepts, and confused notions of profit, common concerted action of the entire nation, the workers' right to organize, supposed duties toward one's own family, crazy opinions about the administration in general, and the malignity and depravity of capitalism in particular. But as clear, unambiguous purpose there emerged the firm, unshakable determination not to settle until the union was reinstated, along with the old pay rates, though with perhaps a few adjustments, for, as they were saying in the union, the earlier rates, apparently so high, were already short of meeting the many fixed and ever-increasing demands of daily life. And here, too, it was impressed on the reporters that the workers were prepared for a very, very long strike. It wasn't a matter solely of wages any more, but of principles which now had to be settled definitely.

So bold headlines on the front pages of newspapers declared, in keeping with the truth, that a coal strike of unforeseeable length had begun, and that it threatened to cripple the entire industry, perhaps even the entire American economy.

This report could have been composed by Mr. Collins himself, so well did it agree with his plans.

As a part of Mr. Collins's plan, the Anthracite Company had informed the other coal companies that its sales had fallen off and that it had had to build up its reserves. And as a result it had also felt compelled to make significant cuts in pay scales. All the other companies were extremely busy as Anthracite cautiously pulled out of the market. For that matter, they did not understand why Anthracite was so short of sales. But if one of the largest companies had problems, something had to be happening in the marketplace. All the companies understood that at once.

They, too, began to become more cautious. They authorized their salary experts to work out new scales with lowered wages. But for the time being they didn't put the new rates into effect. They still had sufficient orders and couldn't afford any unrest among their own workers.

When the Anthracite strike broke out and the newspaper reports did their job, the New York exchange answered by discounting coal stocks, labeling railroad and steamship stocks insecure, and easing the market for steel stocks. A calm began to settle over Wall Street. After a few days the calm became alarming, drawing nearer to the calm that usually precedes the dreaded storm.

But it hadn't yet come to a catastrophe, to that wild oscillation of stock prices and the senseless dumping of securities that lay nearest the center of the cyclone. It seemed as if everyone was forcing himself to keep calm. Because no one knew what was going on. Everyone wanted to wait a bit until he got the proper tip from someone, from a dream or a fortuneteller. But all the business on the New York exchange went slack. Two days later Chicago responded with a softening of the market that had not been seen for several months.

Still, taken as a whole, the market was steady, because securities bearing little relation to coal remained active and moved in the usual way, a couple of points up and a couple down, moving back the next morning. Strangely, electric utility stocks even began to advance. But their steady rise seemed to indicate that people were beginning to trust coal less and less. It was obvious to every insider that this rise in electric stocks had to be followed by a fall in coal. And then, of course, the storm began to break.

Still, in that same week the hydroelectric stocks, which were independent of coal, suddenly rose sharply, climbing eighteen points in one day.

That was the distant thunder of the coming storm.

The steamship lines, the railroad companies, and the large coal dealers did not make any new contracts; they began to buy only the weekly requirement. A drop in coal prices was imminent, and until they knew the new price and the new lower price had been established, they couldn't enter into new agreements.

At this point the rest of the coal companies began to feel the effects of the tightening market. They were not prepared with large inventories since large reserves require large bank loans, which could not be procured overnight, as they required deliberation and agreements and the revocation of other loans. As a result of the growing uncertainty of the market, the banks became very cautious about issuing credit against coal stocks because their value was insecure. In general, when they did give credit, they did so for scarcely more than the bare cost of extracting the coal. So it happened that the other companies could not accumulate substantial stocks.

They had to mine the coal more cheaply. And by the usual system, that could be done only if the workers' wages were slashed. To be on the safe side they immediately adopted the Anthracite Company pay rates.

What was left for the workers to do? They did what Mr. Collins wanted: they struck at the other coal companies because they wouldn't stand for the reduction in wages.

The smaller companies did not know what to do. They were not so deeply affected by fluctuations on the exchange because, as a rule, they had a small but steady clientele. Some reduced wages and forbade union membership whereas others wouldn't accept any risk at all and simply locked their workers out and shut the mines down to see first what the large companies would do.

All this happened without any planned and organized co-operation and interaction among the various companies. Co-operation would have disrupted Mr. Collins's plan. But he had worked it out so cleverly that not one company felt it had been deliberately excluded from the great robbery. Indeed, Mr. Collins had told everyone beforehand that the Anthracite was building up its inventories and had to reduce wages. By doing this he made it seem he was working together with all the companies. No one could blame him. But at the same time he had perfected his plans with every message and drawn a veil over his intentions. This he needed to do in order to work undisturbed.

Two hundred and forty thousand miners were now on strike. Two hundred and forty thousand men and their families had to live on the meager strike funds paid to them by the union, and this support diminished with every week the strike lasted. Since the families had less money, they could buy less. And that swept away thousands of business people and small craftsmen who also were earning less, and because they had less to spend, wider economic circles were affected. Every week thousands more went to the bank to withdraw their savings because they had to live and obligations to meet. As a result money in the bank grew short. With every passing week credit became more difficult to get. Interest rates were raised. Everything that had to be pawned was worth less and less. People had to sell their expensive furniture for a tenth of its value to raise money for the necessities of life. Among those who suffered were the furniture makers and furniture dealers, as well as all the other people who made or dealt in items now being sold at far less than their value.

On the picket lines the workers fought with the police and received bloody heads for their courage. And in their meetings they disputed with their fists the question of which of them was a strike-breaker and which an essential worker needed in the pits during the strike to keep the mines from flooding. They squabbled with their wives, who wanted to have some money. They accused the union secretaries of being corrupt agents of capitalism. They tore up their union cards and spat on them. They whined for mercy to their foremen to take them back again and not to forget them when the strike ended. They swore never to strike again, even if wages were cut sixty percent. And they went to the revival meetings of the Methodists, Baptists, and Episcopalians and threw themselves down in the dust of the church floor, moaning that their souls were cleansed and saved, and that, at last, through this severe ordeal, they had found their way home into the arms of their Redeemer Jesus Christ. And there were the eternal optimists, the eternal pessimists, the eternal grumblers, the eternal whiners, and, finally, the defiant, who gritted their teeth and muttered under their breath: "Ten thousand times better to croak than yield a penny to these thieves!" Everyone was represented, every type that is found in a revolution, in every revolution. Men who want to eat and have nothing. Men who would sell their souls for a regular meal. Men who would rather gnaw their fists than say: "At your service, Sir!" All kinds of men. And among them the all-righteous, the pharisees of the proletarian movement.

The storm arrived.

The New York exchange rattled. If you were only a neutral bystander owning no shares, you might have enjoyed it.

It made the feathers fly.

It hailed and thundered. The walls of the buildings of this unbreakable system shivered.

The telephone booths of stockbrokers crackled.

Ten points up. Sell quick. But before this is done, down twenty, and no one is buying it down thirty. Down forty. Up four. Hope. Up a point. Cables around the globe. The market is beginning to firm up. Down fourteen. The market again volatile.

Three shots in three separate booths in Wall Street, each renting for two thousand a month.

Up twelve points. Down three. Down seven. Down four. Up two. Telephone operators are going into convulsions. Telegraphers are going mad. In the offices of banks and tiny rooms of brokers the small white tapes spew out through the jaws of tickers at incomprehensible speed bearing sentences of death and the rebirth of hope.

Four men are standing around and reading. And reading, reading the rushing figures that change constantly, like wraithes. Reading and grasping with a slender thread of their subconscious the sense and significance, the complete economic relation, of every little letter preceding the figures and explaining to those who are among the initiated the names of companies whose stocks were flying to and fro. To the outsider the letters are just as hard to decipher as old Egyptian hieroglyphics. But the men standing around the ticker read and read, tearing at the tape with the right hand in order to pull it from the tireless spewing jaws even faster, and with the left raising the telephone to quivering lips to give orders. To give orders as quickly as the splitting brain can make head or tail of the figures, situations, and stocks at hand. Brains, jaws, ears, mouths, letters, and tearing hands are pursued by invisible powers that are neither seen nor felt here, but only sensed.

And the endless, long, narrow white tape pops out, rushes along, and flutters about.

The narrow white tape bubbles and fizzes up, deciding in a

second the fates of tens of thousands of willing and able workers whose human personality, individuality, is extinguished and whose value scarcely equals a few points up or down in a stock. And the tape decides the destiny of hundreds of comfortable citizens, determining plans for educating their sons and marrying off their daughters, and providing the comforts of old age.

The long narrow white tape runs over the spools. After it has spoken, it coils up under the small table on which the ticker stands. It is the ticking clock of Doomsday for thousands and thousands of people. The tape forms into a ball in a heap that grows ever larger.

The excited men stand in the heap that winds itself increasingly around their feet like a long slender snake.

After giants and pygmies have sought to decide, as quickly as the rushing figures allow, the tape prances away, useless and forgotten, into the wastebasket, coiling itself into a tangled heap. No one even has time enough to break the tape. It coils and swells and twines along restlessly.

And at last the heap looks like a skeleton, a skeleton with a thousand long, intricate, twisted, thin little bones, the corpse of financial thought.

There is an earthquake on Wall Street, an earthquake of the economic system.

Every day there are suicides of men who yesterday seemed to be great, powerful, unassailable, indomitable pillars of an economy that seemed to the world healthy and bursting with vigor.

No one can control the catastrophe any longer.

It grows and grows.

What seemed to be a powerful, unbreakable, well-organized, cleverly thought out, calm and collected economy cracks down to the foundations—all because a single branch has grown shaky: coal, the sustenance of industry.

No one can halt the wheel. It turns, faster and faster, and tears deeper and deeper wounds into the body of the economy.

Runs on the banks begin. The depositors have been seized with panic. They fear—no, they're sure—the money they've saved, for which they slaved, is lost. In endless long lines they are already standing in front of the banks, each wanting to be first when the tellers' windows open. The earlier they arrive, the greater the chances they'll still salvage something. The orderly life of the banks is disturbed. All efforts have to be spent in paying out. Nobody deposits anything. All credit is suspended. Banks in other countries are cabled asking them to help out with cash and checks. All the reserves of the national bank association are called in. But the lines in front of the banks grow longer.

And then the banks begin to fail because they cannot pay. Their money is on loan, because a bank that cannot lend money cannot pay interest to its depositers. First the small banks fail, and the big ones help themselves a lot by reducing the tellers' hours to two a day, and then to one.

Then the large banks begin to collapse.

And all this confusion has not caused the sudden disappearance of a continent or a gigantic natural catastrophe annihilating irreplaceable values. Behind this breakdown of the economic order and economic security, which is perpetually menaced by agitators, there is nothing but the deranged imagination of those who have something—the insecurities of those who own a lot and of those who own only a little. All that is happening now in Wall Street depends on nothing other than a single thought, a thought that has suddenly taken a course opposite to the one laid out by the usual mass hypnosis: "I can lose!" It rips to tatters this pretty economic system allegedly devised and ordained by God. And yet all values remain the same. The values haven't changed. There is just as much coal as there ever was. The money is all there; not one cent has spun off the earth into space, where it can never be fished up again. All the houses are still standing. Forests. Waterfalls. Oceans. Ships and railroads are still intact. And hundreds of thousands of healthy, vigorous people are willing to work and produce and increase the earth's existing wealth. No engineer has lost his talent for building new machines. No coal pit has been buried in an avalanche. The warm sun is shining in the sky as it always has. It rains as it always has. Grain stands in the field and ripens as usual. The cotton fields grow in splendor. Nothing, nothing at all, in existing earthly wealth, has changed. Mankind, seen as a whole, is just as rich today as it was yesterday. And for this reason, and this reason alone—that the possessions of a few people threaten to shift and change—a catastrophe sweeps over all mankind. It is a catastrophe like those of ages past when famines broke out in one district and adjustments couldn't be arranged with other districts that were choking on plenty because telegraphs and transportation were lacking.

It is an economic system, an economic order, created by men who profess themselves to possess intelligence, by men, however, who in spite of all the highly developed technology they've created have still not fully overcome the primitiveness of uncivilized man—so far as it concerns a well-thought-out and well-ordered economic system.

A great economic crisis now shook the country, and it was followed by a huge depression. Communists and socialists, in the manner of prophets who always claim to know things in advance, had announced its coming, with threatening index fingers, and the people had viewed it fearfully as a divine punishment.

For ninety-nine percent of mankind there is something mysterious about an economic crisis. Whether religious or irreligious, people see in an economic crisis the scourge of a supernatural force that seems ineluctably bound up with the capitalist system, a force that obviously is to be averted or avoided. These people suffer in an economic crisis, some more than others. And practically all people today face a depression with as little hope as, thousands of years ago, people faced plagues, famines, and mongol invasions.

Yet these economic crises are not in any way produced by supernatural and mystical powers. They are produced this way: an individual person or a group of individuals violently interferes in ordered economic life to exploit it for a great private gain. So long as economic life goes along its tranquil way without panics being produced artificially, fluctuations can well arise within the economy, but never a severe crisis. The capitalist system is really not at all so chaotic as it frequently appears. Capitalists make mistakes at times, but they aren't fools. Only fools produce recklessly, without keeping both eyes steadily focused on the market and its capacity to absorb goods. Inventions and new designs of better machines can easily supplant one another, but even they cannot produce a crisis. Something at least has been learned on our continent: the higher the pay, the shorter the day, and the greater the education of the worker, the surer is the peaceful course of economic life and the harder it is for the powerful to bring about a serious crisis.

If hundreds and hundreds of millions of tons of the best coal are cleverly and inconspicuously withheld from their intended purpose without mankind's being able to prepare itself, the result has to be exactly the same as when an earthquake or a stupendous flood destroys a large region of the earth. But a natural catastrophe cannot disrupt economic life as a far-reaching speculation can. With a natural catastrophe you know what has happened, you know what is missing, and where and how to begin to repair the damages. But with a speculation no one knows what really has happened. No one knows whether the cause is coal or money, or the lack of iron or other ores, or speculation in grains or cotton or oil. Thus no one can know the source of the trouble, because it is usually known only to a single person, and he isn't telling because he intends to take his profits in the confusion.

Now a lively debate sprang up across the country.

Economists, industrialists, bankers wrote learned articles in the newspapers. Everyone reached the conclusion that the lack of coal, which was now severely felt, was the cause of the crisis that had arrived so unexpectedly, and that if the coal problem could be relieved, the crisis would soon be at an end. As a matter of fact, a coal shortage was now really at hand. For when all the coal miners strike, every lump of coal has to be used up in a few weeks.

In bold headlines the newspapers called on the government to settle the strike at any cost. But hundreds of large companies and leading industrialists opposed this suggestion, because any government interference in the strike encroaches on the freedoms of business and labor, and thus is against the Constitution.

But the government showed not the least intention of intervening. It did the only thing a government seems to be capable of doing today: It sent troops and machine guns into the strike districts. Stones and insults were hurled at the soldiers, for their presence aroused the strikers. And with that the miners were peppered to a fare-thee-well. Here today, gone tomorrow. And all the people who feared the specter of a lack of coal said: "That's good. The government is establishing order there, blowing those anarchists' brains out."

Even workers, unionized workers, were not entirely kindly disposed to the striking miners. If the coal strike continued for very long, all the factories would have to close by and by, and then there wouldn't be any work for anyone. They sent money to the miners, to be sure, but they did so with sour expressions and gnawed on every penny before finally turning loose of it.

The slowly developing coal shortage soon turned into a hunger. And this hunger quickly began to become a mania. People began to hoard coal, buying it for years in advance so that they would be prepared for any eventuality with a cellarful. And when the cellar was full at last, the happy owner could say: "So far as I'm concerned, the strike can go on for five years. I'm ready for it!" It didn't matter to him whether his neighbor ever laid hold of a pound of coal.

Those were the little people, who needed coal only for their homes.

The large outfits, the railroads and the steamship lines, were waiting, because they still could not see exactly what was happening and for the time being could still draw down their own stocks. But the little companies were driving the price up.

To guarantee themselves coal, the large companies began to enter into agreements with English, German, and French companies.

And that was exactly what Mr. Collins was waiting for. The purchase of foreign coal would arouse the transport workers and stir up their feelings of proletarian solidarity for the striking coal miners.

They did Mr. Collins a favor, acting exactly as he wanted. They even did better than he expected. Use a well-tested recipe and you're bound to bake a good cake.

The transport workers convened giant meetings. From the thunderous debate there emerged a resolution, passed unanimously: "The miners must be supported. They must not lose this strike. Therefore, no coal ship arriving from England or Germany or any other foreign country is to be unloaded on our shores. If need be, there will be sympathy strikes in every business served by transport workers, railroads included."

B. TRAVEN

The magnates did not wait around to see whether this threat was real. What they needed least of all at this time was a transport workers strike. In America that usually involved extensive and very expensive sabotage of every means of transportation. And that would have confused the situation even more. They would have lost all control, and been unable to tell what it would lead to in the end.

They did not sign the contracts with the English and German coal companies, and no coal ships arrived in America. And that was exactly what Mr. Collins wanted.

From that time on everything went like clockwork.

Mr. Collins was working according to the Biblical formula, developed by Joseph, the son of Jacob, which raised him from a forgotten prison inmate to the wealthiest man of Egypt and then to viceroy. To the dismay of many at that time, he was another foreigner. As everybody knows, Joseph accumulated grain at low prices in the so-called fat years and sold it in the lean years—at usurious prices. Of course, the Bible, as it so often does, does not tell us the whole story, but trims it.

Mr. Collins was not a descendant of Joseph. If he had had any say about it, he would have forbidden Jewish immigration to the States. But it must be admitted, he was greater than Joseph, greater than the Earl of Beaconsfield, who understood and worked his way up from Benjamin Disraeli to become British Prime Minister.

Mr. Collins was greater. And more modern. He did not make use of another person's dream: he used proletarian solidarity, of which so much is said but which is seen so seldom when a mobilization order is posted on the walls and the soldiers march out.

The odds were on Mr. Collins's side that the moneyed people would be scared to death that a united proletariat could become a mighty force capable of shaking the world.

Mr. Collins was not sentimental. He collected. He skimmed the cream of the nation. How the nation had to bleed! The price of a ton of coal doubled, then tripled, and then quadrupled. At that point Mr. Collins opened the sheds and helped the dying industries to their feet again. He became the savior of the nation.

The company cashed in. It had no expenses. The mineworkers' union had all the expenses, and its ample funds were drained, right down to the last copper penny. Only the proletariat had expenses, as grumbling and groaning, they took up collections for the starving miners. Kings make war, and the proletariat bleeds and dies. Magnates pull off a great haul, and the prole sacrifices his last penny and goes hungry. Always the proletariat! And ever and again the proletariat. Hang it all, prole, what an ass you are.

As the battle was fought and economic life and Wall Street began to calm down again, Mr. Collins had earned for his own pocket a neat million, four hundred thousand dollars.

He no longer had any use for the workers. They had only been chess pieces, worse than chess pieces, for even a wooden chess piece knows that it is a chess piece. But the workers did not know, and to this day they have not discovered they were only pieces moved here and there by Mr. Collins. The workers raised a great shout about having won the strike when they were permitted to go back into the pits again with their wages reduced only ten percent and were allowed to have their union back again to be used as a play thing.

For what did the companies really care about the union? Union or no union, a worker will starve if he doesn't have a job. And the union doesn't determine whether or not he has a job; the person who decides does not rant and rave, but acts without sentimentality.

Mr. Collins did not count the fallen. He did not post a list of those who were going to sit in prison for years to come, of those who were killed or committed suicide, of those who had gone insane, those who were lying in hospitals.

Only bad generals care about the dead.

We are busy enough with the living.

And while the prole is burying his dead, mourning and eulogizing them, his opponent gains time to plan and prepare for the new battle.

CHAPTER EIGHT

MR. COLLINS was now at the top. He was a full-fledged member of the general staff of the nation's economic life.

But the men who formerly had worked side by side with him—the directors of the Anthracite Company—began to be afraid of him. They all were lacking in sentimentality, but they still were fastidious enough not to go the limit.

Everything the company had done had stayed within the limits of the law. In all its actions the company was protected by the law. Everyone had the right to stock up when and where and how he wished. And everyone had the right to reduce his inventories whenever it seemed most propitious. The Anthracite Company had never operated with lies in their great raid. It had openly announced it was filling its dumps up. And it carried out the entire maneuver without violating any clause in the antitrust laws. It had not entered into any trust-like arrangement with any other company in order to control the market. The business was as clean, as respectable, as upright, as any business within the capitalist system can be. The Anthracite Company cannot be blamed if people allow themselves to be thrown into a panic. For that the good Lord is responsible. He created everything, and not even a mouse may perish if it isn't in his plans. If people didn't allow themselves to become frightened, no one could ever make millions. If people had more self-confidence and greater courage, if they were not afraid of a few days of hunger or of growing old, they could never be used by other men for their private purposes.

Though the business had stayed entirely within the law, the members of the board shrank from any new deals of a similar kind. There are always prying newspapers that can somehow get wind of such a maneuver and expose it. And the people who suffer from this coup turn into complainants. And where there are complainants, judges also turn up right away. A man is considered respectable only so long as no one can look through his affairs. None of the directors could be sent to the penitentiary, but every one of them could be reviled as a destroyer of the state and an advocate of socialistic ideas. Any capitalist who supplies material for socialist propaganda by an entirely too strict capitalist maneuver is worse than an anarchist.

The directors realized this in due course. This spared them the storms which the great oil scandal, the so-called Teapot Dome Scandal, gave rise to a few years later. These storms thoroughly rattled American capitalism and supplied dynamite to the socialists. The storms so upset the President of the Republic, Mr. Harding, that he took ill, lay down, and died, so conveniently that he could not be properly audited—to speak no ill of the dead—to discover how many millions he had made with Mr. Sinclair at the nation's expense while his heir apparent, Mr. Coolidge, lost his voice and has been known, ever since, as "Silent Cal."

So the directors came to the conclusion that it would be best to buy up the shares of this all-powerful person.

Mr. Collins was receiving his share of the profits in Anthracite stock. Because demand was great and coal was again being mined diligently, the stock had risen to its highest. Through his ownership of stock Mr. Collins had a proportionate number of votes, and he would have been able, solely by his votes, to lure the company into another maneuver—and the company wanted to avoid that. It had had enough for a long time; to these men the risk of a scandal was much too high at that time. Mr. Collins was considered an adventurer who did not care about scandals. He certainly did not at the time, because he was still on the rise. Later he would change in this respect. With advancing age a person cares more for his business reputation and social standing than as a youth, when he poses as a bohemian, though he has no contact at all with art.

They offered Mr. Collins a very good price for his shares. Thus they were rid of him. And thanked God. And gave to the church.

A man having a bank account of one and a half million dollars, formerly an influential member of the board of the powerful Anthracite Company, acquainted with and known to every large newspaper throughout the country as a strong, smart fellow, such a man has to turn into a capitalist power—even if he doesn't want to. He is forced into it. He is involved in all the large businesses and all the great maneuvers. The system cannot tolerate his remaining an outsider. The system needs his one and a half million; it needs his experience, knowledge, strength, will power. Large corporations send him stock just to interest him in their affairs and to be able to consult him. Banks will not leave him in peace. He has to participate here and there because he isn't considered so cheap as to be content to make a mere four percent. So no one approaches a man of Mr. Collins's reputation with twaddle. They come to him only with sure things, deals in which eighteen percent is as sure as death. Only the little hucksters are inveigled into stupid mistakes. A Collins never. Anyone who sells potatoes ten pounds at a time and parsley at two cents a bunch may succeed in achieving a modest easy-going prosperity, but he will never be rich. In exactly the same way, a proletarian who always works in a factory, never daring to stand on his own two feet, has just as little chance of collecting fifty thousand dollars for himself. He'd need fifty lifetimes for that, because he constantly receives only a small part of what he produces. The truly great fortunes are made only by those who grab hold of the nation's nervestrings. Unscrupulously.

The vital nerves of civilized man are grain, cotton, coal, and iron. He who controls any one of these four things is omnipotent.

Meat, leather, houses, and land are important, too. But a man can economize considerably on meat, he can wear his shoes till they are in shreds, he can move in with family and friends and get along for years without a new house. But he needs bread, and his cotton shirts and dresses are not so durable as leather. He needs coal so he won't freeze, so he'll have light and power for his workshop. He needs iron for his tools and machines, and, occasionally, for his rifles and howitzers.

All this Mr. Collins had grasped at the right time in life. That's why he had used coal to acquire power.

When he was forced out of coal because he had become too dangerous, he had to find another source of power. If he had power, he could secure all the pleasures of modern life. Playing with power he could taste to the full all the delights that make life interesting and worth living. Speculating and playing with power is more exciting than playing roulette. At roulette influence cannot be exercised. Roulette requires no intelligence. Any blockhead can play, which is why rogues, swindlers, women, and charlatans are found near roulette wheels. They're waiting to take the blockhead's winnings.

Mr. Collins was no fool. He had a good mind. And he constantly endeavored to use it.

It was the age when the automobile had survived its first shuddering trials. But only a few persons recognized the great future of the auto. Belief in the railroad's superiority was still unshakable. The first trial flights of airplanes were also over. Though they had cost the lives of many men, they had succeeded. It was already possible for a man to fly for several miles and stay in the air for a half hour before crashing into the ground and breaking his neck. Advance work on the diesel engine had also succeeded. It showed those who had any intelligence and did not consider the prevailing conditions to be the last expression of human capability the way technology would go. Had to go.

Mr. Collins saw instinctively that coal was beginning to die from hardening of the arteries. There would come a day when coal was unimportant and could perhaps be dispensed with entirely. Even then no one with any sense thought that automobiles and airplanes would run on coal.

So it happened that Mr. Collins latched on to the young, fresh, inexhaustible new commodity—oil.

He also tapped the right places immediately, which at the time were still quite new. He purchased fields in California and Oklahoma, buying in districts where no geologist had suspected oil existed. And he was successful.

He founded the Condor Oil Company. It was very small, very nearly the smallest of all when it came to capitalization.

But as soon as it was born, gave its first cry, and pulled its first long breath, it began to eat. And it ate and it ate. It consumed all the other small and middling companies and gobbled up all the individual entrepreneurs. And it continued to feast until it was so full and so fat that it stood right next to the foremost oil companies, respected and feared. Mr. Collins was so clever that he avoided such maneuvers as entangled a Harry Sinclair, the most powerful oil magnate, in one of the largest and smelliest capitalistic scandals the American people have seen in recent years—and Americans are really immensely rich in capitalistic scandals. That scandal seriously undermined the foundation of the capitalistic system, to an extent communist propaganda will never accomplish. That a system can survive such a scandal, that the people can even laugh about it and listen to satirical vaudeville songs about it, without in the least indicting the system, proves how solidly joined and secure the system still is. That system can scarcely, if at all, be turned topsy-turvy by the means the socialists and Bolsheviks recommend. Quite certainly not in the States. And in any case, not by the widely ballyhooed formulas. Mr. Sinclair is not condemned, but admired, because he was smart enough to purchase the nation's military reserves and turn them into oil and dollars. For years lawyers cudgeled their brains to discover which paragraph in the American statutes could properly be used to pursue Mr. Sinclair and his accomplices right up to the Presidency and into the Cabinet. This is a criminal matter. For anyone who is not a millionaire it is a crime that has to be punished by death since it is a high treason. Indeed, there is no enemy to whom the land might be betrayed. But there might be an enemy, and this belief that there might be must be preserved, nourished, and fed, so that steelworkers will not starve and the tank manufacturers will make enough money to spend in Paris and Berlin with their chorus girls. For in the States immorality with chorus girls and similar hungers for life are forbidden. That's why they're so expensive. And that is why Mr. Collins, in spite of all his millions in profits, always needs money.

His constant need for money was rooted in the difficulties he had with his women. It was partly women in general, and partly the specific women around him.

He wouldn't be able to say, at this point, how he had actually come to be married. Still, he could remember quite well that he had not married his wife: she had married him. She had not brought him any dowry, nor had she raised him up into a superior social class, where he would have influential friends. He was an insurance company clerk when he got married, making thirty-five dollars a week. A person making as little as that cannot expect to marry into a higher social class.

Nothing that might be called love, least of all romantic love, had preceded the marriage. The proceedings had taken place as prosaically and unemotionally as the selling of burglary insurance to a furniture dealer. Subsequently, both husband and wife were rather astonished when suddenly, one day, a daughter was born. Neither one had made any special effort to accomplish this or felt anything especially striking in the three-minute calls that offered, prospectively, the likelihood of a birth.

It never occurred to Mr. Collins to wonder whether he was actually married happily or unhappily. He remained neutral toward his spouse. He fulfilled his responsibilities as the family's constant financial support, and his other marital obligations as sparingly as possible, justifying this inaction with the completely believable excuse that he was overworked and on edge.

Since his lawful wife could not satisfy his sexual hungers—and never had—and he one day opened his eyes and found there were women who really seemed to be capable of something resembling love, he began to look for such a woman. He sought her and found her, and then he found another.

As he was rising to the top of his profession at the time and had sufficient means to select the best that was to be had, his taste improved. Of course, this was quite expensive. And the more expensive it became, the more his taste developed, and the more it developed, the higher he rose and the more he could spend. All this happened as if by itself.

The fact that he had managed to win Betty, and keep her, proved his taste had reached a high degree of refinement, perhaps on the whole the highest a man of Mr. Collins's sort can ever attain. He could not have kept her with money alone, though money had an important function to perform in this venture, of course. She desired more than just money from him. She wanted everything he had acquired in the years when he was on the lookout for the ideal woman and associated with many women, beginning with humble examples and working his way up to the artists of their profession. If he had come to Betty fresh and undeveloped by his wife, he could not have hoped to have any success with her, even if he should have had twice the income he had at the time. Betty would have rejected him in spite of his money, even if she had had to go barefoot. Betty did not sell her affections. She gave and got like a spouse.

The money Collins spent on Betty was in no way wasted or squandered like the money he spent on the chorus girls. The money spent on Betty, in the same amount, in the same way, was one of his best capital investments. He knew this very well, and so did Betty. Nevertheless—and in fairness to Collins it has to be said—he was still far from considering his relation to her a capital investment. In and through Betty he, the mature person, had for the first time in his exciting but unromantic life gained an awareness and understanding of what it is that attracts two human beings to each other in their hearts and keeps them together.

This realization had hit Collins hard. If, by nature, he had not been robust and thoroughly unsentimental, it could have thrown him off the track. But for that, he would have lost Betty again, for it was his lack of sentimentality, his complete lack of romanticism, that made him bearable to her. Sentimental whisperings gave her spiritual and physical nausea.

Betty was amply supplied by nature with an innate sentimentality. This surely was traceable to the dash of Swedish blood in her.

She lost most of it when her first true love disappeared for purely economic reasons. That had been a devilishly hard blow to her. But it freed her from all the dross of bourgeois pieties that had clung to her up until that decisive moment.

In the end she deliberately emerged from that catastrophe as a personality. And she had preserved a great and passionate friendship with her first true love, a friendship that was more lasting and greater than any love, however ardent, can ever be.

Sentimentality is nowhere more of a hindrance than in life. And especially in America, where it is a crime, and in certain instances is heavily punished.

Betty lost the last faint residue of her sentimentality as an editorial secretary. She learned to deal slaps to the face to presumptuous editors and reporters with emphatic severity and startling frequency.

Under the sway of the Holy of Holies, where she now found herself, Betty surpassed the princess. At that moment she became a goddess, a goddess of vengeance, whose glance and gesture conveyed trouble without letup to the mortals who did not comply with her wishes. Mr. Collins had never seen her like this.

But then he had never dared to toy with her and treat her as he had in the last few days when he put her off with the promise he would provide the garage and house and then forgot about it as soon as she was out of sight and hearing.

He could treat his chorus girls like that, but not Betty. Here his judgment, which he displayed so confidently as a leader of the nation's economic life, deserted him completely. Now he swore to himself that he would never try it again.

Without her saying another word, he knew the affair was going to become very expensive, ten times as expensive as it would have been if he had rented the garage and house the very first day she expressed the desire.

Now she was demanding more. She said curtly: "When are you buying the house?" The renting of a house wasn't going to be discussed any more.

"Well, then, when are you buying the house?" she repeated pointedly. "The party is Monday. And it has to be furnished, everything, right down to the last ring on the draperies. Telephone. Lights. I want everything bathed in light. Gentlemen"—she turned directly toward them—"Gentlemen, you'll all do me and Mr. Collins an honor by attending the party. Bring whomever you like with you, any girlfriend whatever. It'll all be completely free and easy. Paris in Frisco. You understand? A preacher will be there, too, to marry people, and divorce them again, later, if the couple finds their characters do not agree. And when you leave in the morning you'll be as free as before. But you'll have to bear the cost of marriage and divorce yourself. Those are private costs. The preacher, though, does it cheap. Imitations are always less expensive. If you get married and divorced two or more times, he'll give you a discount. He's Swedish, but he knows what you like. He really was a preacher in Stockholm. They gave him the ticket to come to America because he couldn't tell them where certain missing church funds had gone. Collins, darling, you'll remind the gentlemen of the party, please."

She went up to him, embraced him, kissed him, and was gone again.

There was no end to the directors' laughter as Betty, in telegraphese, recommended the party. They all agreed they would go. They said it earnestly and passionately. They had only one fear—that something might intervene to prevent their being present at the party. The invitees were being promised all the earthly pleasures the greats of the nation needed to prevent their losing their resilience and thereby be condemned to incapacitation through nerves, headaches, and insomnia: they were supposed to bring with them, not their wives, but their paramours, who were less boring and went along with every joke, understanding it, elaborating on it cleverly, and usually putting it into practice at once. Whosoever works should also play. And whosoever works very hard should partake according to the measure of the value and profits of his work.

Let it be said at once that all the directors went to the party with their women friends and everyone returned home the next morning, long after four o'clock, with the awareness that he had savored everything he expected. Everyone was married and divorced at least once. And if he still felt strong enough in the loins he was married and divorced a second and even a third time. Weddings cost ten dollars, and a divorce the same. There were also bridal suites. Chambermaids who tended to the rooms got ten dollars from the lucky bridegroom for every opening of a room.

Thus in the end each of them went home overwhelmed with gifts.

Only it was seen to that everyone who went home was also properly divorced, since assurances were repeatedly given that the preacher was genuine and the ensuing marriages were valid before the law. What the young brides got in the way of alimony from their former husbands was arranged between them, since they wanted to avoid the expense of a legal determination. Some brides even went so far as to declare in advance of the ceremony how much they expected in case the marriage was annulled in the same evening, or frequently within the hour. All the difficulties, conflicts, and inconveniences were worked out in this way much more smoothly and orderly, and with much less stink and bickering, than in real life, where people take seriously matters that should never be taken seriously. But no, everything has to be treated as if it were for eternity. Well, now, if you believe in eternal pleasure, eternal love, eternal fidelity, then you have to pay for your beliefs.

When Betty was gone, the conference resumed. But no one knew what to say. Everyone had other thoughts—about the princess, his own beloved, the upcoming party, the aura of divinity that for a few minutes had filled the room where everything was ungodly, even if very wealthy. At that moment there was no one present who would not have regarded Mr. Collins as if he were not of this world. How can a thing like that fall into the lap of a man like Mr. Collins, a financier, a powerful capitalist.

And these men, who were so used to concentrating with all their might on any matter whatever, gave up and decided to postpone the meeting. As a result, millions of dollars stuck a few days longer to the hands they were in today.

The fact that all these men had agreed to show up at Betty's party only gave Mr. Collins increased power in the company. For it wasn't just Betty's party, it was surely his as well. He was certainly paying for the entire affair. And he would be getting close to all the

men and to an intimacy that benefited only his plans. For such a
mad party to be a complete, unalloyed pleasure, laws had to be
broken. Bigamy, nude dancing, and the consumption of alcoholic
beverages are severely penalized, and if they had become known,
they would have besmirched the pronounced bourgeois respectability and honor of the powerful. That's why the plotters and allies of
such a celebration are always willing to be plotters and allies in
business, where they intend to earn the money to defray the costs
and pick up enough for another even wilder party.

Mr. Collins could better study his associates at this party than
in a meeting. Here he got to know their weaknesses, which he could
seize hold of to bring them down if they didn't want to follow him in
the development of a great new raid.

Thus it was Betty who once again raised him to greater power.
His wife could never have done this. She lacked the knack for
manipulating and guiding events so that no one saw how and by
whom they were being directed.

Betty's was a daring move. Her invitation caught the directors at
just the right moment. She did it for two reasons, and it was not as
spontaneous as it seemed. She had taken in the situation at a glance
and struck hard immediately. She grasped the essentials. She knew
that if she invited them and they accepted, Mr. Collins could no
longer evade the issue. He would have to buy the most beautiful,
most expensive house to be had; he would have to furnish it lavishly,
and give a party so extravagant that spoiled millionaires would not
be bored and later characterize it as a rotten show.

That was one reason for the invitation. Her other was purely a
business matter. Without his suspecting it, she was helping him to
establish close friendships with these powerful men. This was useful
to his business, and therefore to her: the more he made, the more
she could make out of him.

Once the directors were invited and had agreed to come, Mr.
Collins had in fact to hunt up the house and buy it. It was a mansion,
sumptuously furnished. It had been the estate of a film queen who
had made more as guardian of the temple of Venus than she had in
films, though she received three thousands dollars a week from the

movies. But that was mere pin money, which barely sufficed to pay for her step-ins. The goddess of the silver screen had recently had a new mansion built, and so this one had gone on the market.

It was built in Spanish colonial style. The patio was roofed over mosaic-like with colorful glass. It was a special convenience that the marble pool, which was to play such a big part at the party, was already there in the patio. Its fixtures were finely silvered, and it could be heated. In fact, the entire patio could quickly be warmed to a tropical climate. The bandstands were so well concealed that the musicians could not be seen by the guests and, more important, could not see what the guests were doing. In addition, to avoid extortion through the use of flash photography, there was with each orchestra a trusty blackamoor who took responsibility for the musicians' conduct. The musicians knew what was going on. But they didn't care. They had families, they were paid well, and they knew they would also be drawn upon by other hosts for co-operation in other parties if they behaved. Whatever you may say about the evils of luxury, it has its good side: it allows other people to make money. Thus an arrangement is reached that keeps the earth in balance.

Betty drank only three glasses of champagne at the party. She did this solely out of politeness. She did not get married a single time, not even to Mr. Collins. When he hinted, she sent for one of the available brides, took both by the arm, and led them to the Swedish minister. Mr. Collins let himself be married. Betty congratulated the newlyweds and handed them over to a maid for one of the bridal suites. Betty had learned how to rule world and men. The entire week after the party Mr. Collins sighed in her presence. He wanted to get divorced from his wife and marry Betty. In his madness he gave her written promises—a dangerous thing in America—and nearly choked her in his yearning for her. Before his eyes she tore up the promises and threw them in his face.

From this day on he could commit murder for her.
He fell into a ravening hunger for power. He surrendered to it. That is to say: he did not want to acquire power for himself. He wanted power only so that he could stand before Betty and appear in her eyes as the most powerful, the most intelligent, the most audacious man in the world. In days of old he would have marched out at this point and vanquished continents.

But today continents are not taken by soldiers made of flesh and blood. And generals and field marshals have lost their romantic auras. When Black Jack Pershing, the so-called Victor of the Fields of France, returned home, he was cheered. That was on the day of his triumphal appearance. On the next day he was forgotten. The front page of the newspapers, which yesterday were full of his fame, comparing him to Alexander, Caesar, Washington, and Grant, resounded with the fall of steel stocks and the approaching Bolshevik deluge. No one thought for even an instant of putting his name on the roster of presidential candidates. He had been merely a hired butcher by the nation. Who today has time to worry about an unemployed butcher?

The army sent out by a Collins to rule continents—he doesn't want to conquer them at all—is of another kind. His army consists of agents who receive bonuses. His soldiers are checks. His battle plans are based on tips on the oil race.

The world is no longer ruled by the person with the biggest army, best cannon, and most airplanes, but by the person who controls oil. What can the greatest commander do today if Mr. Collins denies oil to him? In that case there won't be any bomb-laden, gas-spraying airplanes whizzing through the air. Enormous tanks won't creak and rumble over the battlefields. Trucks won't be hauling armies from one front to another. Submarines will remain in port. The giant cannons will not move.

If Mr. Collins says: "I have no oil!", he has to be believed. He cannot be accused of treason, since there isn't any evidence. He owns the plans to the pipelines, access roads, wells, pumping stations. With a few words he can so complicate matters that a hundred thousand barrels of oil would be wasted in producing another hundred thousand.

You can dare to abolish the laws protecting private property so that you can seize all his oil holdings, but if you cannot at the same time seize his knowledge, his very complicated system of delivery, distribution, and transport, the confiscator is as helpless as the French when they seized the transport system in the Ruhr. Traffic moves. Certainly. But so ponderously that the benefits are devoured by the movement.

CHAPTER NINE

TEN DAYS after Betty's party Mr. Collins arrived in his office, as usual, at eleven thirty and found the bills piled up on his desk.

There were bills for the mansion he had bought, the furnishings, the party, and the champagne. The cost of smuggling in the champagne, whiskey, and other sorts of alcoholic beverages was just the beginning. Thousands of dollars in bribes had to be paid to officials of the Prohibition agency, and additional sums were needed for fines. Anyone who does time in prison for someone else also has to be supported so that he will keep quiet and won't talk and so that other persons can always be found to serve new prison sentences. All this is expressed in the price of a bottle of champagne. So at sixty dollars a bottle champagne is cheap. There were five hundred bottles of champagne at the party, not counting the wines, liqueurs, and whiskeys. As at all such routs, scarcely a third is drunk; the rest is spilled and wasted by the party-goers in their drunkenness, merriment, and ostentation.

A rough calculation of the bills—house included—yielded the ridiculously low total of eight hundred and forty thousand dollars. The bills for Betty's costume and jewelry, however, were still outstanding. The suppliers of such articles are always polite about payments to those whose ability to pay is assured.

Mr. Collins's chorus girls, who had only recently come into the magnate's life, had heard about the party, and they were very angry they hadn't been invited. The one knew nothing of the other, but they made themselves heard in their fury and pressured Collins to assuage their anger. They threatened him with scandal, letters to the newspapers, the church to which he belonged, to the agents of Prohibition. They not only detailed it in their chatter with him on the telephone, but said: "I'll make hash of you, dear papa." But he was too good a costumer for either of them to spoil it with him by a rash act. They would strike a conclusive blow only when they had given up hope forever of remaining in his good graces. Mr. Collins estimated the cost of appeasing them with several new outfits, a fur coat, and a diamond bracelet thrown in, at a round twenty-five thousand.

Taken all together, including what was missing from the mountain of bills and still expected to come in, the total came to a round nine hundred thousand dollars. As he reflected on this, he staggered a bit, as if he were going to fall. For though he was used to large sums, such an outlay was nevertheless so strong in its effect that he unconsciously held his breath for several seconds before uttering a deep sigh. This money was coming directly from his pocket, and, strictly speaking, it was spent only on a divertissement.

This enormous sum upset his private budget. His brain was in a whirl. For a moment he didn't know how he could scrape this amount together without ripping such a hole in his fortune that there was scarcely any prospect of plugging it up. It was as if a plate on a seaworthy vessel should suddenly be staved in in the middle of the ocean and water pour in in such a thick stream that it overwhelmed the pumps.

For, in addition to this large sum, there were expenses that went right on at the same time. They could not be halted. His wife wanted to travel to Paris, live there for several months, and then go on to Germany and Italy. His daughter intended to go to England and then to Europe to study for two years. Flossy, too, had to go to Paris, since she needed the skills of a physician who could regularize a careless night of lovemaking with Mr. Collins. In America this operation was too dangerous. And when it was over, Flossy would need a rest trip to the Mediterranean. These expenses could not be avoided or postponed. Altogether, the essential travel outfits—for wife, daughter, and Flossy—came to some three hundred thousand dollars.

A thick book can scarcely hold the thoughts that race through a man's mind in a split second when he is excited, perhaps when he is barely grazed on the arm by a speeding car and becomes aware that he was literally only a hairsbreadth away from death. The brain's ability to think quickly and yet logically when the heart is pounding is enormous.

Of the thousands of thoughts that Mr. Collins had when it dawned on him how much money he had to find, only a few can be detailed here.

First off he thought of shooting himself to escape the job of meeting the debts. But he immediately rejected it. His character was much too strong for him to seek a solution in that kind of escape.

Then he considered annulling the sales contracts or offering the mansion to real-estate agents for immediate resale. But that went away as quickly as it came. Once Mr. Collins has decided something, it stays decided. He is much too proud to admit he might have acted rashly. If he really wanted to sell the mansion, he would sell it when he wanted to and not when he was forced to because he couldn't cover his debts. His job is to make money to pay for what he has contracted.

Then he became furiously angry at Betty because she could somehow overcome him and possessed such a power over him that he lost deliberation, calculation, and judgment. But the anger expired at birth. "What can she do about that?" he thought. "She really can't do anything about it, because if I don't want to humor her, I don't have to. If I'm so soft that I do whatever she wants, then it's entirely right for her to take me for whatever I'm worth." But at the same time he was excusing himself for being weak and a lady killer. He was man enough to know what he wanted and to whom he gave and why. So his deepening anger turned into respect because she was smart enough to manage him so cleverly that he had to do as she wished. He was very proud of himself and considered himself superior to every other man because he was successful in winning and keeping a woman who was so smart, so elegant, so proud. In the very same instant a strong self-confidence grew out of this pride. At the thought of having this woman and of having to suffer through this excitement for her, a renewed feeling of power streamed through his blood. At this his thoughts began to settle down. He began to concentrate. He lapsed into a frantic longing to hold Betty in his arms now, to kiss her, to be certain he possessed her. She alone made life worth living. He began to love her in a whole new way, not just as a woman, but as the sole aim of life, as a genius worth more because she was flesh and could give earthly pleasures. The thought of her, the uncommonly strong love he felt for her, the more fervent because he very much repented having been angry at her, gave him an unprecedented feeling of strength. Every pessimistic thought, every anxiety, vanished. Suddenly he regretted he had to cover only one million two hundred. He wished it were ten million he had to find. The world was too small, too narrow, for him to bring his full powers into play, to allow them to develop in a way that would befit his feeling of strength. Making one and a half million dollars was nothing at all. It wasn't worth mentioning. That was just the job for a duffer. When he got started—really seriously started—the billions swirled. Then the billions had to lose their mystery and be nothing other than helpless play things.

"One and a half million?" he exclaimed. "One and a half million? That's all. It's a cinch. It should be five million. Betty, you shall have the finest yacht the American continent can build. And if, in addition, you still want to have the king's yacht, I'll bust him and buy all his yachts, horses, and castles at the bankruptcy sale. What a lot of talk for a mere pittance!"

He had become so loud that his private secretary knocked on the door, opened it cautiously, and asked softly: "Did you call me, Mr. Collins?"

"Yes. No. Just a second. Come in again in a minute, Ida. I have some urgent dictation."

"Yes, sir." Ida closed the door noiselessly.

Collins picked up the telephone: "Lucky, how are you? Dinner today? Siebert's? Or . . . all right, Siebert's. So, how's the chauffeur? Good. Keep him on a leash. These fellows always want to run things. How're you getting along with the house? Better hire another man to pitch in. Maybe another girl, too. At nine. Right. We'll take your car. The green one? No . . . oh, no. I'd rather see you in pale blue. No, certainly not. Part your hair. I like that better. But why? Better not wear your new shoes. We're sure to be dancing. New shoes always tire me out quick. Later? Can't you guess? I'm sending my things over this afternoon—a business suit, too. And a surprise for you. Something to do with pearls. No, I'm not saying. So. At nine. Kiss. Bye-bye. I'm in the middle of a serious deal. Bye-bye."

CHAPTER TEN

ON THE WAY to dinner Collins and Betty agreed not to go to Siebert's but to visit a more fashionable nightclub. Collins seemed to forget himself and his troubles, dancing often and drinking more than usual. He drank mostly at the bar, but also at the table he had reserved by telephone. He drank everything indiscriminately: champagne, all sorts of cocktails, and a good number of whiskeys. So it was not surprising that, bit by bit, he got soused. Only Betty noticed. All the rest of the patrons would have thought him to be in normal shape.

They returned home together, to the "garage," as Betty still chose to call the mansion. She advised him to lie down. Like a headstrong child he refused to sleep either alone in his room or with her in her room.

He sat up in a chaise longue, elbows on his knees, hiding his face in his hands, and tried to concentrate his thoughts. Betty never intruded on his silences as long as he didn't choose to discuss his plans and ideas with her voluntarily. Tonight, however, she broke with this long-standing custom. With her excellent instinct she felt he had something unusually important to think out and that he had to investigate it to the bottom to find a solution. His head, stuffed with so many whiskeys, so many glasses of champagne, had trouble holding on to the dozens of thoughts that raced through his brain. Not a single idea remained in his head long enough for its usefulness to be established.

"Can I help you, dear? What's bothering you?"

"Nothing important. There's only this confounded business I have to iron out. That's all. And the devil knows, I have nothing to get hold of. I've been struggling with several fellows who are in my way and I don't know how to get rid of them before they get wind of it."

"Ever been in a similar situation before?"

"Bet your boots on it. I've seen worse."

"And you made out all right, or maybe you didn't? And I'm sure you also made a cool million at the same time." She said this in the same drawling accent he had used. The quantity of drinks he had consumed had had a bad effect on his organs of speech.

"Right. Damned right. I scratched around, and at the end there was a nice, neat, tidy sum. . . ."

He suddenly broke off, as if a brilliant idea were taking shape before his eyes and he were waiting for it to assume a tangible form. He saw this idea develop and emerge sharply, as on a movie screen. It was impossible for him to turn his eyes away from the screen for he wanted to see the entire action, every single episode.

Now he leaped up and shouted: "Betty, sweetheart, good God almighty, I've got it! Damn! Why didn't I think of this before? It's really so simple. And the plucking is so quick, I'll be rid of all my troubles. This damned lousy Indian down there may rot for a while longer. He'll get his yet, and then he'll face me. With my nicest smile I'll send him the rope with which to hang himself when and where he likes. But I need the cash now, and can't wait until the lousy cannibal comes to his senses. First thing first. The ranch has to wait."

His idea and the plan for carrying it out engrossed him so completely that he sobered up. A half hour before, he had seen his entire existence tottering. But now he felt himself saved and his life assured better than ever.

He yawned. Then he glanced around and seemed greatly surprised to find himself in Betty's home and in the same room with her. He could not recall how and when he had got there. He could not remember anything except his great idea, which settled more firmly into his mind with every passing second. He thought out its execution from every angle, how to start it, how to manage it, and how to end it.

That made him tired. He yawned again, and still yawning, said: "Well, sweet, it's time to go to sleep. . . . No, not in my room. And not alone. Not today. In yours, with you. Or doesn't Your Grace agree?"

"Quite to the contrary, sir," she said with a smile. "I'm thrilled that Your Excellency is meeting me halfway. Thank you very much."

"The thanks are mine. You really gave me a great idea. And now just you watch how I use it. I'm going to repeat an operation I carried off once before with smashing success. Damn it. Where are my slippers? Well, if they're not here, I can get through the night without them. Do you know," he was already in bed and stretching himself out comfortably, "do you know, I often think there's no greater satisfaction for a real man on this cold lump of clay we call Mother Earth than to have completed a small piece of work successfully and then to go out with his boots on."

Again he stretched himself out, trying to purr like a tomcat. "Of course, you have to understand that this alone doesn't make a man happy. Your love is worth more to me than all the millions I can conjure up when I need them. Want the light on or off? As you like, Your Highness. Your wish is my command. Thy will be done."

From out of the darkness, only faintly lit by the light outside the entrance, whose gleam pierced the thin curtains, their words blended gradually into a loving murmur and, at last into whispers broken by occasional bursts of soft laughter. Now and then their muffled breathing was interrupted by short, scarcely audible syllables that seemed to lack definite meaning.

Then it was he who spoke again: "You know, I'd really like to see whether you could gain about ten pounds. Really, I'd like to see that."

"Man alive! Have you lost your mind? Something must be wrong with you or you couldn't make such an incredible suggestion. I'm eating only quarter portions to lose the three pounds I've gained in the last three months. Honest to God, you men have the funniest ideas about what's good for a woman and what isn't.

In a softer and gentler voice, he said: "As you wish. It's okay with me, just as you like. Sometimes a person would like to have a bit more flesh. Now, for once, let's thoroughly explore the kernel of all wisdom and knowledge. Ah, there we are."

And for the next few minutes they laughed and giggled like two children.

Collins called an urgent meeting of the Condor board of directors. He invested it with such importance that every member was present.

He looked every single one directly in the eye, smiled slyly, and rolled his tongue about his cheeks, as he did when he was planning a haul.

His talk was brief. He recalled once again that Napoleon's shortest speeches were the most effective.

"Gentlemen, I've got a hot tip. Something's breaking. Allow me to warn you not to be thrown into a panic. Whatever happens, whatever you hear—don't sell any stock. Instead, buy Condor. Or buy stock in any other enterprise when our own stock or shares of affiliated companies have hit bottom. Buy everything you can carry. Let me repeat: sell nothing. What you've borrowed and can't hold on to, sell tomorrow. I ask you, on your word of honor, not to let any of this get out to the public. Don't even tell your wives about it, or your sons or friends, much less your—let us say it—your girlfriends. Any word at the wrong time, in the wrong place, to the wrong person, any mistake at all, can send us over the edge. Follow my advice until this is over. Gentlemen, I thank you."

Mr. Collins did not make empty promises.

The very next day, the race was on. As if by magic, it would produce the million dollars he needed so badly.

In the meeting the directors had learned from Collins that

several small independent oil companies, wildcatters who were drilling for oil on their own hook, were beginning to become an inconvenience to Condor. Mr. Collins was asked how he proposed to get rid of these interlopers.

"I've already worked out my plans," he said. "Of course, you'll have to raise the necessary capital for me, and, in addition, each one of you gentlemen will have to support me in my plans."

As in all such cases, Collins got the capital he wanted, and as for the rest, they gave him a completely free hand.

Then he went to work.

The first thing he did was to find a suitable lamb for the slaughter. He was looking for a small industrial enterprise possessing a good, honorable reputation, whose board of directors consisted of upright businessmen, of whom it was known that they did not let themselves get mixed up in risky or shady ventures.

Collins found his innocent in the Laylitt Motor Corporation. The company, which had its headquarters in Laylitt, Ohio, produced gasoline engines for every purpose. In particular, they manufactured lightweight motors which were wanted for power in small shops and small and medium-sized businesses, on farms, and for electric lighting in private homes and motion-picture theaters. The Laylitt motor was a simple, unpretentious motor of a conventional sort. There was nothing much about it to attract a person's attention. Its single virtue was its weight. By attending exclusively to the matter of weight in fabricating it, Laylitt had attained the best power-to-weight ratio in the industry, and as a result, the lowest gasoline consumption. If the company had published expensive newspaper ads throughout the country, they could have plugged the engine as "The Common Man's Motor."

But the company had no reason to lay out good money on such propaganda. Their orders came from people who saw the motor at work for friends or neighbors. They could see for themselves that the motor was exactly what they had been looking for all along. And they recommended the motor to other customers when they were casting about for a relatively cheap, reliable make.

The Laylitt directors and stockholders were apparently content with the dividends they received and could not get excited about expansion of the factory. Expansion might work out quite unhappily and jeopardize the economic security the men were enjoying at the time. Laylitt shares stood at 47. Even when the price on the exchange did bring the stock to the public's attention, the fluctuation was never more than three quarters of a point.

To this day no one has ever explained how Collins discovered this quiet, discreet, and virtually unknown company. Even less clear is how Collins managed to induce two Laylitt directors to go along with his plans. These two men kept him continuously informed of company operations. Not only that, both these men executed his plans cleverly and, true to their word, without any other directors becoming aware of it. No one suspected the true character and actions of these men, even months later, when the whole operation was over and completely forgotten.

Suddenly, on a certain day, the market became exceptionally active only a half hour before its close. For several minutes no one present in the exchange knew what was actually happening, for up till then it had been a quiet day in Wall Street.

Laylitt stock, which for the last few months had been sleeping soundly and shown no fluctuations, not even the slightest, suddenly began to climb. At the opening of the exchange, the price had stood at 47⅜. Now, without any warning, shares fell to 41 inside of fifteen minutes, and, indeed, so it seemed, without any obvious reason. During the next fifteen minutes they slowly rose again, and when the exchange closed, the price stood at 42⅜.

Few readers of the financial pages in the daily papers had ever paid much attention to Laylitt. And those who had were convinced the shares were in the possession of one family, and perhaps factory employees and workers. Nevertheless, all the papers gave one line to Laylitt the next morning: "It is advisable to watch Laylitt Corporation closely today."

On this day, a few minutes after the opening of the market, Laylitt shares were being offered at 41¼. They fell again. After an hour full of excitement they stood at 39¼, a price significantly lower than the lowest level on the previous day. And just as on the day before, the stock suddenly and unexpectedly began to rally, and to the astonishment of the entire brokerage profession, shot up to 52¼. After reaching this level, they fell again. At the close they had settled to 46⅛.

Then Laylitt became front-page news in the evening editions, and even bigger news in the morning editions of almost all the daily papers.

For what was going to happen next everyone had to wait until Monday. Immediately after the opening Laylitt shares were offered at 44. During the next two hours they fell to 38. And then there began a run on the stock so phenomenal that no one who was there has ever forgotten it. This unprecedented rage ended only with the closing of the exchange. Laylitt shares stood at 79¾.

An army of newspaper reporters beseiged the main office of Laylitt. No reports or comments were given out, with the exception of a statement by the company president that the day's events were just as puzzling to him and to the directors as they were to everyone else. He had no idea what had caused the startling rise in the company's stock.

The reporters, of course, would not rest content with this cautious answer. They regarded the president's remarks only as a clever dodge. To them it was new proof that their own explanation was based on solid, unassailable facts.

What they called unassailable facts had been built up bit by bit from rumors and conjectures. These "hot" tips were spread in public against the will of the brokers. They were said to be the biggest secrets in the financial world, though anyone sitting in a café or restaurant, subway or bus, lobby or elevator, could have them whispered in his ear. What was remarkable was that the tip was very seldom passed on by telephone.

On the telephone a voice would say: "Listen, I have to talk to you immediately. I've the hottest tip since Adam went long on apples. No, no. I can't tell you on the phone. Too many people are listening, and if this tip becomes too widely known, it'll lose its value. Where can I meet you? Twenty minutes? Fine. But be sure I meet you there. You can pick up a bundle in a jiffy."

And on the subway train you could overhear their conversation as they clung to the leather straps, pressed together tighter than sardines, banging their heads together on every curve: "Not yet, old boy. The thieves can't skin me. Not me. Certainly not this time. Look here, sonny. There's only one explanation for this. Anybody who can see clearly understands the reason for this to-do about a company that no one ever heard of before. Well, here's the whole thing in a nutshell."

Then, because he noticed a half dozen other riders were pricking up their ears, he began to whisper. "You know, it's very simple. This L-company, now—you know the company I'm talking about—which has made a great invention or purchased a tremendous patent, no matter, it's all the same in the end. These fellows have built a new motor which uses only four gallons of gasoline to generate a horsepower where the rest need forty-eight gallons; that is, twelve times as much. And, my friend, that is something. That's the reason the company's stock is shooting up like crazy. Those shares are going up to two thousand, you've got my word for it, buddy. And today's the day when you have to buy. There's no telling. Maybe you can do it tomorrow. But do it today, while they can be had relatively cheap. Here's my station. Good-by. And don't noise this around everywhere."

This belief that the company had discovered an entirely new motor, based on completely new inventions, and that the Laylitt Company had acquired the exclusive right to build it seemed so reasonable and well-founded that everyone understood why its stock rose so unexpectedly. And this view was so intelligent—and, coincidentally, so in keeping with the American character—that no one took the trouble to examine it soberly.

The sale of motors slowed to such an extent that the weekly figures were the lowest in the history of the American automobile industry. The sale of oil, crude oil, was also influenced. Significant lots of oil, hundreds of thousands of barrels, could not be sold even for the cost of production. Forty small oil companies and refineries and a larger number of small, independent oil-well owners could not resist the onslaught. They were thoroughly shaken, and could be picked up for a wormy apple with a song thrown in.

Collins took pity on eight of these small bankrupt companies. He bought them, at a price amounting to a gift, only out of genuine compassion, or so he said. He did this with such grace, and made it seem such a generous gesture, that the owners felt compelled to praise him for his honesty. He had, in fact, paid more for each small company than its owner had expected under the circumstances. He got them for a fifth of what they were actually worth.

As soon as Condor had acquired the companies and merged them into its own corporation, the Laylitt Company began to find its way back peacefully to its former modest and respectable existence. Its shares fell to 52⅛, and held this price for the next three months, after having gained five points in the excitement. Everyone connected in any way with Laylitt—directors, stockholders, employees, and workers—was highly satisfied with the outcome. The brokers had conducted such a powerful publicity campaign on behalf of Laylitt that the corporation could sell every one of the motors it had in stock. And so many new orders had been received that the company would have to work full-tilt for the next two years just to fill them.

After a period of intense commotion in the stock market some speculators always remain stuck on the track. But this time there were several hundred who had not managed to stay the course. Shorn, wounded, crippled, beaten up, beaten down, they sprawled along the wayside, dissatisfied with the world in general and their own country in particular. Another hundred small, respectable business people and even manufacturers had been ruined. They had lost everything.

This successful operation had brought Condor even more firmly under Collins's control. It had also brought him personally a profit of one and a quarter million dollars. The Condor directors could also be content. They had faithfully followed his advice, bought when he told them to buy, and sold whenever he glanced at them with a grin and a wink. They had amassed tidy little sums. For these very understandable reasons, they believed, more than ever, that Collins was a great magician, a financial wizard capable of making by one trick or another any amount of money he wanted.

CHAPTER ELEVEN

JUST THEN, when Mr. Collins was regarding himself as the greatest financial genius in America, the president of his bank called him on the telephone.

"Would it be possible for you to stop by my office one of these days? I have something important to discuss with you."

"Ah, of course, Mr. Aldrich, with pleasure."

"Shall we say, then, Wednesday perhaps, eleven o'clock on the dot?"

"Very good. Wednesday at eleven. Goodby."

"Goodby, Mr. Collins."

Early on the momentous day the bank called Ida and asked her not to forget that Mr. Collins had an important meeting at the bank at eleven sharp.

Mr. Collins went to the bank.

Grinning familiarly to every side, he projected his boisterous and energetic "Good morning" toward everyone who came within range. At this instant he felt more certain of his power than ever. He thought he discerned in the eyes of everyone he met a profound admiration for his superiority in the financial world. The bank president and all the higher bank officials knew how much he was worth, and it was absolutely a sure thing they would not abstain from pointing him out to all those present in the bank and explaining who he was and what a powerful position he occupied. From his bombastic demeanor and his triumphal march across the great hall of the bank, all the people had to believe that not only did this bank belong to him, but also dozens of others around the country. The least important bank clerks would not forget for a week that they had been considered worthy of a smile and a curt "Good morning, mister."

As he approached the heavy door to the bank president's private suite, it opened, as if he had stepped on a button that opened the door automatically.

That wasn't the case.

The president was standing in the doorway, as though he had just decided to leave. He had obviously been informed of Mr. Collins's arrival by some signal and knew to the second when his visitor would arrive at the door.

"Good morning, Mr. Collins," he greeted him, with a broad smile on his face. "Beautiful morning today, if I may say so. What do you think?"

"Good morning, Mr. Aldrich. How are you? Well? Very good. I can see that. And you're right, it's really a beautiful morning. Well—and, uh—what is it this time, Mr. Aldrich, that you want to see me about. Very important, I guess."

"To tell the truth, Mr. Collins, it is not exactly I who wishes to see you. It is somebody whom I think you ought to know better."

And saying this he threw the large door open wide and invited Mr. Collins to enter.

The president followed him and immediately closed the door.

Mr. Collins noticed a very old, very tired man sitting in a deep armchair. He was studying his pale, bony hands carefully, as if he were concentrating his entire willpower on knowing every single

pore and what role it had to fulfill and on preventing the hands going
to sleep before the rest of the body.

"I'm persuaded you two gentlemen have never met before. Sir,
this is Mr. Collins, Chaney C. Collins, president of the Condor Oil
Company. I guess I can leave you alone now. I'm very sorry, but I
have another pressing matter to attend to, an immensely important
meeting in the matter of the Labine Corporation. You will excuse
me, gentlemen."

Mr. Collins thought that the bank president must really have a
lot of important or worrisome matters on his mind because he had
completely forgotten to introduce the old man to him. He looked so
tired, sitting there, sunk so deep in the armchair that one had to fear
seeing him fall asleep, perhaps forever, in another minute.

As he was speaking, the bank president shoved up another
deep chair for Mr. Collins and with a gesture invited him to sit
down.

Mr. Collins sat and waited for the old man sitting opposite
him to begin the conversation. He studied him for a long while and
came to the conclusion that, so far as he could recall, he had never
met him before in person. Yet he had seen his photograph in the
newspapers several times. However much he tried now, he couldn't
remember in what connection and under what circumstance he had
seen those photographs.

"So then, you are Mr. Collins of Condor Oil." The old man
spoke very slowly, a word at a time. He had a way of speaking that
must have been common eighty or a hundred years ago. It was
broadly accented, with mouth slightly opened, drawling and rolling,
with a nasal twang, as if the man suffered from a chronic catarrh that
had settled permanently in his nose. But he pronounced each word
precisely and deliberately, as if it ought to keep for all eternity.

"That's right, mister."

"I beg your pardon, Mr. Collins," the old gentleman said,
astonished and deeply offended at the same time. "What did you say
just now?"

For more than sixty years, at least, no one, not even the
President of the United States, had dared address the gentleman
directly to his face as "mister." And no one who knew him would
have had the courage to give him such a short, clipped answer. Mr.

Collins quickly blushed, for the words "I beg your pardon" made it clearer to him than a torrent of angry words could have, the kind of slip of the tongue he had committed. And instantly he knew, without needing anyone to tell him, that playing around with this man could only lead to a catastrophe. To be sure, Mr. Collins could not know at this moment what form this catastrophe might take. But his intelligence told him that, since they were sitting in the office of a bank president, it was a matter of finances.

Mr. Collins recovered quickly, and straightened out his answer. The old man had every right to expect this so long as they both weren't dipping up river water and drinking it out of the same cup.

"Yes, that is correct, sir. I have the honor to be the president of Condor Oil Company, Mr. . . . Mr. . . . ? I'm sorry, I didn't catch your name, sir."

"Indeed you did not, my good fellow, for it was not mentioned to you. I thought you knew me."

"I'm very sorry sir, I haven't had the pleasure. But I believe I've seen your photograph in the newspapers several times."

Scarcely had he concluded his statement when Mr. Collins became frightened. His breathing stopped cold, for it dawned on him in a flash. Suddenly he knew when and where he had seen photographs of this man. And in the same split second he knew who this man was. All his blood shot to his head, and he squirmed in his chair as he tried to find a more comfortable position.

Yes, it was old John D., no doubt about it. Mr. Collins knew what everyone in the country having anything to do with oil knew: the entire American oil industry is directed, controlled, and exploited by a half hundred persons who have the manners, methods, and morals of common gangsters and by another half hundred who regularly skulk past the prison, just outside the walls, because they can afford lawyers, as clever as they are lacking in conscience, who know how to find, at the right time, in the right case, every loophole in the laws, even if it is as small as the eye of a needle.

Beyond these two groups there are the actual leading groups, containing some twenty truly royal merchants, a dozen princes, and two kings. These two are as genuinely kings as one could want to see, and their word is as good as their bond—and more secure than a government bond. They were kings who valued their honor and their reputations more highly than their lives and fortunes.

And this man was one of the kings.

Mr. Collins took a deep breath. In the ensuing silence he half rose from his chair to attempt a hint of a bow, and said: "Glad to meet you, sir. How do you do?"

The king nodded sleepily. After a silence he said wearily: "Pleased to hear you know me. That will make the business I'm here on a good deal easier."

Mr. Collins didn't quite know whether or not it was proper to extend his hand in hopes the king would grasp it in a handshake. But since he wasn't sure what the king would do, he thought it better to wait for something to happen. He grasped immediately that his loud, boisterous conduct was meaningless in the presence of this man. In reality, he had already grasped that the moment he stepped into the room and caught sight of the gentleman.

Sensing the proud, haughty, barely civil manner with which the king was treating him, he became aware of one fact he had never noticed before in his life. It came home to him that the bank president, and the vice-presidents, too, displayed the same dignified and reserved manner when they conferred with one of their clients in the bank. On several occasions, he recalled now, he had felt, when in the president's private office, as though he were in the sacristy of a church intended exclusively for the Four Hundred, where the worshipers assume deeply offended expressions when, by mistake, there appears in the church a mere mortal who looks as if he has to work for wages to survive.

It was never possible for Mr. Collins to stick to or practice his loud, hail-fellow manner in speech or gesture on such occasions, or only in exceptional cases. Then he began to think that perhaps, after all, his method of making money was wrong. Perhaps he was wrong to behave like a noisy show-off bursting with energy. He reflected then, as carefully as his temperament permitted, on whether or not the truly great in the industry, those who were considered the true pillars of the nation, perhaps conducted themselves like the old man sitting there before him, or like the bank president. It occurred to him that in spite of his energy, his clever seizing of opportunities as they were presented, and the ease with which he could magically produce a million for his own pocket, in his character and in the way he swept to giddy heights he perhaps rather resembled the ring-master of a carnival or the manager of a prize fight than a sober citizen who had a perfect right to be president of a large oil company.

Anyway, these thoughts flashed through his mind so quickly that he made no effort to record them for calm analysis and study later. To the contrary, he felt more and more confident that his way of doing business was the only proper way. All those so-called merchant princes and industrial barons were wrong. They simply behaved like British diplomats because they were not so richly endowed with talent and were not such go-getters as he was. They were simply trying to make the most of limited mental endowment. At best, these slow-witted and little-talented fellows disguised their defects beneath an elegant, well-fitting top hat and behind the skills of a good tailor.

Mr. Collins's defects appeared at times when it was least convenient for him and suited him not at all. He belonged among those men who are unable to conceal their mistakes with dignity or a raised eyebrow. He had to strike when he thought and felt the time was right. There was no way for him to cloak his mistakes, with greater or lesser success, other than through loud, boastful talk and noisy, constantly excited actions. He knew that if there were a contest to see who could sell the most new or used automobiles at the best price, in the least time, in a slow market, he, without a doubt, would come off ten times better in such a stiff competition than the respected bank president or the drowsy emaciated king sitting there before him. He would bet his last shirt and razor blade that he would emerge the winner.

And so, where are we now? If there was any question about his real standing in the oil industry, it would be disposed of in a few seconds, and right on the spot. The king was world-renowned for not wasting time. Every minute of his life, by day and by night, he added twelve dollars to his immeasurable fortune, and sometimes even twenty. This powerful man, who could cause a riot in the exchange with a simple telegram, had not come here to peruse the rather homely face of Mr. Collins. There was something else behind it. He would not have made the long trip to the West Coast in person if it were only a matter of a sleazy two or three millions. In any case—anything else is inconceivable—it had to be somewhere between thirty and seventy. Perhaps a round hundred. We will surely learn it in a few seconds. Just keep calm, very calm at this time. Don't get excited.

After what seemed to Mr. Collins to be a short nap, which he dared not interrupt, the king said: "It has caused me a few anxious hours—your wild manipulation, I mean. Not because I could win or lose anything by such a disruption of normal business life. I buy and sell stocks, but never on margin in order to buy more. And I never speculate."

"Good grief! That's really the last straw!" Mr. Collins thought to himself. Now this dried-up old rascal is telling me he never speculates in the market or in petroleum or whatever else there is to speculate in. By God, what had he ever done but speculate? I'd really like to know. Liar, that's what he is. And now he's trying to give us good advice—now that he is beginning to be afraid of us and sees we are on to him.

"Yes, as I said, it cost me a few nervous hours, because I didn't see clearly what was behind it, and what the final objective might be. How was I to know you were after a few piddling oil-well owners, just to gobble them up. You could have got the entire cake more easily, without making such a great to-do, with fewer victims, and at lower cost. I could not know that, in addition, you were thinking of picking up some pocket money for yourself at the same time, otherwise I would have understood the entire operation at once. In any case, Mr. Collins, I admit yours was a smart maneuver. Smart, yes, that's the word, smart."

Mr. Collins glowed all over as a consequence of this praise coming from this great, nearly venerated figure. He began to guess at what the proposition was going to be. He resolved firmly not to allow himself to be duped and sold for an apple and a slice of bread and butter. Maybe it was a merger with the king's company. In such a union he would demand for himself a high and extraordinarily well-paid position. He would sell himself dear, very dear, that was for sure. The great, real, and true chance of a lifetime was about to turn up, at last. He would seize it, cleverly, energetically. He would become a general in the king's army, which had regiments and divisions in every part of the world. From now on his income would be at least triple what it was at present.

"Very smart." The steady voice spoke again after a silence during which, apparently, the king had nodded off again. "Very clever. Very intelligent. That is what *you* think. I had to put three of my best agents on the trail to find out in which tree the cat had taken cover. My people found the kitty and its little lair quite admirably. Before you leave this bank, Mr. Collins, don't forget to leave a check with the cashier for four thousand seven hundred and forty-three dollars and sixty-seven cents. That's exactly what it cost me to track you down."

Mr. Collins, astonished, did not know what to say or do. He furrowed his brows, obviously searching for a good answer. But the king didn't give him time for that. "Yes, as I said, my people readily discovered the den. I had not thought of you. I had not believed you were so dumb as to assume such a risk. We had every opportunity to go the other way round and consign you and all your, what you call a company or corporation, to the ashcan. We should have done it. But somehow I think it is better the way it has turned out. Several hundred fools have been retired from the business. That is a great gain for the industry. And now you listen to me, young man. . . ."

"Young man" he calls me, Mr. Collins thought. "Young man. And I'm a good bit past fifty. Good God almighty, I'm convinced he must be nearly a hundred and twenty, to judge by his appearance and the way he dozes off every five minutes. But what the hell? I don't know but that I'd give everything I had to have his phenomenal memory at his age. Knowing exactly what it cost to track me down, to the last penny. And I've already completely forgotten the amount. He didn't even look at a piece of paper to recall the exact figures."

The king again woke up from his nap. "Yes, listen, young man. I'm warning you. Don't try to pull this trick, or anything like it, again. For if you do, I will squash you like a rotten tomato—you and all the nitwits you have as vice-presidents and directors. And I'll smash you to pieces. There won't be so much as a scrap of paper left for you to cling to when the flood sweeps over you."

"With all due respect, sir, didn't you ever in your long and lucrative career try an operation like mine?" Mr. Collins, certain that he knew the king's complete life story, in all its particulars, was asking the question merely to prolong the conversation. He did not expect to get a lecture on business strategy.

"No, you young whippersnapper. I never did anything of the sort. And never tried to. I always played my cards openly. My motto was: Pick them up, if you like, or let them lie. I usually won, but not always. Not because of my daring alone, but in most cases I won because I offered an open and honest game. Everyone who was in the game with me had complete confidence of winning as much as I. Those who got plucked were amateurs, usually gamblers, who use all sorts of tricks to cheat the honest players. It is these parasites who deserve their fate. They are trying to make suckers of all the rest of us who play fair and square, and they employ every kind of dirty trick to cheat us. It is these parasites who cause those devastating panics in the domestic development of honest business and hard-working industry. And while we're at it, young man, I've come to the conclusion that what Alexander the Great did, and what Caesar did, and Attila and Charlemagne in their time, would have been considered despicable crimes if Napoleon had practiced them in his day. What England did in the eighteenth century and Napoleon at the beginning of the nineteenth century would be contemptible offenses against mankind if done today by a nation or a dictator. Every era has its own laws. Mine had its laws, by which we lived and worked and did business. Yours has other laws, which you have to obey if you don't want to be considered a criminal. And so, young man, don't forget my warning. I mean it in dead earnest. I'm not repeating it."

The king stood up and, his shoulders stooped, walked slowly to the door. Without turning round, he said evenly: "Good day, mister."

He touched the door lightly. It opened noiselessly, as if by itself, and let him go out.

Before the door could close, the bank president entered the room again. Smiling his broadest smile, he went up to Mr. Collins and shook his hand enthusiastically.

"Congratulations, Mr. Collins. My sincere, heartiest congratulations. I'm sure the propositions and offers made to you established to your complete satisfaction and more or less fulfilled everything you had expected of this discussion. I knew for some time that this meeting was imminent, but I didn't believe, never even dreamed, it would take place this soon."

The bank president confidently took Mr. Collins's arm as he led him step by step and without haste toward the door.

"I'm convinced, Mr. Collins, that this is a great day for Condor. A red-letter day. A merger, perhaps?"

The bank president broke off pointedly to indicate that he would not pry into a business secret. And he said with a new apologetic smile: "No hurry, Mr. Collins. I can wait for the outcome."

Again he broke off, as they had finally reached the door. "Oh, Mr. Collins, by the by, any loan you may perhaps think you need as a result of the changed situation, whatever the amount, is at your disposal, so far as regulations permit."

They were standing in the open doorway, and the president again shook Mr. Collins's hand: "Again, Mr. Collins, my deepest, most cordial congratulations."

"Thank you, Mr. Aldrich. I can assure you it has really and truly been a great day for us, of that I'm sure." He left the president and other employees who saw him leave with the impression that he might just have closed a deal securing him a ten-million-dollar profit. "And once again, many thanks, Mr. Aldrich, for making your bank available to us for this discussion."

"We are always at your service, Mr. Collins. I need not especially stress that."

Once again the president shook Mr. Collins's hand, and bowing as he had seldom bowed to anyone before, he departed.

Mr. Collins went to the chief cashier. He had only to write his signature, for the cashier had already made out the check, filling in the exact sum to the dollar and cent.

Later, sitting in his limousine and reflecting on the last twenty minutes, Mr. Collins said to himself: "By God, I shall take his warning seriously, and be guided by it, literally. He is precisely the sort to do what he promises. Gosh, this man is old, I mean old. I judge he could just as easily be one hundred and fifty as one twenty. But whatever it is, I'll certainly get down on my knees and thank God every day of my life if I have a memory like his at the age of seventy-five, and a mind so clear, getting right to the point as he was able to do, this dried-up old horse-thief. He's a type whom I'd better respect, a type I'd better steer clear of."

Back in his office and sitting at the desk, Collins went over again the adventure he had had with the big shot scarcely a quarter of an hour before. After considering all the details he concluded that he had behaved like a callow youth: he had—to put it bluntly—allowed himself to be cowed. The thought annoyed him enormously. To rid himself of it, he grubbed about in the drawers of his desk, searching for the photographs of his chorus girls so that he might feast upon those figures unspoiled by bathing suits.

He had scarcely got hold of the pictures and spread them out in front of him before Ida, his secretary, knocked softly on the door. Because she was his confidante, she sauntered in at once, without waiting for him to say, "Come in." Once, as it happened, she had come in while Mr. Collins was entertaining himself with a—let us say, a lady of the chorus, though you don't usually pass the time in an office with a lady in that way. But Ida was tactful. Her presence was not even noticed. Still, Mr. Collins had sensed her. After the woman left, Mr. Collins called her in and said: "Ida, you're one of the most efficient secretaries I've ever had. You know your work, and you're tactful. I value both. Here's an order to the paymaster. Starting on Monday, you'll be getting eighty dollars a week. I'll have some letters for you later."

Up to this time Ida had never made more than fifty dollars a week. From this day on she worshiped Mr. Collins like a demigod. She was won over not by the pay raise but by the way he handled the matter, by his tone of voice, by the fact he hinted at nothing, said nothing, suggested nothing, neither by demeanor nor action, a wink of the eye or a nod of the head, to command discretion. Thereafter he could have done anything he wished in her presence, and she would have taken his every action as a sacrament.

That was one reason for Mr. Collins's success. The moment he met a man, he knew how to win him over. Some persons he shouted down, some he talked down, and others he argued down. And yet others, when nothing else worked, he beat down to the ground. But at all times he displayed a smiling courtesy characteristic of him, a courtesy that was meant to conceal nothing, but which was genuine, and so its effect was always convincing.

Ida said: "The men are here with the report from Mexico. It's the Rosa Blanca business."

CHAPTER TWELVE

WHEN THE conference with the men from the real-estate department was over, the search through all the Mexican land registers was renewed as Condor's agents sought to find a defect in Don Jacinto's title to the hacienda. But the title was old and strong; it had been legally renewed whenever the laws required it.

Once again the governor of Jalapa was urged to compel the sale of Rosa Blanca through a special decree. The argument was that reasons of state had precedence over private rights, and therefore the sale of this farm had to be arranged. Through a deputy whom Condor Oil had won over, they also sought just as cleverly to suggest to the governor exactly what these reasons were.

This representative in the national congress was always short of cash. Besides his wife, he supported two women in Mexico City. He tried to make clear to the governor that the state badly needed the income from export duties on the oil. The duties were essential to the condition of the state and nation. For this reason alone the production and exportation of oil ought to be encouraged in every way possible. And Rosa Blanca contained perhaps the richest oil field in Mexico. A governor ought not to withhold from the nation the revenues from this oil out of consideration for a couple of Indian families that could be settled somewhere else.

The deputy had his verses by heart, better memorized even than the windy speeches he usually delivered in the Chamber of Deputies of the Mexican Congress.

Nevertheless, the governor was not dissuaded from his opinion by this sentimental deputy.

To Licenciado Perez, who was Condor's agent in Mexico, and who had sent the deputy around, he explained, to make matters clear: "I'll go over the case one more time. I don't want to harm the Condor Oil Company in any way or to impede its serious operations. To the contrary, I regard it as my duty, as long as I am governor here, to further production of every kind, whether it is oil or agriculture— sugar or wood or cotton or fruit or coffee. And whether the company is foreign or Mexican makes no difference to me. I respect the constitutional rights of everyone in Mexico—citizen or alien. I promise you, Licenciado, I'll do my best to help Condor with the purchase of Rosa Blanca if I can satisfy myself that Condor absolutely has to have the hacienda to increase oil production. I'll speak to Don Jacinto personally. I think I can assure you I can persuade him to agree to the sale of his hacienda. But I'm not forgetting for an instant that he also has rights and opinions in this matter, and they are as well founded as those of Condor Oil, and maybe better. But without having examined the pros and cons carefully, I can't pass judgment, and I won't. I understand, too, that it's not just Don Jacinto who is involved. The fate of sixty or seventy Mexican families must be taken into account."

"All those people can get jobs with Condor," Licenciado Perez interjected, "or they can be settled somewhere else in the state at the company's expense."

"Certainly. That can be done," the governor said. "Why not?

But it doesn't seem to me to be as simple as all that. More is involved here than the bare necessities of life. There's also something purely spiritual. Don't you see that, Licenciado?"

"I don't know what you mean," Señor Perez answered. "What are you getting at?"

The governor smiled ironically. "Don Jacinto and the other families living there are not giving up just land, bare terrain that can be replaced with other terrain in some other region of the Republic. They are just as surely giving up their *patria*. And that is more than land. This was the home of their ancestors, and it preserves the bones of their revered fathers and forefathers. They are giving up land fertilized with the blood and sweat, the sorrows and joys and aspirations of their fathers and mothers—as well as their own. They are giving up land which, because of these things, is sacred, as sacred as my mother and father, my wife and children, are to me."

There was a long pause during which neither of the men said anything. At last the governor, returning to his desk, said very pointedly: "Well, Licenciado, as I said before, I'll gladly do you a favor in this case, because of our old school connection, and I'm prepared to assist the American company if what it asks is in keeping with what I consider proper. But I'll tell you right now—and I mean it—that if the company does not have extremely good reasons, then I intend to do nothing. It will be entirely up to Don Jacinto. He can do as he likes. He has the right to sell or not to sell, as he chooses. But if I can be assured that the sale of Rosa Blanca is absolutely necessary in the interest of the state, then we will look into it further. If I can't, then so far as the state of Veracruz is concerned, the case is closed. How's the family, Perez? Is Maria already through with medical school?"

"Not yet. She still has two years to do. At the moment the missus is in Guadalajara with her sister."

"My regards to them, Perez. *Adios.*"

The men shook hands in the friendliest fashion. Licenciado Perez left the government offices fully convinced he had won a victory.

He telegraphed a message to the company's San Francisco headquarters: GOVERNOR ON OUR SIDE ROSA BLANCA PATIENCE STILL NEEDED.

The lawyer having left, the governor wrote a few comments in his notebook, and then pressed one of the many buttons of the bell system to indicate that he would now see the rest of the people who had private appointments. There were directors of companies, Mexican, Dutch, English, and American, workers in overalls, delegates and presidents of labor unions, Indians, teachers, architects and engineers drawn from the farthest reaches of the state of Veracruz. And so the governor soon forgot Rosa Blanca again.

That Saturday he journeyed to Mexico City to attend a political meeting convened by the President of the Republic. At the conference the discussions took up, among other things, the question of implementing certain sections of the Constitution resulting from the people's revolution, specifically those clauses that dealt with the intolerable dominance of the Catholic Church and those that defined as the property of the people all natural resources, and, above all else, oil.

At that point, the governor recalled the Rosa Blanca matter. He made a new memo in his notebook and underscored it several times.

When he returned to Jalapa on Monday, he at once had all the documents pertaining to Condor Oil brought in to him. To help him he called in an engineer from the Department of Labor, and together they studied the maps of the lands the company owned, counted the wells, and studied the statistical tabulations of its production, its producing wells and dry holes, studied all the parcels where the company was drilling at the time, calculated the reserves, whether in oil-bearing land the company owned or in suspicious land it had under its control. The governor noted everything down carefully. What he did not understand to his own satisfaction he had the engineer explain to him, for the engineer's special area of expertise was supervision of the oil fields.

On Friday he took three days off for an inspection trip. With his manservant he traveled to the hacienda to get to know Don Jacinto and hear his views and to see the hacienda itself.

For the next two and a half days he stayed there, eating at the same table the same homely fare that Jacinto ate, sleeping in a bed that had for a mattress only two of the usual rush mats spread over boards. Rosa Blanca could offer him nothing more than this, for it had no more, needed no more, had had no more for hundreds of years, and wanted no more. In short, it was happy with things the way they were.

Accompanied by Jacinto and Margarito, the governor visited all the families living on the hacienda. He went into all the huts, spoke with all the people, petted all the children, carrying first one and then another on his arm, giving them coins and candy. When he left one hut to go on to the next, the entire family followed him. So it went from one house to the next until, arriving at the last hut, he had in tow all the families of the hacienda, with all their children, dogs, donkeys, and pigs.

No one, least of all Jacinto and Margarito, wearied him by addressing him as governor at every other word. No one flattered him; no one sought his favor; no one strove to make him smile.

But at every hut he entered, the householder, if he was not waiting for the governor at the door, met him, bowed his head, and said simply: "A sus ordenes, Señor. My house is your house."

The woman of the house, usually with a naked child on her arm, picked flowers at once and gave them to one of the older children to present to the governor. Then the governor, followed by the entourage, crossed the fields of the hacienda to inspect the corn, the sugar cane, the orange and lemon groves, the sugar mill in which the cane was crushed, the coffee shrubs, the papaya and banana plantations, and the pasture where the cows, horses, and mules grazed. He even had to see the quarrelsome parrot with the ugly pig for a friend.

Everything there was to see, the governor saw for himself, as if he were on vacation, and had not left behind in that other world an office that was the source of great cares, a lot of work, much envy, and very little pleasure.

The governor had always lived in cities. He'd been born and raised in a city. He'd studied in Mexico City. He had often been invited by friends to visit the haciendas of rich Mexicans. Living like lords on their great estates, however, they were usually more like city-dwellers than sons of the soil, spending more weeks of the year in the capital than on the hacienda and leaving its management to the major-domo. Now, for the first time in his life, the governor was staying on a hacienda owned by an Indian, and inhabited only by Indians.

Suddenly, to his surprise, there stirred in him the Indian that was in his blood. For though he was an educated person, dressed like an American businessman, and lived in civilized style in the big city, the color of his skin, the color and sorrow of his eyes, the color and lankness of his hair, were so exactly like Jacinto's that they might have been born of the same mother. The white blood flowing in his veins, passed on to him by a Spanish forebear, was not strong enough even to flicker in him. The continent's ancient race was so strong that it had absorbed all his foreign European blood, just as it gradually absorbed all foreign blood born in the Americas. For the foreign blood succumbs not just to the influence of Indian blood by mixing through the generations but also through the same influences of climate, water, diet that in the course of milleniums shaped the uniqueness and peculiar nature of the Indian race.

And because the Indian in him was aroused under these circumstances, he began then and there to think and feel with the Indians. Things he had not understood before he began to understand in his feelings and in his soul.

When he had spoken to Licenciado Perez of the "homeland" and of the rights of Rosa Blanca's people, he was speaking purely theoretically, much as the legal codes dealing with the subjects of nationality and citizenship speak of *patria*. It was a general concept, expressed in documents, confined and circumscribed by extracts from the civil records of births. It was purely an accident, influenced by the changing of residence by the parents and by intentional or unintentional errors in the records.

Here, though, the governor viewed the idea of *patria* in a new way, which, up till then, had been totally alien to him. This homeland was something that could not be fixed or affected by laws, by records. The *patria* was a matter of the heart and the soul. It was something that shaped mankind. City-bred people, and even many farmers and peasants, can be transferred to another city or farm, and they will immediately feel at home. Here, however, the people were so totally at one with the soil that they would cease to be human beings as soon as they were torn away from the land.

So, through his Indian blood the governor came to the conclusion that no oil on earth, no automobile, no diesel engine, was sufficiently valuable to compensate for the loss of native ground. Oil and autos and airplanes are wonderful things, it's true; they are useful and ease man's burden. But what are oil and engines to a man—especially a man of Rosa Blanca—if they make him poorer in heart and soul than he was without them, if to have them he has to part with the native soil that is to him the quintessence of all joy, happiness, peace, contentment, security, love, poetry, art, religion, divinity, paradise.

We all, we poor people, delight in the machine, in the airplane, the radio, precisely because we have lost our attachment to the soil. The loss leaves us apathetic and distracted. That's why we need gasoline—to anesthetize us, to make us insensible of our loss, of our pain, gasoline that deludes us with speed so that we can flee all the quicker from ourselves and the needs of the heart.

All this rose up in the governor's consciousness because he had Indian blood, and in that blood the sense of place was stronger than it was in the white man. The white man had forgotten who he was and where he came from milleniums ago, flitting about, always harried and chased, never having time, never gaining time, whether he was building railroads and express locomotives or wireless telegraph stations. Always there was the restlessness, the harassment. And the more devices he invented to save time, the less he had. Chased from one continent to the next, from Asia to Europe, from Europe to America, from America to Asia again. Involved in military campaigns and world wars—all to find a homeland. And all his scientists try, and try in vain, to find out where his true homeland is.

The governor talked with Jacinto and Margarito and the rest of the men. He talked with them as though he'd known them for ten thousand years. He understood everything they said, and comprehended everything. He began to become intimate with them all. He drank tequila and mezcal with them, swigging from the same bottle as it went from mouth to mouth.

He, the Indian, had found a home. For the first time in his life he heard his soul speak, was consciously aware that he was at home, was truly happy and contented, felt an untroubled, joyful spirit knowing no fears or sorrows.

He removed from his feet his usual stylish brown riding boots and allowed Jacinto to give him a pair of old huaraches. Took off his shirt and tie and slipped his head through the slit of a *tilma*. He rolled cigarettes of corn husks. Ate tortilla and frijoles. He separated the meat from the back of a pullet with his fingers and dipped it into the reddish-brown *mole*. In Indian fashion he took up a pinch of salt with his fingers and pushed it into his mouth. He bit large chunks from the green peppers and drank his coffee black, sweetened only with the raw brown sugar made on the hacienda.

He had to ride all the horses to determine which was best.

In the city, when the governor was with friends, they usually talked politics, because they didn't know anything else to talk about. And so, because they didn't want to talk nonsense or spread gossip and pick quarrels, they always found themselves quite at a loss for words. Then they had to amuse themselves at cards or dominoes or billiards or chess because they didn't know what else to do and they certainly didn't want to seem complete idiots.

On Rosa Blanca it never occurred to the governor to want to play dominoes or cards, not for a minute.

He sat with Jacinto and Margarito in rocking chairs on the portico. All the men of the hacienda were present. A few sat on the wooden steps leading from the patio into the portico; others squatted on the ground; still others hunkered down on the portico's broad plank floor, with the rest sitting on the railing or lounging against the columns supporting the roof. These men did not join in the conversation among the three men in the rocking chairs. They listened. At times one man would whisper to another, or Jacinto or Margarito would call to one of them to ask a question related to the conversation, for information about mules or cattle or about one of the families.

On the whole, the matters the governor discussed with Jacinto and Margarito were as plain and simple as any matters can be. They discussed corn and sugar and salt and the price of cows and hogs; there was talk of woods and forest, good and bad pasture, the yields of other haciendas, the number of children the individual families had, the illnesses of this man and that woman, remedies for cows, horses, and mules. They talked over the condition of local roads and the excessive distance to school for the children, who thus attended irregularly. Jacinto mentioned that he was willing to build a school for the hacienda that very year, and pay the teachers, too. And then there was the weather, the amount of rainfall and the drought. They also talked about the jaguars lurking in the jungle that occasionally carried off a calf or goat, and the mosquitoes. Don Jacinto described the henequen they had begun to raise and how they were now making on the hacienda itself all the linen and lassos they needed and were even selling the surplus sisal. And so they talked over all the goings-on of a large hacienda.

Of politics there was not a word. Not one of the men here cared whether Don Manuel or Don Justo was President of the Republic; no one cared whether the Americans would march into the Republic or show off their battleships and their guns in Nicaraguan harbors. To these men such matters were of no interest whatsoever. The Republic of Mexico was not the motherland; the motherland was La Rosa Blanca. And whatever did not concern Rosa Blanca in some way did not exist.

Still, though it seemed as if the men had no interest in events in the outside world, their talk was full of wisdom and philosophy. The governor listened attentively. More than once he found himself thinking that, in comparison to what was said here, the opinions he had read and heard elsewhere were trifling and insignificant, not worth thinking about.

Here he had to think constantly. A fresh new world was opening up before him, a world of whose existence he had never known, though he thought he had studied all that was to be found, either alive or in books. Here everything was simple and natural. Everything could be understood readily, because everything was rooted in the natural order. Nothing seemed complicated. Nothing was disguised and encased in legalistic jargon, formulas, and parliamentary decisions and court opinions. Here there were no laws, no statutes, no catechisms, no party platforms. And yet the people lived; life ran its course. There was no conflict, no confusion, no vagueness. The women had children, and there was food for all. If the children survived the first year, they grew up into healthy adults. There were no problems, no social questions. There was neither rich nor poor, neither exploiter nor slave. And when, occasionally, there was strife, it was rooted in such simple causes that it was straightened out and decided with a word from Jacinto, with everyone acknowledging that his decision was the only proper one. Here there was no injustice, because justice was natural and self-evident. No one speculated about justice, because the concepts of "justice" and "injustice" were totally lacking and couldn't develop.

After night had fallen, a large woodpile heaped on an old altar-like block of stone lying in the middle of the patio was set afire. Flames leaping into the sky illuminated the broad plaza of the hacienda. So it had been for centuries.

And the families came to the dance.

A few men played dance music on fiddles, guitars, and flutes. Those who did not play or dance sang.

At midnight, or thereabouts, the men and women stopped their dancing and began to sing.

They sang their national anthem, the song of their native land, the song of the White Rose, which has bloomed so cosily and tranquilly near the ravine since time eternal:

> To you, white rose,
> My parting kiss shall fly
> With my last breath
> When death is nigh.

For a time the people stood quietly, lighted by the flickering fire on the altar.

Jacinto and Magarito had joined in singing the song. As the last stanza was repeated, the governor also joined in. And as he sang, he felt that this hymn was just as beautiful as the national anthem. And he thought that their own song said more to those on the hacienda than the radiant hymn to the Republic. Though indeed sweet and spirited, the national anthem certainly did not breathe the peace of this simple song, for it begins with a blaring war cry, a summons to the sons and daughters of the Republic to defend their country against the foe who wants to crush it.

If the Mexicans as a people felt the brotherly love that bound the men here on Rosa Blanca into a united family, they would have no reason to fear the Americans or the British, because they would then be more secure than with soldiers and guns. For no foreign army can go far on Mexican soil if it doesn't find allies among the Mexicans themselves. So it was when Cortez marched into Mexico;

so it was when MacMahon plunged into the country; and so it was when the Americans arrived at Chapultepec and, seventy years later, Veracruz. The enemy of the Mexican people, their greatest enemy, is within and not without. This the governor thought as the song of Rosa Blanca finally faded away and the people began to dance again.

The dance continued until the first twinkling of the morning star.

The governor danced with the women and girls.

He forgot receptions, parliamentary addresses, government business, and oil companies. All that had ceased to exist.

There was only the dancing, the music, and the lovely songs. And there were the people, lighted by the reddish-yellow flickering fire, festively dressed men and women in colorful skirts and white blouses richly embroidered with red, green, and yellow leaves and ornamented tendrils. There were only the laughing, dancing, sweating women with their grave dark eyes, bare brown necks, and strong brown arms. Only women and girls with radiant joyous eyes and with bright flowers and red woolen ribbons intertwined in their thick black hair.

There was only singing, joy, unconcern, contentment, and security, and a blazing fire on a stone altar.

And always there was the sense of belonging to an ancestral home, of attachment to the soil, to the place where one was born and raised, lived, worked, and died.

Back in Jalapa, the governor asked Licenciado Perez to come to see him.

"I've reconsidered the Rosa Blanca matter in detail. Ramirez, the engineer over in the Department of Labor and Industry, has been lending me a helping hand since he's familiar with all the documents and plans. Here's what we've established: The Condor Oil Company is one of the strongest companies in Mexico, when it comes to owning leases to oil-bearing lands. But as of today only a fortieth of these leaseholds are in production or even at the drilling stage. And even if the company should continue at the same speed as before—and I don't for a minute believe it will—it still has enough land on hand, or under its control, to produce as much oil as it needs for fifty years. So there is no need to forcibly thrust more land onto the company to keep it working and productive. They haven't even begun work on five percent of the land known to have oil. We've determined that the company hasn't even drilled where is was bound to drill under the terms of the licenses it has now. You know, we have the right to take those fields away from Condor and turn them over to other companies, or we can keep them for national production. Right now, we're not considering forcing Condor to adhere to all the terms of the licenses. We don't want to create the impression that we're making the operations of foreign companies more difficult. So you see, Condor doesn't need Rosa Blanca. And it's not a case of some other company trying to gain an advantage. All the land around the hacienda is already under Condor's control, whether leased or owned outright.

"Under these circumstances I couldn't argue that the interests of the state justify a decree ordering the sale of Rosa Blanca, even if I wanted to oblige you and Condor Oil. That would be both untrue and unjust.

"Furthermore, the very interests that the company proposes to invoke to raise its production, those very interests compel me to leave Rosa Blanca in the possession of its people, as it has been for centuries. The owner has no intention of selling. Rather than free Rosa Blanca for the production of oil, reasons of state bid us preserve and protect it with everything in our power. The Condor Oil Company is registered in Mexico, of course, but its stockholders are not Mexican citizens. Sure, there's the one exception, the person I would call the statutory Mexican stockholder. On the other hand, all the Rosa Blanca people are Mexican citizens. We cannot take away from them land that is theirs by constitutional right.

"If it really were being argued that the lands under Condor's control could not produce oil in sufficient quantities, and that Rosa Blanca's oil, which according to the geologists' data it has in great abundance, was absolutely needed, then in that case Rosa Blanca would have to be sacrificed. But that is not the case here. Humanly speaking, it won't be needed in the next fifty years. What will have to be done then is not my concern, or the concern of the federal government. The time to resolve the matter will come fifty years from now. I'll leave the decision to those men who will be living and governing at that time.

"And that, my friend, closes the case, so far as I'm concerned, and as long as I'm in office, for the government as well. Still, if the company should manage to buy Rosa Blanca from Don Jacinto by negotiating privately, then the matter is beyond the scope of my power and authority. In any case, the government cannot intervene. There will be no order of any kind."

"Well, then," Perez said, "Condor will just have to abandon the idea. I've done my part."

The governor stood up, walking around the table, and came up close to the lawyer. In a friendly way, he tapped him gently on the chest and said: "What I've said to you so far, Perez, I had to say officially. And that's what's going into the files. That's the final report concerning the case of Rosa Blanca and Condor Oil. Unofficially, I'd like to tell you this: Keep your hands off Rosa Blanca. It would be a shame if it were broken up and converted into a stinking, noisy oil field. I was there recently. It's a jewel. And real men are living there. They are splendid fellows now but they'll become bandits and robbers if Rosa Blanca is taken away from them. We have plenty of cases like this. Who do you think all these bandits and train robbers we find around the country are? They're people who have lost a Rosa Blanca and no longer know what to do with themselves. They end up rotting away in the cities and degenerate into thieves, stealing and murdering as the easiest way to keep themselves alive.

"And there's another thing. The day may come when we'll need this Mexican oil, and won't know where to get it because the gringos have all of it in their hands. In that case, Rosa Blanca may be our salvation—all because our predecessors, especially that coyote Porfirio Díaz, sold and traded our country away. To preserve a larger *patria*, the Republic itself, the native soil of the Mexican people, it may be proper to sacrifice a Rosa Blanca. Yes, that—that's all I wanted to say, Licenciado. If I can ever do anything else for you, you know you can always count on me."

Perez went directly to the Western Union office after leaving the governor and wrote out a telegram for San Francisco: ROSA BLANCA LOST.

As he started to hand in his copy to the clerk, Perez noticed an

American reporter was standing there, handing in a long dispatch for the Associated Press. The newspaperman was discussing the cost, speaking English to the clerk.

Suddenly Licenciado Perez felt himself a Mexican. Perhaps because Condor Oil paid him well, he had long ago forgotten what it was like to be a Mexican.

He tore up the form and wrote out a new message, one intended to communicate unequivocally that the acquisition of the White Rose had been ruled out.

It said: ROSA BLANCA CAN'T BE HAD.

Although Perez had in fact done nothing to save Rosa Blanca, he felt now, nonetheless, a quiet satisfaction that the White Rose was saved for Mexico.

Six days later he received a letter from Condor headquarters. It recommended that he cleverly insinuate into the governor's pockets a hundred thousand dollars; if need be, the company would allow him to spend one hundred fifty thousand. Two checks were enclosed with the letter.

Perez answered at once, advising the Condor Oil Company not to risk any kind of bribery attempt. That could only result in a disaster, for the governor could cause the company the nastiest trouble; he wasn't the kind of person portrayed in Hollywood movies and dime novels.

Then he composed a second letter. In it he informed the company that he was resigning his position as a Condor agent, because he was over his ears in work.

After he had written the letter and stuck in it the envelope, he thought about it for a while.

Then he said to himself: "Resigning would be a mistake. If I want to help, if I'm to have any influence, I have to stay on, and cannot leave. If I don't, I'll be completely powerless. Perhaps the job will be taken by some skirtchaser who fritters his time and money away in night clubs. To pay for his tarts and cognac, he'll be out after the almighty dollar. He'll probably sell his soul, and even the souls of others, to do everything the company orders him to do, honorable or dishonorable."

The lawyer tore up the letter of resignation. Still, he added a postscript to the other letter urgently recommending that Rosa

Blanca be let alone because the national mood at that time was opposed to the foreign oil companies and their manipulations and machinations.

When Mr. Collins read the letter, he commented to the executive vice-president: "This Perez is one of the best lawyers we could have down there. He is first-rate with the administration and the governors we have to deal with. A clever fellow. A diplomat. But he's no good at all for certain matters. We'll do better to retain a shyster who knows how to turn the screws tight. We'll think about it."

.

CHAPTER THIRTEEN

ANYONE WHO didn't know Mr. Collins better might have thought he had forgotten Rosa Blanca and given up trying to get it. For he didn't get upset when Perez's telegrams and letters arrived. The only time he had ever shown any excitement over Rosa Blanca was shown on the day when the report came in from Perez saying that Don Jacinto wouldn't sell even for the fantastic price offered to him. In that excited hour, with an obligation of one and a half million dollars weighing on him, Collins vowed he was going to get Rosa Blanca. This promise settled the matter conclusively, so far as he was concerned. Getting the hacienda was only a matter of the time and labor devoted to it.

In this respect Mr. Collins was like the cold-blooded murderer who shows excitement only when a murder is being decided on.

Once a deed was agreed upon, Mr. Collins became calm and collected. He could reflect on it coolly and clearly, as if he were considering the solution of a mathematical problem. At such times not a trace of emotion influenced his plans. That was another reason for his greatness and his success: He felt a gambler's excitement only at the moment of decision, when a plan, or more precisely, a goal, was decided on. After the goal was set, he never again got excited about the matter, but stayed cool. His mind worked purely mechanically when it came to making particular moves. Once he'd set the goal, there was no escape for his victims. It was as if they were immured in a large room, believing they were still free because they saw doors, although the doors were locked. But the walls telescoped, coming closer and closer together, closing tighter and tighter on the captives until at last the day would come when the prisoners were crushed and removed, shattered and dead, to be cast onto the rubbish heap along with earlier victims.

Mr. Collins had made one and a quarter million dollars on the Laylitt manipulation. Now he was about to make another one and a half million so that he could buy Betty the swellest yacht on earth—plus a few other items into the bargain. He was, at the moment, just as much a prisoner as his victims. But he was a prisoner who had will and freedom of movement. He knew the objective and the way to it, whereas his victims were defensive, passive, and listless. They could not attack, but had to defend themselves as he wished, when he wished. In addition, they were already at a disadvantage because they did not see where the enemy was, who he was, with what weapons he was fighting, which allies he had, and where he was attacking. So their defeat was already assured at the moment he launched his attack.

Collins could have withdrawn the money he wanted from current company accounts, but doing that would have taken more time than he could give to it.

He could order fifty new wells to be drilled at the same time instead of twenty. Of every fifty wells, ten or fifteen would actually yield oil. And based on experience in the fields where they had drilled, the individual wells would produce from two to eight thousand barrels a day.

If Mr. Collins wanted to earn three million dollars more than usual in a comparatively short time, the Condor Oil Company had to earn five hundred million more than before through an extraordinary inflated production so that the amount could go additionally on Mr. Collins's stocks, royalties, and bonuses.

If production is increased by successful drilling and by clever market maneuvers, then not only does Mr. Collins earn more than before, but so, too, do the rest of the stockholders and directors. Therefore all these people are his allies, because they also have their extraordinary expenses—their Bettys, their yachts—and similar necessary and unavoidable diversions. Many of them would perhaps welcome an increased stock dividend with even greater pleasure than Mr. Collins, for in spite of their enormous fortunes, all are stuck, somehow, somewhere. They are involved in speculations, have to satisfy blackmailers, have entered into purchases and obligations. Every one of them is surrounded by a horde of idlers who want to live in luxury and cling to his shirttails and an army of relatives and nonrelatives who cannot be got rid of. Since many of their businesses, even the majority, slink along barely a hairsbreadth away from the toils of the law and even at times, at indiscreet moments, violate the laws, judges and politicians also have to be paid and paid again. Hundreds of thousands have to be paid to the political party, and if things should get too hot, then a church may have to be built, or a library, to extricate them from the clutches of the law. Armies of agents and spies have to be kept on salary. Newspapers have to be bought up or, if not, then paid well.

Mr. Collins's allies are thus the very best a man can have. They need, as urgently as he, a surprisingly high side income. They are also good allies because everyone has connections. The brother-in-law of one is the police commissioner, the brother of another is district attorney, the cousin of a third is a member of Congress, and the sister of yet another is mistress to a cabinet secretary.

With such allies, the battle naturally goes smooth and easy.

The Indian Jacinto Yañez doesn't have such good allies, and so he is at a disadvantage.

Whatever Mr. Collins may do to reach his goals and carry out his plans is sanctioned by all those who share in the pie, as long as those plans are successful, as everyone expects they will be, in extracting higher dividends. So everyone does his best to put the plans into effect. For in the long and convoluted channels there occasionally flow several dozen dollars to that policeman who cannot on his usual salary feed his large family or pay for college for his sons and daughters. Surely they should not have to become, like him, policemen or stenographers, but bank officials, thereby edging up closer to the platter than the father.

At times the socialist and communist newspapers hire editors who serve as fall guys. They serve sentences in any form imposed on the party organs so that the really valuable workers will be able to stay on the job.

The Condor Oil Company also had such a fall guy. At present he was Mr. Abner, the son of a man called Ebner, originally of German extraction. Mr. Abner had attended college and university. If he hadn't, he might have become an honest chauffeur or mechanic, bravely and lawfully slaving his life away. He would have begotten good American citizens and one day died gracefully, to be properly and suitably mourned by his widow and newly begotten American citizens for a week after they had collected on his life insurance.

But Mr. Abner wanted to go around in a white collar even on workdays. And so, after finishing his studies, he joined a law firm as a junior partner. There he had to do all the dirty little jobs that lawyers devise just to keep the office staff busy, to occupy their time so that they don't stare out the windows while chewing on their pencils.

In that law firm Mr. Abner was the one who pulled the chestnuts from the fire. He had responsibility for every dirty, dubious thing that was entrusted to the attorney. Mr. Abner was the foul-smelling attorney while the senior partner kept his hands clean. Of course, the senior partner accepted all the fees, whether they resulted from a squalid divorce or a blackmail attempt or a suit for damages. It was all one to him if a cheat smashed his shin with a stone and threw himself in front of an automobile. No matter that the fellow was never run over, but only grazed, in time three thousand dollars would be ground out of the car owner's insurance company. The senior partner came in for half of that. By all sorts of complicated and devious means, and with the help of a shopgirl through whom he became the bedfellow of a member of Condor's board, Mr. Abner succeeded at last in landing a job at Condor. As a staff lawyer for the company he received seventy-five dollars a week, and an annual Christmas bonus of three hundred.

Mr. Collins, who had a good eye for the talent of most of his important employees, soon recognized Mr. Abner's great ability to do the dirty work. So that he could use him to better advantage, Mr. Collins made him third assistant vice-president, at one hundred twenty-five dollars a week, and gave him two shares of stock and a right to bonuses for matters Mr. Abner had handled. Mr. Collins told him at the time of the promotion that he, Mr. Abner, would have to assume full responsibility for everything he did. He could decide right then whether he wanted to, but if he accepted the job, he would be bound to it.

Mr. Collins was straightforward. He had found that things worked out better if a person was told frankly what he was good at, and what not. And so he told Mr. Abner directly: "If you accept but make a face when things go wrong, you'll be given such a hard time you'll be lucky afterward if you're allowed to shine shoes somewhere."

Mr. Abner was certainly no greenhorn. He knew immediately what Mr. Collins meant. One evening, in some corner, there would be a thrashing. And with a vengeance! And when his wounds were healed, Mr. Abner might head east or west, north, south, or central—and inside of two weeks, his new employer would receive a letter containing the message: Mr. Abner has been guilty of an unheard-of breach of confidence. He is untrustworthy because he has a loose tongue. Even if the company wanted to keep him, perhaps because a wagging tongue could do them no harm, still no company, large or small, would want to incur the displeasure of the mighty Mr. Collins. So Mr. Abner would have to move on. If he were lucky, he could get work as a reporter paid by the line. And that, God forgive me, is a bed of thorns for the thief.

But Mr. Abner was not spoiled. He had no scruples. Nothing could be worse than the job he had had in the law firm. Besides, a company like Condor never allowed anyone who had eaten its dirt to rot in prison. It recognized the value of a job, and it paid full value. So Mr. Abner took the position with all the conditions that were attached to it, or might be attached to it later, without their being mentioned.

It was this Mr. Abner who was now called into Mr. Collins's private office.

After Mr. Abner had sat down and one of the best cigars was offered to him, Mr. Collins sat down opposite him. "Abner, I have a special job for you," Mr. Collins began. "A matter I'd like to entrust to you because I don't know anyone in the company who could handle it more capably than you."

Mr. Abner had never before in his life been addressed in such a fashion. Mr. Collins could now have talked him into traveling solo to Tibet to steal Buddha's statue from a temple and bring it back to America and Abner would have done it, or at least tried.

"The problem is this, Abner. Down there in Mexico in the state of Veracruz, we have under our control large holdings of oil land. Right in the middle of these—and it's very inconvenient to us—is a farm, or, as they call it down there, a *hacienda*. It's called the White Rose. A stupid name for a farm. But we can't help that until we make a firm move there.

"Well, now, we have to have this hacienda, because it hinders our freedom of movement. It's rich in oil. We figure on wells of fifty thousand barrels to perhaps eighty thousand on every tract. The owner, a lousy Indian, is half crazy, like all Indians. Doesn't know what he wants. A barrel of brandy ought to do it. That and a couple of thousand put in the hands of the mayor of the commune to which the hacienda belongs. But since the revolution the people down there are all getting swelled heads. That's for sure. They talk their heads off claiming they ought to keep all the oil for themselves, or as they say, the nation. We've offered that crazy Indian who owns the hacienda about four hundred an acre. Do you think that fire-eater will sell for that? He will not! And an acre down there is worth, on average, less than a dollar. Under old Porfirio Díaz—the Old Fox as he was called—we bought thousands of acres for ten cents an acre. Of course, there were a few thousands for the bigwigs who had anything to say about it officially. But as I said, since the revolution these fellows have become as stubborn as mules. The lawyers we have down there aren't worth a fig. They cost us a fortune and they do nothing. Sit all day and all night in their harems. You know, don't you, they still practice polygamy down there in Mexico."

"I know," Abner confirmed. "I was just reading about it again yesterday in a novella in *Action Stories*."

"Well, then, in that case, you surely know the country and the people who live there. Do you know how many generals they have in their army? You don't know. But I know from Mr. Halburn, who was down there last summer. They have so many generals every single soldier has a general of his own. And when a soldier dies, two generals fight a duel. The survivor gets a soldier to command so that he can remain a general. Our agents down there aren't of any use either. They only telegraph us about their per diems and the bribes they have to pay, but when we want something from them, they write us that nothing can be done about it at present until we send weapons to help the bandits and rebels bring down the government.

"So you see, Abner, you can't get anything there directly and honestly. The people don't see where their good fortune lies. Now I'm convinced that neither the lawyers nor the agents have done anything serious about bringing about the purchase of the hacienda. Those people don't understand the psychology of buying. That's also why they never amount to anything and are constantly begging from us. If we could deal directly with the Indian, we could make clear to him the advantages there are in selling that miserable property for a good price and buying a bigger and more beautiful farm somewhere else in Mexico or Arizona with all the machines and good roads and a first-rate market for his products."

Mr. Abner interrupted hastily and said: "Now I understand what has to be done, Mr. Collins. We have to bring the Indian here to the office. Then we can fire away at him."

Mr. Collins had not thought of that. His first thought had been to try to arrange a meeting with Don Jacinto somewhere in Mexico, perhaps in Mexico City or San Luis Potosí. Then he would let qualified people deal with him, amusing him in the city, getting him drunk, gulling him with presents for himself and his wife, anything to delay his departure until he had agreed to sell. That was the way Mr. Collins imagined it when he said that the Indian had to be dealt with directly.

But Mr. Abner's interjection gave him a better idea. If Abner succeeded in luring Jacinto to the States, perhaps even to San Francisco, then the acquisition was assured.

Mr. Collins immediately changed his plan. "That's exactly what we have to do. We must get him to come here to San Francisco. We can settle the final price with him here and explain to him in peace and quiet the benefits he can obtain by selling. Here we can show some attractive farms to him and offer them to him in exchange. They will surely tempt him. Then he'll be able to see for himself what money can do. He won't want to go back at all to his rotten old filthy hacienda. The people are still so backward there. You won't believe it, Abner, but it's true, they still grind corn on a stone, just like cavemen."

Mr. Collins had been to Mexico quite often, twice a year in some years, to inspect the wells and to gather information. But like all of his kind, he knew absolutely nothing about the land and the people living there. Why should he? He stayed at the Hotel Imperial in Tampico, ate only in American restaurants, and raced from oil field to oil field in an automobile. In the fields he usually paid no attention to the Mexican workers and spoke only a few words to the American drillers about the kind of terrain they were working. And as he whizzed about the countryside in his auto, he flew by the huts of the Indian peasants without so much as a glance into the people's lives. He saw only the palm huts, palm roofs, adobe houses, naked children, barefoot men and women, roving pigs and chickens that were forever in the way of his automobile. But of the land itself he knew only what he read in American newspapers and novels and in the short stories of the thrillers. When he heard Mexico mentioned, he always heard of bandits, rebellions and revolutions, of pistols being fired in the Chamber of Deputies, of filth, of ignorance, of superstitious Catholicism. That was the Mexico Mr. Collins was acquainted with.

Still, there was a balance present in the world: Mexicans hearing of America, of the United States, always thought only of the millionaires and billionaires living there, because there was no such thing as an American who wasn't at least a millionaire. Not to the Mexican. Every American is a millionaire, and if he isn't a millionaire, he isn't an American. To the Mexican mind all Americans live only in skyscrapers because there are no other houses in America.

For this exhaustive knowledge of one people vis-à-vis its neighbors, we owe thanks to the educational efforts of the newspapers. Everyone knows that a newspaper has but one great task to perform: to enlighten the people, telling them nothing but the absolute truth.

And what Mr. Collins did not learn about Mexico and the Mexican people from newspapers and periodicals, he got from anecdotes told in the hotel to kill time, stories that hadn't been fabricated in Mexico but were taken from *Life* and *Judge* and other American humor magazines.

So it was thoroughly understandable that Mr. Collins formed an opinion of the Mexicans, and at this time of the obstinate Indian Jacinto Yañez in particular, that silently conformed to his knowledge of Mexico and the Mexicans. That there might be people on earth who do not understand the value of money, who do not know that a thousand glistening silver dollars are a sacred thing—that was something that Mr. Collins could not understand. He didn't even believe that such a situation could exist. He believed only that a given sum of money could cause a man to do, or not do, certain things. But he did not believe there were people who considered money irrelevant, who valued other things much more highly than money. And when anyone maintained that there was something— material or spiritual—worth more to him than money, worth more even than all the money in the world, Collins smelled a trick, a ruse to extract a greater sum.

"So now your job is clear to you, Mr. Abner," Mr. Collins continued. "You have to bring this man, this Don Jacinto, here to San Francisco. I leave it entirely up to you to determine how you accomplish this. Whatever funds you need for this purpose will be at your disposal. Of course, I have to caution you against one thing: no breaking the law, Abner. I'll not put up with that. Above all, you may not kidnap the man, and, least of all, drug him. That's a mess for which you'll have to defend yourself. I'm telling this to you expressly. That wouldn't help us at all. For then the Mexican government could challenge the contract, and we'd come off badly. The man must come here voluntarily. How you bring this off is your affair. I consider you bright and intelligent enough to do it skillfully. That's why we chose you for this difficult job. When the man arrives in San Francisco, you'll receive a special bonus of ten thousand dollars. Provided, of course, as I said before, you've not used force or committed any crimes to bring him here. Have I made myself absolutely clear, Mr. Abner? Fine. When the man is here, then, the main task will be finished. The rest will be up to other people who specialize in closing deals. Perhaps you'll want to go down there this week to study the matter at first hand and find the right moves. Well, that's it. You know your job. I leave the details entirely to your skill."

Just as Mr. Collins urgently needed his five million dollars, so Mr. Abner needed both the bonus of ten thousand dollars and special recognition from the company for his excellent work.

CHAPTER FOURTEEN

MR. COLLINS's fierce craving for possession of Rosa Blanca was not in any way a mere lust for profits, though he did not for a moment lose sight of his intention to collect an extraordinary profit.

His explanation of his brutal procedure was not quite so unscrupulously capitalistic as it might seem to the outsider. He was not a monster at all. As a man he was neither a murderer nor a rogue; as a man he was lovable and kind. Otherwise Betty would not have tolerated him as a friend and lover for a single day. But if he had visited Rosa Blanca, if he'd had the ability to understand the soul of the White Rose, its owners and inhabitants, if he could have regarded it with affection, instead of as a naked business proposition, he might even have been the person to defend the White Rose with all his might against its plucking and fading. But away from it, far from its heart, he saw in it only an object. He saw in Rosa Blanca only an American farm.

Not a single American farm he knew of was a spiritual homeland. None of the farmers he was acquainted with thought for an instant of turning the farm on which he lived into such a place. Anyone who bought a farm worked himself half to death to improve it. But not with any intention of creating a permanent home. He meant to sell it for fifty to a hundred percent more than he paid for it. The farm was an item of commerce, like a retail store or a lumberyard. No spiritual bond connected the farmer to his farm. The farm was only regarded for its value as a dead, money-making object. So, too, the cattle, and the fruit trees that were there. If a farmer planted seedlings, he did so not with the solemn thought that succeeding generations would want to have apples, pears, nuts, and oranges and that these fruits had to be left behind for them, just as our ancestors planted saplings for us. The farmer cultivated them only because he could sell a farm with many properly tended fruit trees for more than one without them. The saplings promised the new owner a greater profit. Once a farmer had improved a modest farm through his labor, he quickly scurried around to find a buyer who would pay him a good price. Then he could buy another farm at a low price somewhere else, with the intention of improving it and selling it at a higher price.

How could it be expected that Mr. Collins, in such circumstances, knowing only such farmers, could understand the White Rose? He saw it only as a farm, nothing more, and its owner he considered a pigheaded farmer who, having heard of the millions in profits from the oil fields, was now seeking to squeeze out the highest imaginable price for his farm. Mr. Collins was behaving entirely consistently, true to the influences to which he was subject. He could not behave any other way. If he did, he wouldn't be an oil magnate. And if we follow the argument to the bitter end, we may actually arrive at the point someday where mankind won't have the oil it needs so urgently at the current state of civilization. In the end, every parcel of oil-bearing land may be a Rosa Blanca for those who live on it. And in that case, if it should be valued sentimentally, like Rosa Blanca, there wouldn't be any oil at all. What would have to be done then in order to get the needed oil? With perhaps a few modifications, exactly what Mr. Collins was doing now to pluck the White Rose.

Mr. Collins had a justification for everything he did. This made it easier in every single case for him to salve his conscience if his tactics seemed a bit too crude and sometimes even had consequences that he neither desired nor foresaw. In the long run an open yearning for profit cannot shield even the most calloused moneymaker from self-recrimination and uneasy thoughts. There exists in every man a more or less strong fear of retaliation for what he is doing or has already done. This punishment has nothing to do with that punishment after death in which so many people believe. Nor does it have anything to do with the punishment that is inflicted by the legal process, where a person has to give a full account of his actions to a judge.

No, the punishment that is meant here, which all men feel and fear instinctively, is of another kind. They fear that an evil deed they have perpetrated may be avenged on them or on those they love. Many people fear that all the goods they've gained by sordid and improper ways are going to be lost again. Others fear that they will be pursued by bad luck for the rest of their lives, that they'll be sick or infirm and that if they themselves aren't affected, their children and wives or their best friends will have to suffer. Many people go so far in this belief that they expect they'll have to suffer one day precisely what they did to someone else.

That is one of the psychological reasons why nearly all men draw a line they dare not cross. Every man knows he is not the Almighty, the Omnipotent. Everyone knows he can somehow fall into the clutches of a stronger person who may treat him exactly as he has treated others. It is this instinct alone that makes possible social life and human cooperation. It is this instinct that keeps an evil man from ripping out a section of a railroad line under cover of darkness. For at some time there may be someone whom this man loves and would not want to kill riding on the train. Or, quite possibly, an imitator might destroy the tracks when he himself is sitting on the train, and then he might perish. This is why no normal man torments or tortures another man whom he has in his power, and rarely even an animal, out of pure pleasure in the torture.

Every man looks for an excuse to justify to himself the sordid, antisocial things he does and have them appear thereby less sordid and less antisocial.

No king, no president, no group of capitalists, will hatch a war without justifying it on the grounds that it serves the common good and cannot be avoided for this or that reason, and that the nation's standing in the eyes of other peoples, hence honor, requires the war. Without a moral justification no war is begun. And finding a good excuse is the first task of those who think a war is needed. The more believable the excuse, the surer the result in all actions requiring the co-operation or toleration of other men. Of course, that does not prevent the perpetration of countless deeds without anyone seeking an excuse. At times it is too difficult to find an excuse. And at other times the performance of the action cannot be postponed for any reason.

Mr. Collins's justification for his present actions was not farfetched, one he had concocted elaborately so he could stand there unembarrassed before himself and his fellow man.

He said to himself: People need oil. They'll need much more oil tomorrow than they need today. And next month they'll need a hundred times as much. And next year, once an airplane can be bought for five hundred dollars and is so easy to operate that anyone can fly it without danger to himself or to others, five thousand times as much. More and more, diesels are replacing steam engines, and increasingly trains are run on oil. More and more, important new products are made from oil. Thus mankind needs more and more oil, though the need for wheat, cotton, and leather stays the same.

"The Condor Oil Company is one of the most powerful companies on earth. It has in its possession an enormous share of oil-bearing lands—in California, Oklahoma, Mexico, Venezuela, and Colombia. And because this is so, the Condor Oil Company has assumed the responsibility of providing men with the oil they need. At the same time, with this responsibility, it has taken on the obligation to transport it so that mankind doesn't go without oil. Since I'm president of Condor, I have to see to it with all my abilities that more and more oil is on hand than is needed today and tomorrow. For the day after tomorrow even more will be needed. And if I'm not careful, if I should fail to consider that every well will run dry sooner or later and that many wells are drilled but never produce, then it can happen that the day will come when mankind won't have enough oil on hand. Its machines won't run, engines will sputter and die, locomotives will stop, ships won't sail. There'll be no raw materials coming in from abroad, and tens of thousands, even hundreds of thousands of workers will go without jobs. If something like that should happen, they'll blame me, the president of the mighty Condor Company. They'll hold me responsible for all the evil that results from a lack of oil. What can I do about that? I have to supply oil and store it so that people won't suffer. If I profit from it, say profit very well, that is only what mankind owes me for my pains, my concern, my sleepless nights, the skill with which I procure the oil.

"What can I do about it if farmers are driven off the land. I'm not responsible if they perhaps go so far as to commit suicide because they can't get over the loss of their homes. Old stagecoach drivers have even hanged themselves because people no longer cared to listen to them crack their whips and play their songs on the post horn, but preferred to ride on the train because it was quicker and cheaper.

"It's really and truly deplorable that this shyster Abner, a fellow I cannot stand, is now going down there to ruin Rosa Blanca. But, dammit, it will be a thousand times sadder if men run out of oil someday. I didn't create this world. God knows, I'm not responsible for this crazy world. I didn't invent oil and I've never seriously concerned myself about why they want to have it anyway. But they will have it because they need it; and I'm obligated to give it to them because I know where it is. So why hasn't God, who is so wise and so powerful, made all this different and better? Some things I could have done better myself."

Perhaps Mr. Collins is not a remarkable fellow. But in his reasoning there is scarcely a flaw.

CHAPTER FIFTEEN

MR. ABNER had studied Spanish in college. But as so often happens with a foreign language one studies in school, he discovered when he got to Mexico that the Mexicans did not understand their mother tongue.

Still, he picked it up, and one day he arrived in Tuxpan. He thought he'd launch his attack from this small city, and he first wanted to study the ground on which he had to fight.

He spent the first few days hanging around in the cantinas and poolrooms in hopes that he could perhaps pick up all sorts of things that would be useful to him. Here he made the acquaintance of a mestizo named Frigillo. His father was an American who had gradually let himself go in this land of the easy life, going completely to pot, becoming a drunkard and siring a child on the Indian woman he was living with.

As a boy Frigillo had gone to the States. There he worked at every job imaginable. He was jailed several times for theft, and at last the American authorities shipped him back to his native Mexico. His English was adequate, and that helped him quite a bit in finding a well-paid job as a foreman of Mexican peons working in the oil fields.

This regular work in the fields did not suit him, so he got to his feet and became a recruiting agent for the oil companies. For every worker he recruited he got a fixed fee. Depending on the circumstances, the fee varied from three to twelve pesos for each man. He made good money at this, for the workers changed jobs frequently. And when they didn't move often enough to suit Frigillo, he knew how to lure them away on one pretext or another. Then the companies had to reorder workers for him.

At the moment Frigillo was idle because all the fields were full up with people, and wages were so good that everyone thought it best to stick to his job and not move so often.

Frigillo, of course, had a personal interest in the laying-out of new fields. New production meant renewed demand for workers. And that meant easy profits for him.

Feeling himself lucky to have met the mestizo, Abner said not a word about Rosa Blanca on the first day of their friendship, but within the week he had begun to talk about the hacienda. He did not say that he was in Mexico on account of Rosa Blanca. He told Frigillo he was there to buy oil-bearing land. It was widely known that Rosa Blanca was rich oil territory. Even better known was the fact that a large American oil company wanted to buy it, and Don Jacinto had refused the deal. There were rumors that the company had offered five million dollars.

"That man is really out of his mind," Frigillo said to Abner when they discussed the matter. "What a splendid life the man could lead! And just think how many hundreds of workers could find good jobs out there, people who now have to emigrate to the States. Your turn, mister."

Abner and Frigillo were playing pool, and Abner was letting the mestizo win so that he would be friendly and talkative.

"That's it. You win again," Abner said, as he watched Frigillo's last shot and chalked his cue to show that he was looking forward to a new game.

The new game began, and both men spoke casually of Rosa Blanca and Don Jacinto, with occasionally a few words about the game.

"Selling the land could only be a blessing to those poor fellows out there on the hacienda who have to work themselves half to death for a couple of centavos," Abner said. "Those poor people get absolutely nothing from life. They can scarcely afford shoes. And they're never gone to a movie."

"That's almost exactly what I was going to say, mister. Think what the people can earn, and how well things might go. They could pick up their four or five pesos a day with a laugh, and do it in eight hours. What do they have now? Seventy centavos a day. If, in fact, they get that much. I don't even believe they get seventy centavos a day. And it runs from cockcrow to the deepest night. Well, you know, mister, that shot you just took—I could do better with the little toe on my left foot. Where'd you actually learn to play? Take a good look at how we play such a ball here in Mexico. As easy as pie."

"Well, señor, that isn't so. We also know how to play pool. Just you wait and see how I treat you. Then you can perhaps go from New York to Los Angeles and never get to see such a fine shot. Have you seen this, *hombre*? That's how we play with Mexicans. And I can do it again, slick as a whistle. Tarnation! The cue slipped. What sort of filthy chalk is it you have down here? This isn't chalk at all! It's lipstick. Why, then, isn't this Don Cazimpo . . ."

"Jacinto, he's called. J-A-C-I-N-T-O. Jacinto Yañez. Yes, why doesn't he sell? *Quien sabe?* Perhaps because he's not been offered enough and means to get his price."

Abner knocked the cue stick against the floor and rechalked. As he was doing this he said: "Maybe the lawyers who're dealing with him don't know how to handle him. Maybe they don't know how to convince a man of his own interests."

Frigillo leaned over the table as he tried to sink a difficult shot. After made it, he said: "That'd be it. These lawyers don't care whether he sells or not. They get their money, and as for the rest they don't care."

"I really have a good mind to buy some land," Abner said as he watched Frigillo play. "I have some big financiers supporting me, and they will pay whatever is necessary."

"Listen," Frigillo broke in, "if you have so much money behind you, then, you know, mister, why don't you invite Don Jacinto to go to the States. Pay him plenty for the trip, and when you get him up there, your backers can discuss the price with him at their leisure."

"That's an idea. But do you think he'd make such a trip?"

"No, I don't think so," Frigillo said. "Certainly not. Not without something else, not without a reason. But if you find a good reason, why not? Certainly every man readily makes a long trip once. But Jacinto? No, I don't believe he'll go that far. Not without a reason. In fact, he doesn't even know what far is. I don't think he's ever been farther than Jalapa in his entire life."

"Could you find a reason, señor, so good he'll agree to go? I'll readily pay for the trip up and back—even if he still doesn't want to sell. But then, at least, we'll have tried everything."

Frigillo looked the table over as he studied how he could best pocket a ball and said absentmindedly: "A reason? Sure. I don't know. Well, I'm taking the first ball from the left and putting it over there in the corner pocket. Scratched! I really think this chalk is positively worthless. But, mister, no, if you don't get yourself together, you aren't going to take a single game today."

"The table doesn't seem to be set up properly. It's quite definitely not in balance. It dips at one side. I'll bet five dollars on it." Abner walked round the pool table and examined it from all sides with great seriousness, as if the fate of the world depended upon the table's being precisely in balance. After he had come back to the scratch line, he chalked his cue again and said: "You really know this fellow well?"

"Certainly, I know Jacinto," Frigillo answered. "As if he were my own brother."

"Then you shouldn't find it hard."

"What?"

"To find a reason for his trip to the States. If you manage to find a good reason for his going along with me, you figure to make some money out of it, too."

"How much?" Frigillo asked as he pocketed a ball.

"Say, a hundred pesos."

"One hundred American dollars." With that Frigillo stroked the ball as though the hundred dollars depended on his making the shot.

"Agreed, Señor Frigillo. One hundred American dollars when Don Jacinto is sitting on the train with me."

"But not by this time tomorrow, of course. Things don't happen that fast," Frigillo said. "I also figure that when you buy the land and lay it out for production, I'm going to get the commission on the workers who are needed."

"No question about it. You'll certainly get the commission."

Frigillo looked at Abner, rested his head first on his right shoulder and then his left, and said at last: "Perhaps we ought to put that in writing. But I'm no sucker. I know a piece of paper also has its drawbacks. But for my own security, I'll tell you here right now—if you don't stick to the agreement we've made, I can make such a stink that you and all your people won't even be able to say spit. Understand? Good, then we're clear on everything."

"There's not the slightest intention of evading the terms," Abner protested. "Anyone who helps us is helped in return. And we need an agent to recruit workers. So why argue? It doesn't matter to us whether you get the commission or Señor X or Señor Z. But we know you, and so we prefer you. That's quite clear and logical."

"It's your ball, mister. Perhaps you can cut it quite sharply from the bottom right and draw it back here to the spot on the cushion. Here where I'm pointing. That's how I'd play it. Well, I really thought you'd go broke earlier. The devil only knows where you learned to play what you call pool. People really have very curious ideas about pool sometimes."

Frigillo took his time in the matter. He had to figure everything out fully, so he told Abner. He also had little interest in seeing it go quickly. Because as long as the gringo was in town, he could win fifteen to twenty pesos a day from him at pool. Making money wasn't always that easy, so once you found a lucrative occupation, you stuck to it for a while.

But then one day, about a week later, Frigillo seemed to be ready with his plan. In the meantime, Abner had also learned the reason for the delay. Thereafter, he made a greater effort, and soon Frigillo was not making so much at pool and lost interest in keeping the gringo in Tuxpan. He had devised a plan, and now he discussed it with Abner. Abner found it suitable. One morning they rented horses and rode off to visit Don Jacinto.

On their arrival at the hacienda, the mestizo introduced Mr. Abner: "Don Jacinto, here is an American who would like to buy some good, strong saddle horses, born and bred in this region, because he'd like to use them on inspection trips around the oil fields."

Jacinto studied Abner's face, and when Abner returned him a level gaze and smiled, Jacinto took a liking to the stranger.

"I have horses. Strong, sound horses sired right here on the hacienda. They're small, rough-looking *caballitos,* but they are very strong, and tough as mules. Well nourished. Not a single sore on their backs. Broken in. I can sell you four, five, perhaps even six. Do you want to see the *caballos?* In that case, I'll call Margarito, and he can bridle the horses and bring them in from the pasture."

Abner had been leaning against a post on the portico. Now he said wearily: "It's already quite late now, Don Jacinto. We're also tired out from the long ride. Maybe I can stay here a day or two and we can discuss the business quietly. I'd also like to ride the horses around a bit to see what they're like under the saddle."

Abner knew absolutely nothing about horses.

"*Es su casa,* Señor," Don Jacinto said. "My home is your home. I'm glad to welcome you, Señor."

He called across the wide patio: "Miguelito, take these gentlemen's horses down to the river and water them. Then bring them back to the enclosure. Watch out that the stallion doesn't nip you. And smear some salve on the saddle sores to heal them up, and there on the neck of the dark one brush some disinfectant to kill the screwworms."

He slapped the horses on the flanks and grasped them by the nostrils with this thumb and forefinger. The horses sniffed and whinnied as they smelled companions in the pasture.

"*Muy bien, patron,*" Miguel said, attending to the horses.

The men entered the house.

A boy brought a bowl of water, and the two newcomers washed their hands. Another boy brought out a wooden tray with two glasses of water, and the guests rinsed their mouths out, gargling their throats clear of the dust of the road.

Don Jacinto had meanwhile fetched a bottle of mezcal, poured three glasses full, and with a *"Salud!"* they drank welcomes to themselves.

"Excellent mezcal," Frigillo said, as he inspected the bottle and its label.

"It is," Don Jacinto said. "It's from Tabasco."

Abner put in: "This is really good. I didn't know you could make such a good drink here in Mexico."

"Care for a chaser, Señor?" Jacinto asked with a laugh and in good humor.

"Well, yes, one more. But only half a glass, Señor."

So they drank another three-quarters of a glass and a chaser, and then, so that the first one wouldn't lie alone on the stomach, another full glass was added at the end.

Three crudely wrought rocking chairs were dragged out onto the portico.

The mestizo was first to bring up the subject of the States—how rich the people were there, how tall the houses were, what all could be seen in the theaters. According to the mestizo, the railroad in New York ran under the ground and away up over the houses, and in other places it even ran along under the river. A person sitting in his own living room with a radio could hear music that was being played ten thousand miles away in Russia or China. Doctors in America could slice a man's body open from stem to stern, take everything out, wash it, put it back in again, and sew the body up, and the man could get up and be walking around again the very next day. Don Jacinto knew of course that all this was not true, that this was being said only to make conversation. Still, he knew as a fact that some part of it was surely true, because he had seen an airplane with his own eyes when it buzzed over the hacienda one day.

But Mr. Abner produced pictures of the States, and Jacinto could see for himself that the houses were really tall, and that to get to the train racing along underground one actually had to crawl deep into the ground. So maybe everything that was being said was true. Maybe the doctors could cut off a man's head, repair it, and sew it on again. If people could fly through the air like birds and hear what was being said in China, then anything was possible. He surely would not take Mr. Abner's word about such things as readily, since he was a foreigner. It was impossible to know whether he was telling the truth because he didn't even speak properly and one always had to guess half of what he was actually trying to say. With Frigillo it was somewhat different. Frigillo didn't always stick entirely to the truth. That was all right, for Jacinto knew about it. No wonder, because Frigillo's father had certainly been a foreigner. Still, Frigillo was half Indian. Jacinto had known him since he was a boy, and so he could believe Frigillo much sooner than the stranger. And Frigillo had also been in the States for a long time and spoke that foreign language just as well as the gringo did.

When the gringo said something that didn't seem to be quite believable, Jacinto looked to Frigillo. If he confirmed it with a nod or by verbal agreement, then Jacinto knew that what was said was true.

At last they sat down to supper. Mr. Abner was not entirely satisfied with the meal. Once, out of curiosity, he had gone to a Mexican restaurant in Los Angeles. At the time he'd thought that the dishes served to him there were fanciful creations given to diners just to satisfy their curiosity. Now he realized that Mexican people really ate what was served to him in that restaurant. The tortillas did not please him, and the heaps of green and red peppers in the dishes caused him to drink whole pitcherfuls of water during the meal. In Tuxpan he ate American food in the restaurants. Here, however, he had to observe the customs of the country for once. He yearned for white bread, butter, ham, beefsteak, and soda crackers.

After supper, they returned to the chairs on the portico. To provide light an immense heap of wood was burning on the altar stone in the middle of the spacious patio before the hacienda's main house.

Crickets were singing in the nearby jungle and in the fields. Now and then a cow lowed and a horse snorted. A mule trumpeted and a donkey brayed in complaint. Farther away, in one of the huts, where the light from the oven shone through the latticed walls, a dog barked. Others answered. Like creeping shadows young men pressed up against the walls of the courtyard, and the girls giggled in the corners. From the kitchen there came the prattle of the cooks, and in among them the deep, calm, full voice of the mistress of the house. She was sitting in a rocking chair on the beaten-earth kitchen floor, watching the girls, giving them directions, and laughing with them, joking and jesting at the same time. When the baby of one of the cooks began to whimper, the wife called out: *"Dame el pobrecito.* Give me the poor thing. You're holding him carelessly. He really has to cry, the poor little beggar." In the woman's lap the baby quieted down at once. Softly she blew tobacco smoke into his face to keep wandering mosquitos away. Pigs grunted, jostled each other, squealed. The sky was a deep blue-black with golden buttons tightly fastened to the vaulted dome of the universe.

Meanwhile Mr. Abner was thinking and brooding and calculating how he was going to spend the ten thousand dollars that were surely his.

The men had a look at the horses next morning. Following Frigillo's advice, Abner praised the horses to the skies, although they were, in fact, ordinary Mexican ranch stock.

Hearing the foreigner praise his horses in this way made Jacinto happy. He was very proud of his horses and mules.

He was so delighted by the praise that he made Mr. Abner a gift of all six horses, and steadfastly shrank from accepting a peso for them.

"How can I take money for these horses you've praised so highly, if you believe them worthy of your admiration? That would make my heart ache. I can't sell them to you. Take them as a souvenir of Rosa Blanca."

Frigillo poked Abner hard in the side at that moment, as Jacinto was stroking one of the horses and patting it good-naturedly on the muzzle.

"Don Jacinto," Abner began, speaking in a trembling voice as though he had trouble controlling his emotions. "The honor you do me with these horses, these marvelous horses, I can—I really don't know. No, I cannot accept such a gift. The horses are too valuable for me to accept them as a gift."

Jacinto answered simply: "Please, Señor, would you cause me

sorrow by refusing an honest gift offered to you by Rosa Blanca? I don't believe you could be so discourteous. That would be an insult. Knowing that you love and cherish these horses so much, I can never sell them. I can't take them back. The horses, Señor, are yours."

Now it really wasn't true that Jacinto was giving the horses for keeps. In accordance with the custom of his country he expected to get a present in return. Courtesy required it, a courtesy that the foreigner in Mexico usually forgets to observe—whether intentionally or unintentionally cannot always be easily determined. The Mexican who has taken a liking to someone will honor him by giving him the shirt off his back, and he'll never think he's owed anything in return. Never. But if a present fails to arrive, he'll get a bad taste in his mouth. This is so not because of the gift's material value, but because of the feeling that a process has developed only halfway. If the courtesy and honor he has sought to show are not returned with like courtesy and honor he feels that he has been misunderstood. This disrupts the harmony of the world. The world is out of balance. He begins to feel that he is not respected and honored as much as he respects and honors others. And even among men who do not give gifts but only express their feelings in empty words, such a feeling always hurts. An offer of money in return would be an insult leading to a mortal enmity if the Mexican did not know that the foreigner is following customs different from his own. Mr. Abner received a second poke in the ribs.

At this he remembered his role. "Señor Yañez, the honor you do me is so heartfelt, so sincerely meant, that I feel compelled to accept the horses. I can only say to you that these horses will always be worth more to me than mere animals alone. They shall always remind me of you and of Rosa Blanca and of how you have shown me, a foreigner, such great kindness, which I would never have expected to find here. To have found you here as a friend makes your beautiful land of Mexico as dear to me as my own. I thank you a thousand times for this valuable gift, which I don't believe I can ever repay in any way."

Jacinto clasped Abner in his arms and held him in the embrace for a long time, repeatedly slapping him on the back. Then they shook hands. And that, so far as Jacinto was concerned, sealed a friendship pact of such importance that the Indian considered it binding on Abner's children as well.

Abner paced back and forth, before at last stopping in front of Jacinto. He said: "It's difficult for me to find anything with which to repay you for your friendship and hospitality, Señor. I would consider it the greatest honor and pleasure that you can give me if you would be my guest in my country for a week, or even better, two. I would show you everything we've talked about here—houses as high as the sky, trains that whiz along underground—we would ride on them—movies that talk, radio sets that play music from China. And we would take a ride in an airplane so you can see the earth for once from way up high. You must allow me to repay your own noble hospitality, which you showed me in your house, with this trip. Of course, I will pay for you to go there and back. In California, I, too, have a ranch . . ."

With this Abner began to lie.

". . . and I have a strain of mules, too. But I don't raise the small animals you have here. No, I breed those gigantic mules you use in the Mexican artillery and machine-gun divisions." Jacinto had seen such mules in the illustrated Sunday supplement of a large Mexico City newspaper given to him by a shopkeeper in Tuxpan. He had cut out the pictures of the enormous army mules and pasted them to a wall in the living room. Seeing the pictures there, Abner knew how to use them very cleverly for his own purposes.

"Until I saw those pictures, I never would have believed that such a race of mules existed," Don Jacinto said. "Breeding such mules here on Rosa Blanca would really give me a lot of pleasure."

"That's for sure, Don Jacinto," Abner nodded. "Breeding such animals is a pleasure, in and of itself, even if you forget what you can get for them. I don't think there's any better way to repay you for your gift. Will you do me the honor of accepting from me a present of three mares and a jackass? With them you can start a strain of mules that will be both a joy and a delight and a memento of our friendship. Not only will you have the pleasure of owning the mules, they'll always be a lasting reminder of the priceless days we have spent here on your beautiful ranch in the friendly interchange of our thoughts and experiences."

171

Mr. Abner knew how to talk. You have to grant him that. He was better than a rag merchant on New York's Lower East Side. Abner could have wheedled Old Nick into giving him Hell itself if he'd taken an interest in it.

Because of the friendship pact which now bound him to Abner, the Indian abandoned all caution and mistrust of the foreigner.

The mestizo Frigillo knew his people to perfection. That's why the scheme he had worked out for Abner was so effective. He knew it would earn him his hundred dollars.

For just as Abner would have badly insulted Don Jacinto by declining the horses, now Don Jacinto would insult Abner if he refused to accept Abner's gift of the trip, the hospitality, and the breeding stock. In fact, he would have inflicted an even greater insult, for the foreigner had already accepted his gift. Thus the friendship permitted no refusal. And in any case Don Jacinto was not well trained in the art of subtle evasions and perfect excuses. He simply did not know how to justify a turndown without wounding or insulting his friend. And what sort of friendship was it that fell apart at the first token?

Of course, if Don Jacinto had known that the trip to and from San Francisco cost nearly two hundred and fifty dollars, if he had known how expensive good breeding animals are in the States, he might have been more cautious. Then he might first have thought it all over carefully. But he was already so enmeshed, with the help of the mestizo, that there was no escape. Even if he had known the total cost of the gifts, he would have concluded only that Mr. Abner valued his horses so highly that they merited a sizable present in return. And this valuation of his horses would have vanquished Don Jacinto even more decisively. Don Jacinto was proud of his horses, and an acknowledgment of the value he saw in them signified respect for the man who had bred them.

So Don Jacinto was trapped by his own customs, his own character. No man on earth is more bound up than the man caught in these things. Hold a man to his honor and he will give you his God and his world view—and throw his eleven-year-old daughter in for good measure. Even so stupid a thing as a duel in which the injured party is shot and killed by the person who insulted him proves more than the psychologists seek to prove in enormous fat tomes.

Frigillo knew the spot where a person like Don Jacinto is vulnerable. It doesn't take a swordthrust to kill a hero. The bite of a gnat raised on a dunghill will do as well.

In three days Jacinto was ready to leave.

Mr. Abner was now so sure of the Indian that he had already paid Frigillo the money. And because everything had gone so well, he paid him not just the hundred dollars, but two hundred.

When they arrived in San Francisco, Abner rented a furnished house. Its condition and location seemed suitable, and he informed Mr. Collins of Jacinto's arrival.

At once they debated what they intended to do.

Don Jacinto was taken by Abner to the Condor Building. There they worked at him might and main to get him to agree to sell Rosa Blanca.

But in this matter Don Jacinto knew exactly what he wanted. So the negotiations came to nought. Their last offer to him, a million dollars, made no impression at all. It might just as well have been ten million, for to him Rosa Blanca was a treasure that couldn't be sold, any more than one could sell the need to have to eat and drink.

When at last everything had been tried, when it emerged that any further attempts and offers to induce Jacinto to make the sale would also be fruitless, Mr. Collins summoned Mr. Abner to a private conference, without witnesses.

In San Francisco Don Jacinto had run into an old acquaintance. This man, born in the vicinity of Tuxpan, had married there and shortly afterward moved with his wife and son to San Francisco. Espinosa, so he was called, had opened a small shop. For some reason Don Jacinto had said nothing about this to his friend Abner. Later, Espinosa could supply information about Don Jacinto when he told the Mexican consul what he knew. Perhaps fortunately for him, Don Jacinto did not mention his name. For Espinosa was to be quite an embarrassment to the Condor Oil Company in the future. But by the time Condor heard of him, it was too late to silence him in one way or another. If the Condor plan had not been prepared and carried out all too well, it wouldn't have come unstuck on this Espinosa. Espinosa didn't know much, but what he did know confirmed everything suspected by the Mexican consul in San Francisco and by the Mexican officials in the Republic.

One day Don Jacinto was invited by Mr. Abner to drive with him in his automobile to Abner's ranch. Abner didn't have a ranch.

Late in the evening, when they were on the open road, they were flagged down by people who had been waiting for them. Don Jacinto received a hard blow on the skull with a club. In the buzzing that raced through his brain perhaps he was thinking about the White Rose, the old cartwheel in the patio, the gigantic mules, the horses, Margarito, the parrot, and Domingo, his grown son. Perhaps he was thinking of other matters. But those mentioned may well have been what he was actually thinking about. He was not completely knocked out. He raised himself up halfway, as though he wanted to say something to Mr. Abner, who was sitting next to him. At that moment he received a second tremendous whack, which caused him to collapse. He was dragged out of the car and Abner drove away. Jacinto was stripped to the skin and then dressed in tattered clothing. A second car, in which Abner's accomplices had come, drove up. The ragged-looking Jacinto was laid out in the middle of the road. The car was driven off for some distance and then raced at full speed over the body, paying careful attention that the wheels on one side ran over Jacinto's neck. The auto turned around and ran over Jacinto a second time. The men got out and shone a flashlight on Jacinto. After examining him carefully, and seeing he was dead, really dead, they got in again and rushed back to the city. Abner took a different route.

Don Jacinto's corpse was found the next morning. The coroner issued his report, and Don Jacinto was buried at the state's expense.

The report said that a poor man dressed in rags, evidently a Mexican, and judging by his hands a bracero who had undoubtedly crossed the border illegally to work in the States, had been run over at night by an automobile. Neither the name of the man nor the license number of the automobile could be determined. To facilitate later identification, the corpse was measured, the hair and eye colors were ascertained, identifying marks were sought and found, and, finally, the face and profile were photographed. The report was delivered to the Identification Division of the Los Angeles Police Department, since the corpse was found within its territory. There the report lies, and there it will lie until the day an earthquake destroys the city and all its official documents. For no one on earth has the slightest interest in the corpse of a ragged Mexican bracero who has entered the States illegally.

CHAPTER SIXTEEN

Two weeks later the documents for the sale of Rosa Blanca were submitted to the government of Jalapa by the Condor Oil Company for approval, and the change of ownership was entered in the land register. The papers consisted of a contract for four hundred thousand dollars and supporting documents. Condor had paid the taxes, the tax stamps, and the recording fee. The contract was signed by Jacinto Yanyez, by Condor's executive vice-president, by two witnesses and a company agent. Annexed to the contract was an affidavit of an American notary who confirmed the sale and the authenticity of the signatures. All the documents were duly attested by the Mexican consul in San Francisco, along with their Spanish translations. In fact, the consul had nothing more to verify than the signatures and the official authority of the notary.

A month passed.

Then company engineers turned up at Rosa Blanca to survey.

At once there was trouble on the hacienda.

Jacinto's oldest son, Domingo, and Señora Yañez, Jacinto's wife, resisted the engineers' rooting about, and the people who lived on the hacienda closed in. If the engineers hadn't withdrawn quickly, there would have been a vicious fight.

When the engineers asserted that the company had bought the hacienda, the son, the wife, Margarito, all the men, disputed their assertion. They all knew that Jacinto never intended to sell. And since the engineers hadn't any copies of the documents with them, they could do nothing but go away again.

The company telegraphed the government in Jalapa requesting military protection during the hacienda's takeover. With that the governor learned of the situation for the first time, since he really had nothing to do with the recording of deeds. "Something's wrong there," he said to his secretary. He had the documents brought to him and examined them carefully. "The documents are in order, signed and sealed by our consul. But I don't understand this Yañez. He never planned on selling. True, this contract calls for payment in dollars, whereas Don Jacinto was offered pesos earlier. After all, that is such an enormous difference in price that it may have made the difference. How can anyone know what else they may have promised him." And the governor sent the file back to the Register's office.

Other matters intervened. When he had finished with them, he stood up and went into the next room, to speak to his secretary. It was as though he wanted to get his thoughts together by talking and guiding them in a definite direction.

"I still don't understand," he began. The secretary still didn't know that the governor had thought uninterruptedly about the Rosa Blanca matter while he was handling other business. "I don't know why military protection is needed out there. If Don Jacinto sold the hacienda, and for so much money, why don't the people just hand it over? Is it possible that Don Jacinto himself isn't there on the hacienda?"

A horrible thought flashed through his mind. His whole body tautened, as if he had received a violent shock.

Trembling with anxiety he ordered the secretary to send an official telegram to the station nearest to Rosa Blanca. "I want to see the oldest son and Señora Yañez, too, if possible, at once. They're to come here at the first opportunity. Tell them to bring with them any letters or telegrams they may have received from Don Jacinto while he was in San Francisco. If he comes home in the meantime, he's to come along with them, of course. I'm convinced," the governor said in his usual voice, "he's not there. If he were there, there wouldn't have been any trouble. But if he isn't at home, where is he?"

"Perhaps with all that money he's having himself a good time," the secretary said with a laugh.

"Possibly. But I don't think so. All right, a couple of days, maybe. You can never really know a man after he suddenly comes into a lot of money."

At that the secretary said: "It could be he saw a good ranch there in California and decided to buy it for himself."

"Maybe," the governor responded. "But it seems that his family hasn't had any news from him, not a single word about the sale. That's curious, to say the least."

Once again the governor had to leave to deal with official business. Later in the afternoon, he returned to the secretary's office. "There's still the matter of that affidavit filed with the papers. Why in the world was an affidavit needed? Surely it wasn't necessary."

"Sure it was, or so it seems to me," the secretary broke in. "Since the contract wasn't concluded at the Mexican consulate—as it should have been—the two parties have substituted the affidavit of an official notary. Perhaps the consul wasn't present."

"Surely there is always a deputy at the consulate."

"Of course," the secretary said. "But perhaps he didn't have the same authority."

The governor shook his head: "Still and all, this was an important matter. Not only was this contract being executed in a foreign country, but it was transferring ownership from a native Mexican citizen to a foreigner. In such a case, one might even wait a few days for the consul to return. Or they could all have gone down to Los Angeles to close the deal in the consulate there."

"The company is domiciled in San Francisco," the secretary protested. "The San Francisco consulate was the right one to use."

"All right. The company wanted to be entirely on the safe side. That's the reason for the notary's affidavit," the governor said. "But if it wanted to avoid all such risks, it would have been safest to go to our consul and execute the contract in his presence. That's just what seems so strange to me. Why did the signers avoid looking up the consul?"

"Sorry, governor," the secretary protested, "but our consul has authenticated the documents."

"What, exactly, did the consul authenticate? According to what is said in his certificate, the consul only verified the accuracy of the signatures of those persons who seemed to be known to him personally. Not to put too fine a point on it, the consul is only saying that this is the signature of the notary. Of course, he also states that the notary who drew up the affidavit is a notary whose office and power are valid. Nothing more than that. But there's nothing I can do about it. All right. Send another telegram, this one to Condor. Tell them the militia is being got ready, and it will be set to go, if necessary, in a few days. As long as the contract cannot be contested the company has the law on its side."

A few days later Jacinto's son and wife arrived in Jalapa. They were ushered into the governor's office at once.

From his visit to Rosa Blanca, he knew them both personally.

They looked haggard and worried and showed on their faces the sorrow they felt and the sleepless nights.

The governor made them feel they could have confidence in him. He offered a cigarette to the son and to Jacinto's wife he presented a box of chocolates that he took from a drawer in his desk. As he extended the box to her so that she might take a few morsels, he began to chuckle. "Forgive me, Doña Concepcion, you'd prefer cigarettes, too. Here, please try one of these." And he held out to her his own leather cigarette case. Smiling through the tears glistening at the corners of her eyes, she took one.

"Where is Don Jacinto?" the governor asked.

"We don't know. We're very worried about what might have happened to him. Since he went away with that gringo, we've heard nothing at all from him."

"He has sold Rosa Blanca."

"That's a lie!" The mother and the son screamed in unison. "He did not. Not ever! Not for a hundred thousand million pesos," the woman added.

The governor picked up the sales documents, which had been brought to his office, and handed them to her. "Here, look at the documents for yourself."

Taking the papers, Doña Concepcion scanned the contents, without actually reading every word. When she came to the signatures, she cried out: "This name! Jacinto didn't write this!"

Quickly the governor asked: "What makes you think Jacinto didn't write it?"

"Simply because he can't write at all!" she cried out in her excitement. "Not one single letter!"

The governor leaped to his feet. For a moment no one said a word. The governor stared at Señora Yañez as if he weren't seeing her.

At last Señora Yañez broke the silence: "He really cannot write. He never learned how. And he cannot read either. Everything that has to be written on the hacienda—I write it. I learned in school. I went to the Escuela Mixta in Tuxpan for seven years. Domingo here, we also sent him to school, and he writes. But Jacinto? He cannot write."

"So," the governor said, and he sat down again.

Doña Concepcion, still holding the papers in her lap and looking forlornly over the signatures again, noticed the signature on the receipt for the four hundred thousand dollars. She compared the signature and said: "Besides, the name is spelled incorrectly. We don't write our family name with a 'y' in the middle, but with an 'n' with a tilde over it. The 'y' comes only at the beginning in our name, never in the middle."

The governor took the documents out of the woman's hands, and he likewise examined the signature. "That's right," he said. "It didn't strike me at all to begin with. The Americans write 'Yanyez' with a 'y' because their alphabet doesn't have an 'n' with a tilde. But Mexicans never write the name that way. I'm surprised the consul didn't notice this."

"It's not so strange," the secretary put in. "People spell their names the way their fathers do. And spelling rules simply don't apply to the spelling of personal names. No matter how the name is spelled, it's pronounced the same."

"Now listen to me carefully, Doña Concepcion," the governor said in a friendly way. "We will conduct an investigation at once to see what is genuine and what is fake. Officially I cannot say to you what I think, for these documents are legally incontestable, no matter what error may be contained in them. As governor, I'm obliged to recognize the validity of these documents, and to assist the person who, on the basis of these documents, has the right to call himself the owner. If necessary, with armed force."

"What you are saying," Doña Concepcion said in dismay, "is that we don't own the hacienda any more, that we and all our people have to get off our own land."

"That's correct. Temporarily, the Condor Oil Company has the advantage, and we can do nothing about it. On the basis of these documents the company could appeal to the American government. Then they would use diplomacy to compel our government to turn the hacienda over to the new owners and to enforce his rights in every way, even against the rights of Mexican citizens. If, Doña Concepcion, you could produce similar documents for a ranch in the States, the American government would have to help you just as our government has to help Americans here when valid documents clearly state ownership. International rules govern here. We can only intervene and postpone the takeover of the hacienda until ownership is established incontrovertibly if we can prove that the sales documents were obtained fraudulently or in some criminal manner. Which means we can step in only if the documents do not reflect the actual facts. In such a case, those in possession of the property would keep possession. That would be you and your son. But we cannot do that here, since we have to consider these documents to be authentic. Putting it bluntly, those documents are genuine in and of themselves. We—you and I, the three of us— doubt the authenticity of Don Jacinto's signature. But first we have to prove that it is not genuine."

"Jacinto really cannot write," the wife repeated stubbornly.

"I know that, Señora. But we have to prove it. And that is going to be difficult to do."

"Difficult?" the wife cried out in astonishment. "When I had to write everything for him because he couldn't write?"

"It's possible somebody guided his hand, Doña Concepcion. Right now we don't know one way or the other."

Señora Yañez hadn't thought of this. All her hopes began to dwindle away.

"You have to remember, Señora, that there were several witnesses to these signatures and to the closing of the sale. And every one of them is a respectable person who holds a responsible position. Furthermore, the contract and the signatures are officially attested by a sworn notary."

"They're all swindlers."

"You may say that, Señora. I can't."

"All notaries and lawyers are cheats."

"Maybe." The governor laughed. "But if I say the American notary is a swindler—or if our consul in San Francisco says it—there could be diplomatic complications. The matter cannot be solved to your satisfaction in such a straightforward way. Unfortunately. I don't believe for a minute that Jacinto has sold Rosa Blanca. That's for sure. But what I think means nothing officially. I come thus to what I have to say to you, Doña Concepcion. I'm sorry to have to say it, but it's my duty as governor. The company now has nominal possession of the hacienda. That means you have to yield. All the people have to go. There's nothing to be done about that. If this is a swindle, and if we can prove it, you'll get Rosa Blanca back and you'll be compensated for all the damages you have suffered materially. But, for now, you're at a disadvantage. I'll get in touch with the company at once and try to persuade it that you be permitted to stay on the hacienda with as many families as possible until you've harvested all the crops. Since the company doesn't begin drilling on all its property at the same time, there'll be enough land available for you and for many other families.

"For all these reasons I would like to request you not to make trouble for the engineers. They are totally blameless. They are merely workers who are paid by the company, and they have to do what the company orders them to do. Will you promise me, Doña Concepcion, and you, too"—he turned toward Domingo—"to obey my request and, for the time being, accept the change in ownership?"

"Never! We don't accept any such thing!" the wife cried out excitedly. "And we've never seen the money. Only if Jacinto himself tells me he has sold the hacienda, then I'll believe it—even if all the money was lost or stolen from him. But so long as he doesn't tell me himself, I'll admit nothing, I'll believe nothing. I'm telling you this is an infamous crime by those gringos who want to have our hacienda." She fell silent.

The governor sat looking at her calmly, without saying a word.

And under the gaze of this man who had spoken to her so affably and clearly, who had been her guest, who had been so lighthearted in her home, she began to calm down. It was as if she were sitting before her father, who desired only good things for her.

She swallowed several times, as though she had to suppress the swelling tears and hold back words she didn't want to utter.

At last, holding still under the governor's calm gaze, she said, quite softly: "Very well, Governor. The engineers can come and work as much as they want. I'll tell all the families to let them alone."

The governor stood up, walked around his desk, and went over to Doña Concepcion. Grasping her hands like those of a child, he shook them, and, finally, kissed them. Then he said, just as gently as she had spoken: "Thank you, Conchita"—using her pet name— "thank you for making my job easier. Never forget that you have a friend in me. Not only as governor, but as a personal friend to you and Jacinto. I promise you I'll do everything in my power to discover the truth. And I promise you that when I've found the truth, the White Rose won't have been plucked for nothing. If, perhaps, it can never bloom again in all its beauty, it shall certainly not fade away, never. It shall bear fruit that will ripen. And that shall be the beginning of the liberation of the country and its citizens. We will have a country in which every single rose, white or red, shall have freedom to bloom, to be as beautiful as it was meant to be, and to flourish for as long as it was intended to flourish."

Doña Concepcion did not entirely understand these words. Yet she sensed their significance, and she carried them in her heart, as she carried mankind's undying belief in eventual deliverance from every torment.

CHAPTER SEVENTEEN

THAT WEEKEND the governor traveled to Mexico City. He sought out Licenciado Perez, but found he wasn't in his office.

Late in the afternoon he went into a restaurant where he was to meet with some senators and discuss several political items with them. As he entered the large dining room he glimpsed the lawyer sitting and drinking tea with his wife in a corner. He went over to him at once and asked him to a quick conference. They went over to another small table and sat down together.

Without preamble, the governor said: "Don Jacinto has sold Rosa Blanca."

"Right," Perez answered. "As the agent, I've just sent the documents to be recorded."

"Was there anything about those documents that struck you as unusual?"

Perez glanced up sharply: "Why, Governor? Sure, there was something. It was obvious to me that the papers weren't signed in the consul's office. But there may be a good reason for that. The documents are properly notarized by an American notary. However, all the signatures and the translations are certified by our consul, and he knows all the signers personally."

"Did our consul by any chance know Don Jacinto personally when he certified those signatures?"

"I've no way of knowing that."

"Have you already received official confirmation that the documents were recorded?"

"No. I don't have that in my hands yet. But Señor Jazmines in the Registry office let me know when I asked him that the recording has been done," Perez said.

"He's telling the truth," the governor confirmed. "Before you tell the company of this, however, I'd like to talk to you some more. Tomorrow, if possible, because I've got to go back early day after tomorrow."

"Fine," the lawyer replied. "Tomorrow is Saturday, it's true, but I'll be in your office at eleven, and we can talk alone there undisturbed."

"*Bueno*. Tomorrow at eleven then," the governor said. "If you'll excuse me now, Licenciado, here are the gentlemen with whom I'm supposed to meet."

When the governor and the lawyer sat down together the next day, the governor immediately said what was on his mind: "Didn't it strike you as curious that Don Jacinto sold the hacienda so quickly once he arrived in San Francisco?"

"No, that didn't occur to me. All the less so, since they were paying him in dollars what I had only offered in pesos. He could never resist such a high amount."

"Don Jacinto signed the contract—the original and all copies," the governor said.

"Yes, he did.

"Do you know, Licenciado," the governor was now asking with apparent calm, "that Don Jacinto cannot write?"

"What?" Perez cried. "He can't write?"

"Not a single letter."

After a little while for calm reflection, Perez said: "They might have guided his hand. That's legally permissable."

"Correct. But in that case it has to be expressly stated by the notary. This is true of any important document, just as it has to be done when someone who cannot write signs with his mark or with three crosses."

"You're right, Governor," the lawyer said. "To be valid legally, that fact would have to be sworn."

The governor thought for a while. At last he said: "Now then, a few other questions, Licenciado, a few questions of law."

"Go ahead."

"Do you think it's possible that the witnesses who signed those papers—the agent, the notary, and the vice-president—are all scoundrels?" the governor asked.

Perez broke into loud laughter. "But, Governor, what sort of question is that? How can I know whether all those people are rascals? In the eyes of the law and, of course, to the public, they're highly respectable people. What they're like in reality, in private, no one can know, of course. And we are not allowed to concern ourselves with that, no matter what we may think of them privately."

"My question is really not that unusual," the governor pleaded. "I'll put it more clearly. Imagine that a crime has been committed in this case. Or let me put it more charitably—an illegality. Do you think that so many respectable men could lend a hand in such an illegality, having such grave consequences?"

"No, I don't. Every one of these men may commit a crime individually. Why not? But no one of them is ever going to do something illegal in the presence of others. That would be dangerous. Such a lawbreaker is always at the mercy of witnesses. These men are too intelligent and too cautious for that."

"That's exactly what I thought," the governor replied. "If this is a case of illegality, then it's entirely possible none of the witnesses knows what happened."

"I don't follow you, governor."

"All right. Here's what I'm getting at: Were all the witnesses present when Don Jacinto signed the contract and the copies?"

"I've no way of knowing."

"Indeed, Señor Perez. You certainly were not there yourself. Tell me, what usually goes on at the closing of a contract?"

"Ah, Governor, now I get what you're driving at. A contract, especially an important one like this, where a lot is at stake, should really be executed in the presence of all the signers if it is to meet all the conditions of the law. Should, but usually isn't. And the law actually says very little on the subject that is precise. In many cases, I can even tell you this from my own experience, in most cases, this is what happens: A representative of the company—in this instance the executive vice-president—signs the contract when it is submitted to him by a staff lawyer or by someone in the contracts department. Most likely, he'll sign it in his office at the same time he signs hundreds of other documents, letters, and contracts. Usually, he doesn't even look at what he's signing, because he depends on his staff. After he's signed, the contract is submitted to the other contracting parties—Señor Jacinto Yañez in this case. He, too, signs the contract wherever it is submitted to him—at home, the office, perhaps in his hotel room. Then the contract goes first to one witness and then to the others, to each one individually. Usually, all these signers know one another personally. They recognize their various signatures. The contract then goes, if necessary, to a notary, who notarizes the signatures because usually the signers or the signatures are also known to him personally. He has no qualms because the contract is being submitted to him by a well-known, reputable company whose integrity cannot be questioned. The signing is done in this way—it usually has to be done this way—because it's often impossible to get all the signers together in the same place at the same time. One may live in Chicago, another in Albany, yet another in Phoenix. Now if a contract bearing the signatures of such respectable, well-known gentlemen and the authentication of a notary sub-sequently comes to our consul, or to any other consul, he will have no qualms about giving it his official endorsement. He generally doesn't have enough time to review the contract carefully and to ponder for long over whether something might be wrong with the signatures. Today we have to trust one another. If we didn't, so much time would be lost that business would come to a standstill."

"So it's possible then that someone other than Don Jacinto signed."

"Of course, it is possible," Perez conceded. "And not only that.

In the entire process of closing a contract, only one person really needs to know the truth, and all the rest of the signers may in fact be innocent. Under the circumstances they cannot be reproached with the accusation that they have acted negligently, when the whole business was conducted in the usual and customary way."

"Just as I thought," the governor said. "Let's take this a bit further, now. If one of the most important signers—let's say, Don Jacinto—disappears from the face of the earth, then evidence can never be produced to prove he didn't sign the contract."

"To the contrary, Governor," the lawyer retorted. "The experts can compare Don Jacinto's signatures on the contract and the copies to his other signatures. At one time or another he has signed something that is known, without a doubt, to bear Don Jacinto's authentic signature."

"But such proof cannot be produced," the governor demurred, "if earlier signatures do not exist."

"In that case, certainly not."

The governor thought for a while. Then he said: "The man who signed for Don Jacinto was probably a Mexican who could prove, perhaps, that he really was named Yañez. The name Yañez is not exactly the most frequent; still, it's met with often enough that someone bearing the name might be found. Most likely this imposter hadn't the slightest idea what was written in those documents and understood nothing of their contents. They laid a few dollars in his hand and the poor devil did what they wanted him to do, was even delighted that he could make twenty or fifty dollars so easily. Possibly this man vanished after the signing. What does a poor Mexican worker amount to up there? They're slaughtered by the dozens and no one hears about it. Here in Mexico, if one American is killed by bandits, the whole world hears of it immediately and everyone becomes indignant over the instability of Mexico."

Suddenly, the governor lashed out at the lawyer, his voice like a thunderbolt: "You do know, don't you, Perez, that Don Jacinto still hasn't come back from the States?"

Señor Perez started in alarm: "What are you saying? Not returned?"

"No, he's not back yet. No one on the hacienda has received any word from him. No one knows where he is. No one knows where the money is that he is supposed to have received."

"That's surely not possible, Governor," the lawyer said, becoming even more excited. "That surely cannot be!"

"But it is." The governor nodded. "And now I'll tell you what I think. Don Jacinto didn't sign that contract. In the first place, he didn't want to sell Rosa Blanca. In the second, he couldn't write. Don Jacinto has not sold the hacienda. Some Mexican worker falsified the signature for a few dollars. That was a clever stroke, since in our handwriting the letters are slightly different in form from the American style. If an American had signed the contracts, then everyone would have seen at once he was not a Mexican. And it would have to be a worker, or possibly a schoolboy, so that the signature would be clumsy and awkward, since that is the way the signature of a peasant having little practice at writing usually looks. I'm firmly convinced that Don Jacinto has been murdered because he could not be persuaded to sell the hacienda."

"But what you're saying is really shocking," the lawyer exclaimed.

"Not at all. You've just confirmed to me how such contracts are signed. The signers do not need to get together in the same place at the same time to sign because everyone places his trust in the integrity of the others. I admit that this is legal because, as you explained it to me, it would be impossible to do business otherwise. I, too, sign contracts and letters as they are submitted to me by my associates, relying on my secretary's trustworthiness. Indeed, in the case of Don Jacinto, there was the possibility of obtaining a contract by trickery. I'm convinced that Don Jacinto has not received the money due him, and if he did, it was taken away as soon as he was killed."

"I can't believe this," Perez said. "I know the president of the company personally. Mr. Collins has never given me the impression that he would have agreed to such a monstrous deed."

"As an attorney, dear Perez, you really must be more cautious about judging people by the impressions they make on others. It's not a question of an ordinary murder in the usual meaning of the word. Such a man does not commit an ordinary murder, of course. But here, in that man's opinion, a murder is necessary in his company's interest. Such a murder he regards rather like a political murder. And conscience usually takes a different view of a political murder than it does of a murder serving a purely personal interest.

Perhaps the murder was not set out in the president's plans. They aimed only at gaining possession of Rosa Blanca. Then he gave an order to some fellow to arrange the purchase at any price. That fellow, lacking the president's intelligence and nerve, chose the shortest, crudest way to accomplish the mission given to him. That fellow may have been the man who visited the hacienda and lured Don Jacinto away to the States. But that is only a guess."

"Isn't it perhaps possible that everything you've said is a guess?" Perez asked.

"Yesterday, everything was guesswork. Today, after this talk with you, I'm sure my guess is correct, or, at least, it comes close to the truth. Only now we have a chance to discover the truth. For in every crime some mistake is always made. And one will have been made here, too. And I suspect—this time I'll emphasize the word, I only suspect—the contract was signed after Don Jacinto was already murdered. Or after he was left to die because of an accident—a clever trick sometimes used in the States—hunting or fishing, swimming or sailing, along some byway or in a car. We have to try to find his corpse and determine when he died. If we can establish that the contract was signed after Don Jacinto was dead, we have proved the fraud."

"Something like that may be difficult to do," the lawyer said.

"That I know, Señor Perez. It's only an idea of mine. But I'll pursue it, and I'd like to ask you to help me. You're surely not just a representative of the company, you're still a Mexican, too, isn't that so, Señor?"

"With my whole heart, Governor. I really don't need to assure you of that," the lawyer said sincerely. "And in a case like this, a shabby deed, where it involves an open robbery of our country, I am a Mexican first of all, and in spite of everything. In spite of his pigheadedness and his obtuseness, I've learned to respect and cherish Don Jacinto during my repeated visits to his hacienda. And I openly admit to you that when he definitely rejected the sale, in spite of the heap of gold coins on the table, I developed a deep respect for the man. Though I lost a large commission, deep down I was really pleased that he wasn't going to sell the Americans that beautiful tract of land. Such a hacienda, bearing men like Jacinto and the others who live there, men whom I got to know, should not be transformed into a stinking, noisy oil camp. And that is my honest opinion, Governor."

"Very well. Now we can go into action. Write to the company and tell them you haven't received the registration notice yet, which just happens to be the truth. Then add that according to a private informant, the recording has been taken care of. Then write, in addition, that doubts have arisen about the transaction in the government here. Say frankly that it turns out Don Jacinto cannot write. And, finally, say that the government is interested in finding out where Don Jacinto is so that it can question him about some details in regard to the contract."

"Wait a minute!" the lawyer broke in. "I can't write that. Just suppose that Don Jacinto is still alive. When they read that, they'll try to get rid of him even after the event. They're certainly not going to want to have such an embarrassing witness around."

"That's true. I hadn't thought of that," the governor said. "Simply say Don Jacinto hasn't returned yet and his family is interested in finding out where he is, and whether something could be learned about him up there."

CHAPTER EIGHTEEN

ENGINEERS WERE now working at full strength on Rosa Blanca.

The cornfields, sugar cane, and citrus groves were hacked down to make room for the derricks. A road was carved out and graded so that the heavy trucks could deliver materials, steam boilers, and machinery. Every family that was compelled to leave the fields and cabins without delay received two hundred and fifty pesos each to hasten their departure. This money, regarded as compensation for the loss of the ripening crops, was paid out in one peso coins so that it would seem like a lot, as if a pile of silver could alleviate the pain of the loss of their native home. After only a few days Don Jacinto's family also had to leave the hacienda.

The engineers were kindhearted. They saw the people's sorrow at being uprooted. To do them a favor and show them they were not to blame for this destruction, the engineers carried the families' possessions in their empty autos to wherever the people wanted to go.

Because the compadres had received good-paying jobs in the newly built camp—they were being paid four and even four and a half pesos a day—they took their families to the little towns lying along the borders of the hacienda.

Frigillo, of course, got his commission as a recruiter. He had never before in his life had such a pleasant, easy assignment. He didn't need to travel to find workers or pay their travel expenses. In general, he had no difficulties at all. The people were right there at hand, since they really didn't know where else to go. And now that this year's harvest, and all future harvests, had been taken away from them, they were delighted just to find another source of income so quickly.

Don Jacinto's family settled in Tuxpan. As compensation for home and harvest they had received the sum of two thousand pesos. Doña Concepcion didn't want to accept this money. Out of pride. She had no intention of taking money from robbers and murderers, she said. But Domingo was wiser. He knew his mother was certainly not young any more, and his sisters could really use the money. So he accepted it. After buying a small store in Tuxpan so the mother could have a job and a small but steady income, he gave the rest of the money to her.

The son himself worked for a while as a gang boss in the new camp. The engineers, always careful to mitigate evil whenever they could, trained him after a few weeks as a chauffeur. So, for a time, Domingo drove supply trucks from Tuxpan to camp. For this he got ten pesos a day. Since he was willing and able, the engineers soon trained him to be a tooldresser, and for that he made fifteen pesos a day. Later he advanced even higher, becoming a skilled driller. At this he earned five hundred dollars a month. He also got excellent bonuses for every oil-producing well he drilled.

The teller of this tale has no intention of producing false sentimentality and achieving impressive effects so that the reader can speak of a pretty, touching story about the plucking of a fair white rose. So it has to be said, in keeping with the truth, that not only the engineers, but also the Condor directors, helped the former inhabitants of the hacienda, at least in the material sense, to suffer the loss of their native soil with less distress. Furthermore, the truth requires us to say that many of the men, if perhaps not every one of them, became so well accustomed to the new circumstances within a few weeks that they were hardly ready yet to swap their new life that quickly for the earlier one. They all were wearing good clothing and new shoes and boots, even the women. All the children were going to school, and the women were not working as hard as before. And all the people, without exception, especially the children, were following better rules of hygiene.

From a purely material point of view, all those affected by the move were now better prepared for life than before. They were no longer merely the inhabitants of a little spot of earth where what they knew of the world was only what they could see with their own eyes. Increasingly they were becoming men who consciously lived in a larger world, a greater homeland, the Mexican Republic. They sensed the magnitude and extent of human cooperation the entire world around. Earlier, the only enemies had been their neighbors on a nearby hacienda. But with the expansion into a larger world this enmity vanished. They became aware of the first stirrings of the thought that all men on earth are one, that everyone is part of a great brotherhood. In the movies that eager entrepreneurs showed in the camps they saw what other people far from Mexico were doing. They saw how those people behaved, thought, worked, loved, and treated their children, and how they cheated and lied. They saw that other men were not so very different from themselves. And this strengthened the fraternal bond to other men and other peoples. They listened to the radios brought into the camps by the American engineers and oil people. They heard music and words from other lands, heard the speeches of the President of the Republic, heard the lectures of doctors, teachers, instructors, artists, health inspectors—of all those people who were bearers of culture, knowledge, and advice, into the most remote regions of the nation. They met other workers. These men, coming from other regions of the Republic, had seen and experienced a lot. Thus a whole new world of whose existence they had never known before opened up before their physical and spiritual eyes. And they were seeing that new world, living in it, understanding it, and feeling almost like members of that wider world, and not just tolerated, but legitimate and essential fellow-inhabitants of that new world. For as soon as they had learned their way about in this large world, they found they were needed, that they were essential, even if they only carried iron pipe about and helped to heave it into the drill holes. This work was important, for if no one unloaded and carried the pipe, there would be no gasoline for automobiles, which then couldn't go. So they sensed, almost instinctively, that they were just as important as the engineers and drillers. They had lost a beautiful home, a beloved home, and they had believed they couldn't survive the loss. But as they learned to see and began to snap out of their daze, their time-honored customs, they discovered they had gained in place of the small narrow homeland, a larger one that also had its attractions. And whereas the little old homeland seemed always to remain what it was, the new larger homeland was of a different kind. The new homeland did not end at the horizon. It grew and grew. It became with every day's new perceptions an ever greater homeland that seemed to have no limit, comprising every man, every nation, every thought that was ever thought. Certainly at the core, with the destruction of the older smaller homeland, much had been lost. They missed much of what had once made them rich in their feelings, in their quiet natural happiness.

Indeed, the spiritual feelings were now often less rich, but they learned increasingly to make these feelings clear to other men in words, and by the words of their fellow men, who could talk again about their own feelings and experiences, to gain new treasures that completely made up for the loss of the earlier, more beautiful feelings. Of course, there frequently entered into their lives here, as well, in their dealings with other people, coarse, unfeeling, foul-minded people, and many an ugliness and evil. But whoever knew how to shake it off, to muster up sufficient robustness to pay no attention to the elbowing of his crude co-workers, was affected less by the ugliness, and he took part only in the good and the beautiful.

Seen as a whole, without prejudice, and setting aside every foolish sentimentality, it can be asserted with confidence: The people of Rosa Blanca had lost a lot, but they had also gained a lot.

And a day was coming when everyone could rightly say: We have become richer than we were; we have become greater than our fathers were. Today we are citizens of the world. What is more, we are conscious citizens of the world, because we understand the earth and the other people in it, and we understand more and more. And because we understand more, our love has become greater. What greater thing can a man gain than a greater love for his fellow man!

CHAPTER NINETEEN

LICENCIADO PEREZ had addressed his letter directly to Mr. Collins to avoid the contents becoming known to subordinates.

Mr. Collins sent for Mr. Abner immediately.

"What did I say to you, Abner?" he snapped. "Didn't I tell you not to make a mess? I told you I wouldn't accept responsibility for your blunders, that I'd hand you over to the authorities without a second's thought if you did things I can't conceal. We show no mercy for mistakes. I'll drop you into the hands of the hangman as you deserve if you can't carry out an assignment properly."

Mr. Abner turned pale.

"Has something come out?" he said apprehensively, in a low voice.

"Yes. Everything." Mr. Collins spoke the words coldly, cruelly.

"In that case, I'd better buy myself a revolver," Mr. Abner said helplessly.

"If you have the time, Abner. Man, you have barely twenty-four hours, so buy yourself a good one, one that won't misfire at a convenient moment. The Mexican consul has the matter in hand."

Mr. Collins was working as only a genius knows how.

He had had his agents and detectives on the plan throughout. And those people were efficient.

The Mexican consul also had good detectives, Mexicans born in the States. In the main they were used by the consul to observe countrymen who had settled in the American border states and were plotting revolution and smuggling weapons into Mexico. They called themselves patriots. And some were decent people who seriously believed they were serving their homeland when they caused the present government embarrassment with revolution and rebellion.

Most of them were Porfiristas, followers of the overthrown dictator Porfirio Díaz. They believed they were honest. They were of the opinion that their country could only be served by returning to power the old conservative system of Díaz. They were of the opinion that Mexico could prosper only if Americans, English, Germans, foreigners generally, would bring in capital in order to extract Mexico's natural wealth. For more than thirty years this system had operated successfully in Mexico. In its heyday, in 1910, ninety-five percent of the Mexican people were barefoot and dressed in rags. An entire people, apart from a narrow upper class, was enslaved as seldom before in history. So little had been done in education that eighty-five percent of the people could neither read nor write when the revolution broke out.

Then there were those patriots who wanted to incite revolution because they disliked those holding public office in the Republic. That is, they wanted those jobs themselves, since the present officeholders had not passed on to them lucrative, money-making opportunities.

Then there were those patriots who were ignorant tools of American and English capitalists.

And finally there were even those charming patriots who were openly paid by American companies and magnates to foment the revolutions so welcome to them, since they enabled them to carry out successful financial speculations.

To protect the country from mischief the Mexican government had to have all these patriots watched.

A single instance like the criminal theft of Rosa Blanca could very well lead to a rebellion or, if the Mexican government did not act very cautiously, to an armed incursion into the country by American troops. Diplomatic discussions of the legality or illegality of sales contracts could lead to painful complications if someone lost his temper. Relations between the countries were strained enough after the revolution so that a single spark was enough to set off a conflagration.

One day a Mexican visited the Mexican consulate in San Francisco to register the birth of a son so that he would keep his Mexican citizenship.

The consul was crossing the hall just as a staff member, taking down the particulars, asked for the man's birthplace. Hearing the man answer, "Tuxpan, State of Veracruz," the consul stopped and spoke to the man: "You come from Tuxpan, Señor?"

"*Si*, Señor, *a sus ordenes.*"

"Do you know of a hacienda named Rosa Blanca there in the vicinity?"

"I know of it, Señor."

"Do you know Don Jacinto Yañez?"

"Yes. He's the owner."

"That's the one," the consul said.

"He's here in San Francisco right now. Or at least he was here not long ago."

"Did you talk to him?"

"Yes, we got together at various times. Had lunch together twice. At Palido's restaurant."

"Did Don Jacinto tell you he was going to sell Rosa Blanca?"

"He told me he'd come here with an American named Abner.

This fellow invited him here to give him some breeding stock in return for six horses Don Jacinto gave him. This Abner had tried to persuade Don Jacinto to sell Rosa Blanca, and at last offered him a half million dollars for it. I have to say, Señor, Rosa Blanca's not worth that."

"Very good," the consul interrupted. "Go on. Tell me what else you know."

By this time the consul had learned all the details from the governor in Jalapa, and he well knew how to ask the right question when a propitious occasion arose.

"He told me," the man continued, "he'd never sell Rosa Blanca, not even if he were offered two million dollars. I told him he must know what he's doing. For my part I'd sell the hacienda if I were in his place. He wouldn't listen to a word about it, saying he never considered selling Rosa Blanca because he couldn't. Too many families lived on it, and he didn't want automobiles driving around over the graves of his father and mother."

"Did you ever see him drunk while he was here?"

"Kind of. Seemed foolish to me, since he doesn't drink much. But he said Mr. Abner was always offering him something, and he didn't want to be impolite and turn it down."

"Did he say anything about going to Mr. Abner's ranch to look the animals over?"

"In a way. According to Don Jacinto, Mr. Abner never had time to drive to the ranch. Don Jacinto was beginning to believe Mr. Abner didn't have a ranch at all—and no animals either."

"Did he stay with you or in a hotel?"

"He was living in a house with Mr. Abner. That must be somewhere in Brenton Street."

"Did he tell you he would be getting a lot of money?"

"To the contrary, Señor Consul. The last time I saw him he . . ."

"Wait! When did you see him last?"

"Four, five, . . . eleven weeks ago come Wednesday."

"You remember the exact day?"

"Yes. I bought a money order at the bank to send to Mexico for serapes I was importing. I've never carried serapes here before. But I though maybe they'd be a good sideline."

"And on that day——" The consul hesitated.

"Yes, that was the day. I met Don Jacinto in front of the bank and we went in together so he could see how you go about buying a money order. He didn't have much money then. He told me he might have to borrow money from me for the trip back, since Mr. Abner wasn't saying anything about the return trip he'd promised to pay for."

"Have you seen him since then?"

"No. And he's probably left by now. But I'm really quite surprised he didn't come round to say goodby. We were good friends, from way back when. He's acquainted with all my friends and relatives in the Tuxpan area."

"That's fine. Let me have your address. I may still need you. I'll even tell you why. Don Jacinto hasn't returned to Mexico. He never recrossed the border. And it now appears that he signed the contract to sell Rosa Blanca five days after you saw him."

"I don't believe that. He wouldn't sell. And in any case, he couldn't write. He couldn't even sign his own name."

"That's right. Did he tell you perhaps that he learned to write his name on the journey with Mr. Abner or at Mr. Abner's house? Perhaps Mr. Abner taught him."

"I don't think so. Something like that would've been so important he would've told me about it."

"That's what I think, too," the consul said.

"And Jacinto is not a person who could learn to write so quickly, in such a short time. One letter, or two or three. But not his full name. Not Jacinto."

"Good. I'll have you notified if I need you again. A boy, eh?"

"And healthy, Señor."

"What are you naming him?"

"Emilio, Señor, *a sus ordenes. Adios.*"

The consul went directly to his office and telephoned one of his agents. After lunch he dictated a report to Jalapa.

Mr. Collins looked at Abner sharply. Abner seemed not to have recovered from his fright. "Did you know that that fellow Yañez couldn't write? Not even his name?"

Abner sat down to keep from falling down.

"Damn! I never thought of that," he said, perspiring.

"That is precisely what I mean," Mr. Collins said. "Never thought. Tell me, who ordered you to forge his name?"

Abner felt an inner jolt. His face, which had begun to lose it composure, hardened, and he said: "I taught him to write on the way up and at my house."

"Very clever, Abner. But it won't wash. You've not been paying attention. He met a landsman here—talked to him a lot—and that fellow has yapped to the consul. It's all in the files already. Perez has even put it in a letter to me. This man Yañez told this fellow here that he couldn't write."

What Mr. Collins was saying was not entirely accurate. The compatriot, according to Perez's report, had said only that Don Jacinto had not told him he had learned to write in the meantime. "The name alone is not all that important," Mr. Collins said. He was setting Abner up for a larger issue. Since Yañez had not specifically said he had not learned, the signature could be salvaged, and therefore the contract.

"The name is not that important. You'll give us an affidavit that you taught Señor Yañez to write on the way here, and we'll get it notarized."

"Yes. I'll confirm that," Abner said, thinking that the knot in his stomach would now go away.

"No, the name, by itself, is nothing," Mr. Collins repeated. "A worse problem is the gardener at the house you rented. He saw you go off with Yañez in the automobile, and he saw you come back alone the next day. Furthermore, the Mexican consul's agents, unknown to us, were rummaging about in your house, your garage, and your car, too. And guess what they found? Blood and a couple of bloody black hairs, Indian hairs. As you might expect, they have photographs of this. The hair has been analyzed chemically. The analysis, as well as the hairs, are now in the Mexican consulate, for further investigation, so our agents tell me. So, you stupid blunderer, which is what you are, you listen to me, now."

Abner saw cowering in his chair, seemingly unable to listen to any more.

Calmly, icily, Mr. Collins continued with what he had to say: "We have receipts showing that Yañez got the four hundred thousand dollars in eight checks. Those eight checks have been cashed. The Mexican consul knows we have the canceled checks. He knows you were the last person with Yañez. He knows Yañez was staying at your house. He knows Yañez didn't send the money to Mexico. Now, think carefully, Abner, who do you suppose has the money? Don't you suppose that the district attorney will wonder about this man who brought Yañez to San Francisco, who lured him here from his farm, who knew how much money Yañez was paid, and perhaps even where he kept it?"

Abner said nothing. He could not budge. He had turned gray and old, and his disheveled hair was damp with perspiration.

Mr. Collins pressed a button.

In came a notary, the executive vice-president, a secretary, and the company's chief counsel.

The notary drew up an affidavit in which Mr. Abner declared under oath that he had taught Señor Yañez to write his name on the trip up.

After the gentlemen had left, and the two were alone again, Collins said calmly: "You're fired. Here's a letter. It says you've resigned to take a job in Japan."

"Thanks," Abner said curtly as he took the envelope containing the letter.

"Do you need any more money, Abner?" Collins asked. Intentionally or not, he had laid a light ironical stress on the question. "Or do you have enough with what you've made already?"

"I could use another fifty thousand, thank you." Abner's usual stony calm had returned to him while the notary was drawing up the affidavit.

"You are as, as—I don't know what to compare you to," Mr. Collins said.

"Why not say, as greedy as the president of an oil company?" Mr. Abner responded impudently.

"You might have spared yourself that, Abner," Mr. Collins said. "Yes, really. That's too cheap. It only shows me, once again, you lack imagination. If you had even a trace of intelligence, you wouldn't have made such a series of blunders. Anyone can make a mistake, but making more than three dozen requires an abundance of stupidity. But it's really not my job to train you. Still and all, I'd like to give you just this one bit of advice. I don't know what you're planning to do—use a revolver or make a quick departure—but whatever it is, do it within twenty-four hours, because if Huerta doesn't take the field in Mexico soon, you won't be able to get away at all. You won't even have time to load your revolver."

Mr. Abner was lucky. Adolfo de la Huerta went into action as the oil companies had expected. Whether they had actually ordered the campaign won't be discovered so soon.

The Mexican government had no time to concern itself with such a small matter as the sale of the White Rose. The homeland of those who had saved the country for the people in a long and bloody revolution was in danger of being lost to the Porfiristas, to all those who mourned the demise of the old rotten conditions and hated everything that did not bear pasted on it the phony glitter of Porfirism.

With the help of generals who could not obtain in the new era those sinecures they had under the old regime, Huerta succeeded in taking and holding Veracruz. The governor of Jalapa had to resign. He became colonel of a battalion fighting on the government side against Huerta. Brother against brother. Father against son. Citizen against citizen.

The Huerta forces occupied Yucatan as well. There they shot the Labor Party governor and, to be on the safe side, his son as well. Wherever Huerta went they began to shoot and hang union leaders and syndicalists.

Oil tankers brought weapons in, deep in their holds, to stir up the country even more.

But Tampico, which Huerta could easily have captured, remained unoccupied, because oil, the wealth of the country, around which the fratricidal strife revolved, was shipped from there. This harbor had to stay open to show who was in control.

CHAPTER TWENTY

ROSA BLANCA had become lots 119 through 176. Work went on, and production started. Here millions were being made while the Mexican people seemed to lose their senses, smashing their heads and mangling their bodies, so that, very quietly and without the government's inconvenient supervision, the rich black oil, the pulsing lifeblood of the Mexican soil, could be shipped off in unprecedented quantities.

What did the Mexican care that in this period of internecine warfare the large companies might do, and did do, whatever they wanted. Licenses were not respected, contracts were not observed. Right and wrong vanished. Whatever could not be gained voluntarily was exacted by murder, robbery, and kidnapping. The Mexican, ever obliging, did what the companies wanted. He fought with his brothers while the sneering foreign magnate calmly stripped from his body his last tattered shirt. To the Mexican the land and the welfare of his people were unimportant. It was much more important that Señor X *not* be governor, that Señor Y *not* be President, that Señor Z *not* be mayor. The question of who *should* be governor, president, or mayor was irrelevant. The only thing that mattered was that the person who was in office at the moment should not stay there. They hadn't yet become mature enough to realize that they served only as tools of the magnates with their mangling of their own people. They believed they were honest patriots, liberating their country, and yet they were only slaves of the foreign capitalists. In the end it wasn't the foreign capitalists who suffered the consequences, it was the Mexican people.

So it happened that Rosa Blanca was forgotten, and Condor Lots 119 through 176 became known the world around. Rosa Blanca was now smeared over, oiled up, smoke-filled, filthy. The groaning, creaking, throbbing, clattering, and puffing of machinery, pumps, trucks filled the air. Monotonously, in an untiring rhythm, the drills clanked up and down, day and night, night and day. Drillers were killed by swinging pipes, tooldressers were crushed by collapsing jacks, part-time workers were struck down by heavy steel cables and wound up piecemeal in the winches. But the drills clanked up and down, up and down, day and night, night and day. Anyone who was maimed did not count and was immediately forgotten. At once another person stepped up to serve the driller-god. For the man who ran the drill was paid thirty dollars a day. And for thirty dollars a day a man ought to risk something.

Work went on at a frenzied pace that, till then, was unprecedented. For it was necessary to exploit this tremendous opportunity while the Mexicans were carving themselves up and blowing themselves to pieces. During this period no one at all was attending to the legality of contracts and mining concessions. And that explained the haste to extract every drop of oil that could be pumped. For if the Mexicans should ever make up, then the good times of lawlessness would end. And then even the contract for Rosa Blanca could be checked.

So get the oil out!

And the compadres all were carrying pipe, living like slaves running around in chains. Everything looked just as it had in Jacinto's vision.

Then, at last, the first well came in.

One hundred and twenty thousand barrels a day. The news was telegraphed around the world. Everyone soon knew about it. Everyone but the Mexicans. They were still fighting over who shouldn't be President, and had no time to read telegrams and find out what was being done to their country.

Four days later, the second well came in at ninety thousand barrels a day. And every barrel was a beautiful new American greenback for the pockets of Condor shareholders.

That same week, a third well began producing a hundred thousand barrels a day. And so it went every day—a hundred thousand barrels a day here, sixty thousand there, twenty thousand over there.

Mr. Collins was sitting in his office reading reports on the incoming wells. They seemed to be participating in a self-arranged contest to see which of them could produce the most oil.

"The King of England's yacht for Betty?" he mused. "Not for me. Not for Betty. Compared to the yacht Betty is going to get now, the King's will look like a worn-out shrimp boat."

He picked up the telephone and spoke to her, calling her "My Empress." "Princess" didn't satisfy him any more, so he elevated her in rank. He lacked only the cathedral in which to crown himself, with her at his side. But, he recalled, he had promised a church to the Baptists. It really was a pity that a person couldn't be crowned Emperor in the States.

As he put the telephone down, Ida brought in a newspaper. Excitedly she held it out to him and said: "News, Mr. Collins."

He read the boldface headline: AMERICAN MURDERED IN SINGAPORE GAMBLING DEN—CHEATING ALLEGED.

Mr. Collins stared at Ida. What did he care about an American who got himself shot. That happened in Chicago and New York and San Francisco. If he was going to worry about things like that, he'd have to read newspapers twenty-four hours a day. He didn't understand Ida. Since when had she bothered with sensational newspaper stories?

But when Ida said: "Just read the story, Mr. Collins," he took the newspaper from her and scanned it. Ah, well: "From a baggage check found in the victim's pockets it has been determined that the slain man is a Mr. Abner, of San Francisco."

"A pity," Mr. Collins said regretfully to Ida. "It's really a pity. This man really had no business being in the oil industry. He did a lot of stupid things. But he could have become a first-rate president of a steel corporation. He had the nerve for that. But he lacked the poise and a bit more steadiness of character. Showed in his cheating. More cables from Mexico there? Lots 119 and the rest?"

"Eight," Ida said tersely, giving him the telegrams.

"How many dead?" he asked as he leafed quickly through the telegrams.

"None."

With that brief reply Ida proved she was not just an ordinary secretary any more. She had become something more in the meantime. She had become oil, she thought only in oil, she understood the language of oil—thoroughly and completely.

In the camps on lots 119 through 176 the scorching work had become constantly more furious. The bonus to the leading driller, the one who brought in a producing well, had been raised even higher to spur the workers on in the most savage frenzy. The driller handed over a part of the bonus to the rest of the people working on his well. Live and let live. But only to those who raced along with him. Show a worker a twenty-dollar bill and he becomes a capitalist on the spot. You don't believe it? Try it. A bonus has more effect today than a whip used to.

When the drilling of four or five wells began at the same time, the driller who brought his well in first received an additional bonus of one thousand dollars. But owing to this dimwitted frenzy not a day passed without one, two, or even three peons, and maybe even a tooldresser or driller, being struck down on the battlefield of oil, to say nothing of the many who were injured or crippled.

And if one man was crushed or another was snatched up by a twisted loop of steel cable and his body shattered, it gave rise to long haggling, interspersed with hellish oaths, about the delay, which could mess up the bonus, because the corpse had to be hauled away first.

And that was why, when Mr. Collins asked, "How many dead?" Ida did not for an instant think he was asking about the number of men who had died in return for bringing in those eight wells. She understood immediately that he wanted to know how many of the wells were dead, that is, nonproducing. Ida understood the language of oil.

The dead men were not mentioned in the cables, where every word cost thirty-five centavos. They were listed in the monthly report, which could be stuck into an envelope with other lists, all for only ten centavos.

They really could be more careful, those people. An oil camp's no kindergarten. There's no room in this world for people who don't look out for themselves.

What do we care about people? All that matters is oil.